The woman was stubborn as well as gorgeous, Dave realised.

And not above pulling rank over him. Well, that pretty much fitted in with what he'd heard about Lieutenant Commander Kate Hargrave.

The sexy hurricane hunter couldn't know it, but her ex-husband had had a few things to say to Dave about the woman who'd just dumped him, none of them particularly flattering. She was, according to the still-bitter aviator, ambitious as hell, fearless in the air, a tiger in bed and a real tough cookie out of it.

Dave thought three out of four was good enough for him.

Yes, sir, he thought, as he caught a last glimpse of turquoise spandex in the mirror. This assignment was looking better and better by the minute.

Ruling Passions
by Laura Wright

ꙮ ꙮ ꙮ

'Have I proved myself, Your Highness?'

Jaw as tight as the rest of him, Alex released her. 'You are very bold, Sophia.'

She nodded. 'I'm going in now. You'll be all right out here by yourself?'

'I always have. I always will.'

Alex saw her flinch slightly before saying, 'Good night, then.'

He watched her go, all the way up the sandy beach and into the house. His mind was blistered from their silly game of seduction. But it wasn't merely madness and unrequited pleasure that plagued him. Those two shackles he could deal with.

No, it was something far more dangerous.

For the first time in six years, he felt connected with life—open to lust, to need, to pain and to want.

And Sophia Dunhill was his keeper of the keys…

Full Throttle
MERLINE LOVELACE

Ruling Passions
LAURA WRIGHT

SILHOUETTE®
Desire™

First published in Great Britain 2004
Silhouette Books, Eton House, 18-24 Paradise Road,
Richmond, Surrey TW9 1SR

The publisher acknowledges the copyright holders of the
individual works as follows:

Full Throttle © Merline Lovelace 2004
Ruling Passions © Laura Wright 2003

ISBN 0 373 60109 3

51-1104

Printed and bound in Spain
by Litografia Rosés S.A., Barcelona

FULL THROTTLE
by
Merline Lovelace

MERLINE LOVELACE

spent twenty-three years in the air force, serving in Vietnam, at the Pentagon and at bases all over the world. When she hung up her uniform, she decided to try her hand at writing. She's since had more than fifty novels published, with over seven million copies of her work in print. She and her husband enjoy travelling and chasing little white balls around the fairways. Watch for the next book in the TO PROTECT AND DEFEND series, *The Right Stuff*, coming from Silhouette Sensation in December 2004.

To my buds on the RomVets loop—
women who all served their country and are now
turning out great novels! Thanks for sharing your
expertise on aircraft malfunctions, explosive devices
and general all around fun stuff.

One

Kate Hargrave was a good five miles into her morning jog when she spotted a plume of dust rising from the desert floor. Swiping at the sweat she'd worked up despite the nip September had brought to the high desert, she squinted through the shimmering New Mexico dawn at the vehicle churning up that long brown rooster tail.

A senior weather researcher with the National Oceanographic and Atmospheric Agency, Kate had logged hundreds of hours of flight time as one of NOAA's famed Hurricane Hunters. The pilots she flew with all possessed a steady hand on the controls, nerves of steel and an unshakable belief in their ability to look death in the eye and stare it down. So when she gauged the speed of the pickup hurtling straight toward her, she had no doubt who was at its wheel.

USAF Captain Dave Scott—a seasoned test pilot with hundreds of hours in both rotary and fixed-wing aircraft. Scott had been yanked off an assignment with Special Operations to become the newest addition to the supersecret test cadre tucked away in this remote corner of southeastern New Mexico.

He was supposed to have arrived last night but had phoned Captain Westfall from somewhere along the road and indicated he'd check in first thing this morning. No explanations for the delay, or none the navy captain in charge of the supersecret Pegasus project had relayed to his crew, anyway.

That alone was enough to put a dent in Kate's characteristically sunny good nature. She and the rest of the small, handpicked cadre had been here for weeks now. They'd been working almost around the clock to conduct final operational testing on the new all-weather, all-terrain attack-assault vehicle code-named Pegasus. The urgency of their mission had been burned into their brains from day one. That Captain Scott would delay his arrival—even by as little as eight hours of admittedly dead time—didn't particularly sit well with Kate.

Then there was the fact that the air force had pegged Scott to replace Lieutenant Colonel Bill

Thompson, the original air force representative to the project. Everyone on the team had liked and respected the easygoing and highly experienced test pilot. Unfortunately, Bill had suffered a heart attack after being infected by the vicious virus that attacked him and a number of other members of the test cadre some days ago.

Now Bill was off the Pegasus project and probably off flying status for the rest of his life. His abrupt departure had ripped a gaping hole in the tight, close team of officers and civilians plucked from all branches of the military to work on the project. Dave Scott would have to scramble to catch up with the rest of the test cadre *and* prove himself worthy to fill Bill Thompson's boots.

"Sure hope you're up to it, fella."

With that fervent wish, Kate lengthened her stride. She'd just as soon not come face-to-face with her new associate out here in the desert. Her hair was a tangled mess and her turquoise spandex running suit sported damp patches of sweat. With luck and a little more oomph to her pace, she could veer off onto the dirt track that ringed the perimeter of the site before Scott hit the first checkpoint.

She should have known she couldn't outrun a sky jock. The speeding pickup skidded to a stop at the checkpoint while Kate was still some distance from the perimeter trail.

The dazzling light shooting through the peaks of

the Guadalupe Mountains off to the east illuminated the vehicle. The truck was battered. Dust streaked. An indeterminate color between blue and gray. She couldn't see the driver, though. He was still too far away and the bright rays glinting off the windshield formed an impenetrable shield.

She'd get a glimpse of him soon enough, Kate guessed wryly. From the bits and pieces of background information she'd gathered about Captain Dave Scott, she knew he wasn't the type to cruise by a female in a tight jogging suit. Or one in support hose and black oxfords, for that matter. Rumor had it Scott was the love-'em-and-leave-'em type, with a string of satisfied lovers stretching from coast to coast.

Kate knew the breed.

All too well.

So she wasn't surprised when the pickup cleared the checkpoint, roared into gear and kicked up dust for another quarter mile or so. Scant yards from Kate, it fishtailed to a halt once more.

Dust swirled. The truck's engine idled with a low, throaty growl. The driver's-side window whirred down. A well-muscled forearm appeared, followed by a rugged profile. With his creased straw cowboy hat and sun-weathered features, Scott might have been one of the locals who'd adapted so well to life here in the high desert. The hat shaded the upper portion of his face. The lower portion consisted of the tip of a nose, a mouth bracketed by laugh lines and a blunt, square chin. The rolled sleeve of his white cotton shirt showed a sprinkling of hair bleached to gold by the sun. Mirrored aviator sunglasses shielded his eyes, but the grin he flashed Kate was pure sex.

"Well, well." The drawl was deep and rich and carried clearly on the morning air. "This assignment is looking better by the moment."

Kate had heard variations of the same line a hundred or more times in her career. Her ready smile, flaming auburn hair and generous curves had attracted the attention of every male she'd ever worked with. She'd long ago learned to separate the merely goggling from the seriously annoying and handle both with breezy competence. Edging to the side of the dirt road, she jogged toward the idling vehicle. Her voice held only dry amusement as she offered a word of advice.

"Pull in your tongue and hit the gas pedal, flyboy. Captain Westfall's expecting you."

His chin dipped. Eyes a clear, startling blue peered over the rim of the sunglasses and locked with hers.

"The captain can wait," he replied. "You, on the other hand…"

He didn't finish. Or if he did, Kate didn't hear him.

She'd kept her gaze engaged with his a half second too long and run right off the edge of the road.

Her well-worn Nikes came down not on hard-packed dirt, but empty air. With a smothered oath, she plunged into the shallow ditch beside the road. Her right leg hit with a jar that rattled every bone in her body before going out from under her. A moment later she landed smack on her rear atop a fat, prickly tumbleweed.

So much for breezy competence!

Scott was out of the pickup almost before Kate and the tumbleweed connected. His low-heeled boots scattered rock and dirt as he scrambled into the shallow depression. When he hunkered down beside her, she expected at least a minimal expression of concern. What she got was a swift, assessing glance followed by a waggle of his sun-streaked eyebrows.

"And here I woke up this morning thinking the next few weeks were going to be all work and no play."

Kate cocked an eyebrow. Best to set him straight right here, right now. "You thought right, Captain."

"I don't know about that." Dipping his chin, he gave her another once-over. "Things are lookin' good from where I'm squatting. *Very* good."

Kate sucked in a swift breath. Behind their screen of sun-bleached lashes, his eyes were electric blue. The little white lines at their corners disappeared when he smiled, which he did with devastating effect.

Thank heavens she'd been inoculated against Scott's brand of lazy charm and cocky self-assurance.

The inoculation had been painful, sure, but once administered was supposed to last a lifetime.

Unfortunately, she hadn't been inoculated against the effects of sharp, stinging barbs to the backside. The prickly weed had penetrated right through her spandex running tights. Now that Kate had recovered from the initial shock of her fall, she felt its sharp, stinging bite.

"How about unsquatting," she suggested dryly, "and helping me up?"

"My pleasure."

Rising with the careless grace of an athlete, he reached for her hand. His palm felt tough and callused against her skin, his skin warm to the touch.

Of course Kate's blasted ankle had to give out the moment she gained her feet. With a grunt, she fell right into his conveniently waiting arms. This time he had the decency to show some concern. At least that was the excuse he gave for swooping her up.

"You must have come down hard on that ankle."

Hefting her not-inconsiderable weight, he cradled her against his chest. His very solid, very muscled chest, Kate couldn't help noticing.

"I'd better get you to the base."

He was already out of the ditch and striding around the back of the pickup before she could tell him she had a more pressing problem to worry about than her ankle. She tried to think of a subtle way to inform him of her dilemma. None came immediately to mind. Sighing, she stopped him just as he opened the passenger door and prepared to deposit her inside.

"Before you plop me down on that seat, I think you should know I'm sporting a collection of needle-sharp stickers. I landed on a tumbleweed," she added when he flashed her a startled look. "I need to remove a few unwanted thistles from my posterior."

"Damn!" His mouth took a wicked curve. "And I was just thinking my day couldn't get any better."

His leer was so exaggerated, she didn't even try to hold back her sputter of laughter. "Let's not make this any more embarrassing than it already is. Just put me down and I'll, er, perform an emergency extraction."

He set her on her feet and gave her a hopeful look. "I'll be glad to assist in the operation."

"I can manage."

Making no effort to hide his disappointment, he watched with unabashed interest while Kate grabbed the door handle to steady herself and twisted around. It took some contorting to reach all the thorny stickers. One by one, she flicked them off into the ditch.

"You missed one," Scott advised as she dusted the back of her thigh. "A little lower."

Removing the last twig, she leaned her weight on her ankle to test it. The pain was already subsiding, thank goodness. Pasting a smile on her face, she turned to her would-be rescuer.

"I'm Lieutenant Commander Kate Hargrave, by

the way. I'm with the National Oceanographic and Atmospheric Agency.''

As a lieutenant commander in NOAA's commissioned-officer corps, Kate outranked an air force captain. The fact that Scott had just watched a senior officer pluck thorns out of her bottom appeared to afford him no end of amusement. His eyes glinting between those ridiculously thick gold-tipped lashes, he introduced himself.

''Dave Scott. Airplane driver.''

To her profound disgust, Kate discovered her inoculation against handsome devils like this one wasn't quite as effective as she'd thought. Or as permanent. Shivers danced along her skin as she gazed up at him. He was so close she could see the beginnings of a bristly gold beard. The way his cheeks creased when he smiled. The reflection of her sweat-sheened face in his mirrored glasses.

She got an up close whiff of him, too. Unlike Kate, he still carried a morning-shower scent, clean and shampooy, coated with only a faint tang of dust. No woodsy aftershave for Captain Dave Scott, she noted, then wondered why the heck she'd bothered to take such a detailed inventory.

This wasn't smart, Kate thought as her heart thumped painfully against her ribs. Not smart at all. She'd learned the hard way not to trust too-handsome charmers like this one. If nothing else, her brief, disastrous marriage had taught her to go with her head and not her hormones where men were concerned.

Added to that was the fact that she and Scott would be working together for the next few weeks. In extremely close proximity. Despite her flamboyant looks and sensual figure, Kate was a professional to her toes. A woman didn't acquire a long string of initials after her name and the title of senior weather research scientist at the National Oceanographic and Atmospheric Agency without playing the game by the rules.

"Do Not Fool Around With the Hired Help" ranked right up there as rule number two. Or maybe it was three. Within the top five, anyway.

Not that Kate was thinking about fooling around with Captain Dave Scott. Just the opposite! Still, goose bumps danced along her spine as he took her elbow to assist her into the pickup's passenger seat. Once she was comfortably ensconced, he rounded the front end of the truck and climbed behind the wheel.

"So how long have you been on-site?" he asked, putting the vehicle into gear.

"From day one."

When his boot hit the gas pedal, Kate braced herself for the thrust. Instead of jerking forward, however, the pickup seemed to coil its legs like some powerful, predatory beast and launched into a silent run. Obviously, Scott had installed one heck of an engine inside the truck's less-than-impressive frame.

Interesting, she thought. The captain was a whole lot like his vehicle. All coiled muscle and heart-stopping blue eyes under a battered straw cowboy hat and rumpled white shirt.

"So what's the skinny?" he asked. "Is Pegasus ready to fly?"

Instantly, Kate's thoughts shifted from the man beside her to the machine housed in a special hangar constructed of materials designed to resist penetration by even the most sophisticated spy satellites.

"Almost," she replied. "Bill Thompson had his heart attack just as we were finishing ground tests."

"I never met Thompson, but I've heard of him. The AF lost a damned good pilot."

"Yes, it did. So did Pegasus. You've got a lot of catching up to do," she warned him, "and not much time to do it."

"No problem."

The careless reply set Kate's jaw. She and the rest of the cadre had been hard at it for weeks now. If Scott thought he was going to waltz in and get up to speed on the top secret project in a few hours, he had one heck of a surprise waiting for him.

Unaware that he'd just scratched her exactly the wrong way, the captain seemed more interested in Kate than the project that would soon consume him.

"I saw your career brief in the package headquarters sent as part of my orientation package. Over a thousand hours in the P-3. That's pretty impressive."

It was, by Kate's standards as well as Scott's. Only the best of the best got to fly aboard NOAA's specially configured fleet of aircraft, including the P–3 Orion. Flying into the eye of a howling hurricane took guts, determination and a cast-iron stomach. Honesty forced Kate to add a qualifier, though.

"Not all those hours were hurricane time. Occasionally we saw blue sky."

"I went up once with the air force's Hurricane Hunters based at Keesler."

Kate stiffened. Her ex-husband was assigned to the Air Force Reserve unit at Keesler Air Force Base, on Mississippi's Gulf Coast. That's where she'd met John, during a conference that included all agencies involved in tracking and predicting the fury unleashed all too often on the Gulf by Ma Nature.

That's also where she'd found the jerk with his tongue down the mouth of a nineteen-year-old bimbette. Kate had few fond memories of Keesler.

"So how was your flight?" she asked, shoving aside the reminder of her most serious lapse in judgment.

"Let's just say once was enough."

"Flying into a maelstrom of wind and rain isn't for the faint of heart," she agreed solemnly.

He cracked a grin at that. When he pulled his gaze from the road ahead, laughter shimmered in his blue eyes.

"No, ma'am. It surely isn't."

Kate didn't reply, but she knew darn well Scott was anything *but* faint of heart. When the air force had identified him as Bill Thompson's replacement, she'd activated her extensive network of friends and information sources to find out everything she could about the man. Her sources confirmed he'd packed a whole bunch of flying time into his ten years in the military.

Flying that included several hundred combat hours in both the Blackhawk helicopter and the AC–130H gunship. A highly modified version of the air force's four-engine turboprop workhorse, the gunship provided surgically accurate firepower in support of both conventional and unconventional forces, day or night.

Kate didn't doubt Scott had provided just that surgically accurate support during recent tours in both Afghanistan and Iraq. After Iraq, he'd been sent to the 919th Special Operations Wing at Hurlburt Field, Florida, to fly the latest addition to the air force inventory—the tilt-wing CV–22 Osprey.

Since the Osprey combined the lift characteristics of a helicopter and the long-distance flight capability of a fixed-wing aircraft, Scott's background made him a natural choice as short-notice replacement for Bill Thompson. If—*when!*—Pegasus completed its operational tests, it might well replace both the C–130 and the CV–122 as the workhorse of the battlefield.

Thinking of the tense weeks ahead, Kate chewed

on her lower lip and said little until they'd passed through the second checkpoint and entered the compound housing the Pegasus test complex.

The entire complex had been sited and constructed in less than two months. Unfortunately, the builders had sacrificed aesthetics to exigency. The site had all the appeal of a prison camp. Rolls of concertina wire surrounded the clump of prefabricated modular buildings and trailers, all painted a uniformly dull tan to blend in with the desert landscape. White-painted rocks marked the roads and walkways between the buildings. Aside from a few picnic tables scattered among the trailers, everything was starkly functional.

Separate modular units housed test operations, the computer-communications center and a dispensary. The security center, nicknamed Rattlesnake Ops after the leather-tough, take-no-prisoners military police guarding the site, occupied another unit. A larger unit contained a fitness center and the dining hall, which also served as movie theater and briefing room when the site's commanding officer wanted to address the entire cadre. The hangar that housed Pegasus loomed over the rest of the structures like a big, brooding mammoth.

Personnel were assigned to the trailers, two or three to a unit. Kate and the other two women officers on-site shared one unit. Scott would bunk down with Major Russ McIver, the senior Marine Corps rep.

Kate directed him to the line of modular units unofficially dubbed Officers Row.

"You probably want to change into your uniform before checking in with Captain Westfall. Your trailer is the second one on the left. Westfall's is the unit standing by itself at the end of the row."

"First things first," Scott countered, pulling up at the small dispensary. "Let's get your ankle looked at."

"I'll take care of that. You'd best get changed and report in."

"Special Ops would drum me out of the brotherhood if I left a lady to hobble around on a sore ankle."

He meant it as a joke, but his careless attitude toward his new assignment was starting to seriously annoy Kate. Her mouth thinned as he came around the front of the pickup. Sliding out of the passenger seat, she stood firmly on both feet to address him.

"I don't think you've grasped the urgency of our mission. I'll manage here, Captain. You report in to the C.O."

Her tone left no doubt. It was an order from a superior officer to a subordinate.

Scott cocked an eyebrow. For a moment, his eyes held something altogether different from the teasing laughter he'd treated her to up to this point.

The dangerous glint was gone almost as quickly

as it had come. Tipping her a two-fingered salute, he replied in an easy, if somewhat exaggerated, drawl.

"Yes, ma'am."

Dave took care not to spin out and leave Lieutenant Commander Hargrave in a swirl of dust. His eyes on the rearview mirror, he followed her careful progress up the clinic steps.

The woman was stubborn as well as gorgeous. And not above pulling rank on him. Well, that pretty well fit with what he'd heard about her.

The sexy Hurricane Hunter couldn't know it but her ex-husband had piloted the mission Dave had flown with the reserve unit out of Keesler. The man had had a few things to say about the wife who'd just dumped him, none of them particularly flattering. She was, according to the still-bitter aviator, ambitious as hell, fearless in the air, a tiger in bed and a real ball-breaker out of it.

Dave figured three out of four was good enough for him.

Yes, sir, he thought as he caught a last glimpse of turquoise spandex in the mirror. This assignment was looking better and better by the minute.

Two

Showered, shaved and wrapped in the familiar comfort of his green Nomex flight suit, Dave tracked down the officer in command of the Pegasus project. He found Captain Westfall at the Test Operations Building.

"Captain Scott reporting for duty, sir."

The tall, lean naval officer in khakis creased to blade-edged precision returned Dave's salute, then offered his hand.

"Welcome aboard, Captain Scott."

The man's gravelly voice and iron grip matched his salt-and-pepper buzz cut. His skin was tanned to near leather, no doubt the result of years spent pacing

a deck in sun, wind and salt spray. His piercing gray
eyes took deliberate measure of the latest addition to
his team. Dave didn't exactly square his shoulders,
but he found himself standing a little taller under
Westfall's intense scrutiny.

"Did you take care of that bit of personal business
you mentioned when you called last night?"

"Yes, sir."

Dave most certainly had. Fighting a grin, he
thought of the waitress who'd all but wrapped herself
around him when he'd stopped for a cheeseburger in
Chorro. The cluster of sunbaked adobe buildings was
the closest thing that passed for a town around these
parts. The town might appear tired and dusty, but its
residents were anything but. One particular resident,
anyway.

Dave would carry fond memories of that particular
stop for a long time.

Although…

All the while he'd soaped and scraped away the
bristles and road dust, his thoughts had centered more
on a certain redhead than on the waitress who'd de-
layed his arrival at the Pegasus site by a few hours.
Kate Hargrave was still there, inside his head, teasing
him with her fiery hair, her luscious curves and those
green cat's eyes.

As if reading his mind, Westfall folded his arms.
"I understand you brought Lieutenant Commander
Hargrave in this morning."

Word sure got around fast. Dave had dropped off the gorgeous weather officer at the dispensary less than twenty minutes ago.

"Yes, sir. We bumped into each other on the road into the site. Have you had a report on her condition? How's her ankle?"

"Doc Richardson says she'll be fine. Only a slight muscle strain." A flinty smile creased Westfall's cheeks. "Knowing Commander Hargrave, she'll work out the kinks and be back in fighting form within a few hours."

"That's good to hear."

The smile disappeared. Westfall's gray eyes drilled into his new subordinate. "Yes, it is. I can't afford to lose another key member of my test cadre. You've got some catching up to do, Captain."

"Yes, sir."

"I've set up a series of briefings for you, starting at oh-nine-hundred. First, though, I want you to meet the rest of the team. And get a look at the craft you'll be piloting." He flicked a glance at his watch. "I've asked the senior officers and engineers to assemble in the hangar. They should be in place by now."

The hangar was the cleanest Dave had ever seen. No oil spills smudged the gleaming, white-painted floor. No greasy equipment was shoved up against the wall. Just rack after rack of black boxes and the sleek white capsule that was Pegasus. It took everything Dave had to tear his gaze from the delta-winged craft and acknowledge the introductions Captain Westfall performed.

"Since Pegasus is intended for use by all branches of the military, we've pulled together representatives from each of the uniformed services. I understand you've already met Major Russ McIver."

"Right."

The square-jawed marine had just been exiting his trailer when Dave pulled up. They'd exchanged little more than a quick handshake before Dave hurried in to hit the showers and pull on his uniform. From the package headquarters had sent him, though, he knew McIver had proven himself in both Kosovo and Kabul. The marine's function was to test Pegasus's capability as a vehicle for inserting a fully armed strike team deep into enemy territory.

"This is Major Jill Bradshaw," Westfall announced, "chief of security for the site."

A brown-eyed blonde in desert fatigues and an armband with MP stenciled in big white letters, the major held out her hand. "Good to have you on board, Captain. Come by Rattlesnake Ops after the briefing and we'll get you officially cleared in."

"Will do."

The petite brunette next to Bradshaw smiled a welcome. "Lieutenant Caroline Dunn, Coast Guard. Welcome to Project Pegasus, Captain Scott."

"Thanks."

Dave liked her on the spot. From what he'd read of the woman's résumé, she'd racked up an impressive number of hours in command of a Coast Guard cutter. He appreciated both her experience and her warm smile.

"Dr. Cody Richardson," Westfall said next, indicating a tall, black-haired officer in khakis. The silver oak leaf on Richardson's left collar tab designated his rank. On the right tab was the insignia of the Public Health Service—an anchor with a chain fouling it.

A world-renowned expert in biological agents, Richardson held both an M.D. and a Ph.D. His mission was to test the nuclear, biological and chemical defense suite installed in Pegasus. He also served as on-site physician.

"Heard you provided ambulance service this morning," the doc commented, taking Dave's hand in a firm, no-nonsense grip.

"I did. How's your patient?"

His patient answered for herself. Stepping forward, Lieutenant Commander Hargrave gave Dave a cool smile.

"Fit for duty and ready to get to work."

He sure couldn't argue with the "fit" part. Damned if he'd ever seen anyone fill out a flight suit the way Kate Hargrave did. She, too, wore fire-retardant Nomex, but hers was the NOAA version—sky blue instead of the military's pea green. The zip-

pered, one-piece bag sported an American flag on the
left shoulder, a leather name patch above her left
breast and NOAA's patch above her right. A distinctive unit emblem was Velcroed to her right shoulder.

It featured a winged stallion on a classic shield-
shaped device. The bottom two-thirds of the shield
was red. The top third showed a blue field studded
with seven silver stars. Captain Westfall saw Dave
eyeing the patch and reached into his pocket.

"This is for you. I issued one to the entire test
cadre when we first assembled. The winged steed
speaks for itself. The stars represent each of the seven
uniformed services."

Dave's glance swept the assembled group once
more. They were all there, all seven. Army. Navy.
Marine Corps. Air Force. Coast Guard. Public Health
Service. And NOAA, as represented by the delectable
Kate Hargrave. The four military branches. Three
predominately civilian agencies with small cadres of
uniformed officers.

Dave had been assigned to some joint and unified
commands before, but never one with this diversity.
Despite their variations in mission and uniform,
though, each of these officers had sworn the same
oath when they were commissioned. To protect and
defend the Constitution of the United States against
all enemies.

Dave might possess a laid-back attitude toward life

in general, but he took that oath very seriously. No one who'd served in combat could do otherwise.

Captain Westfall took a few moments more to introduce the project's senior civilian scientists and engineers. That done, he and the entire group walked Dave over to the vehicle they'd gathered to test and—hopefully!—clear for operational use.

Pegasus was as sweet up close as it had looked from across the hangar. Long, cigar-shaped, with a bubble canopy, a side hatch and fat, wide-tracked wheels. Designed to operate on land, in the air and in water. The gray-haired Captain Westfall stroked the gleaming white fuselage with the same air of proud propriety a horse breeder might give the winner of the Triple Crown.

"You're seeing the craft in its swept-wing mode," he intoned in his deep voice.

Dave nodded, noting the propellers were folded flat, the engines tilted to horizontal, and the wings tucked almost all the way into the belly of the craft.

"The wide-track wheels allow Pegasus to operate on land in this mode."

"And damned well, too," Dr. Richardson put in with a quick glance at the trim blond Major Bradshaw.

"We encountered some unexpected difficulties during the mountain phase of land operations," she told Dave. "You know about the virus that hit the site and affected Bill Thompson's heart. It hit me, too, while I was up in the mountains conducting a prerun check. Cody... Dr. Richardson and Major McIver rode Pegasus to the rescue.''

She'd corrected her slip into informality quickly, but not before Dave caught the glance she and the doc exchanged. Well, well. So it wasn't all work and no play on the site after all.

''Glad to hear Pegasus can run,'' Dave commented. ''The real test will be to see if he can fly.''

He saw at once he'd put his foot in it. Backs stiffened. Eyes went cool. Even Caroline Dunn, the friendly Coast Guard officer, arched an eyebrow.

''Pegasus is designed as a multiservice, all-weather, all-terrain assault vehicle,'' Captain Westfall reminded him. ''Our job is to make sure it operates equally well on land, on water *and* in the air.''

There was only one answer to that. Dave gave it.

''Yes, sir.''

He recovered a little as the walk-around continued and the talk turned to the specifics of the craft's power, torque, engine thrust and instrumentation. Dave had done his homework, knew exactly what was required to launch Pegasus into the air. By the end of the briefing, his hands were itching to wrap around the throttles.

The rest of the day was taken up with the administrivia necessary in any new assignment. Major Bradshaw gave Dave a security briefing and issued a high-tech ID that not only cleared him into the site but also tracked his every movement. Doc Richardson conducted an intake interview and medical assessment. The senior test engineers presented detailed briefings of Pegasus's performance during the land tests.

By the time 7:00 p.m. rolled around, Dave's stomach was issuing noisy feed-me demands. The sandwich he and the briefers had grabbed for lunch had long since ceased to satisfy the needs of his six-two frame. He caught the tail end of the line at the dining hall and joined a table of troops in desert fatigues.

Like the officer cadre, enlisted personnel at the site came from every branch of the service. Army MPs provided security. Navy personnel operated most of the support facilities. Air force troops maintained the site's extensive communications and computer networks. The marine contingent was small, Dave learned, only about ten noncoms whose expertise was essential in testing Pegasus's performance as a troop transport and forward-insertion vehicle.

He scarfed down a surprisingly delicious concoction of steak and enchiladas, then returned to the unit he shared with Russ McIver to unpack and stow his gear. McIver wasn't in residence and the unpacking didn't take long. All Dave had brought with him was an extra flight suit, a set of blues on the off chance he'd have to attend some official function away from the site, workout sweats, jeans, some comfortable shirts and one pair of dress slacks. His golf shoes and clubs he left in the truck. With any luck, he'd get Pegasus soaring the first time up and have time to hit some of New Mexico's golf courses before heading back to his home base in Florida.

Changing out of his uniform into jeans and a gray USAF sweatshirt with the arms ripped out, he stashed his carryall under his bed and explored the rest of the two-bedroom unit. It was similar to a dozen others he'd occupied at forward bases and a whole lot more comfortable than his quarters in Afghanistan.

A passing glance showed Russ McIver's room was spartan in its neat orderliness. As was the front room. Carpeted in an uninspiring green, the area served as a combination eating, dining and living room. The furniture was new and looked comfortable, if not particularly elegant. The fridge was stocked with two boxes of high-nutrition health bars and four six-packs of Coors Light.

''That's what I admire most about marines,'' Dave announced to the empty trailer. ''They take only the absolute necessities into the field with them.''

Helping himself, he popped a top and prepared to attack the stack of briefing books and technical manuals he'd plopped down on the kitchenette counter. The rise and fall of voices just outside the unit drew him to the door.

When he stepped out into the early-evening dusk, the first thing that hit him was the explosion of color to the west. Like a smack to the face, it grabbed his instant attention. Reds, golds, blacks, pinks, oranges and blues, all swirling together in a deep purple sky. The gaudy combination reminded Dave of the paintings he'd seen in every truck stop and roadside gift shop on the drive out. Black velvet and bright slashes of color. But this painting was for real, and it was awesome.

The second thing that hit him was the silence his appearance had generated among the officers clustered around a metal picnic table. It was as if an outsider had crashed an exclusive, members-only party. Which he had, Dave thought wryly.

His new roommate broke the small silence. Lifting an arm, McIver waved him over. "Hey, Scott. Bring your beer and join us."

"Thanks." Puffs of sand swirled under Dave's feet as he crossed to the table. "It's your beer, by the way. I'll contribute to the fund or restock the refrigerator as necessary."

"No problem."

The others shifted to make room for him. Like Dave, they'd shed their uniforms. Most wore cutoffs or jeans. Kate Hargrave, he noted with a suddenly dry throat, was in spandex again. Biker shorts this time. Black. Showing lots of slim, tanned thigh.

Damn!

"We were just talking about you," she said as he claimed a corner of the metal bench.

No kidding. He hadn't been hit with a silence like that since the last time he'd walked in on his brother and sister-in-law in the middle of one of the fierce arguments they pretended never happened. As always, Jacqueline had clammed up tight in the presence of a third party. Ryan had just looked angry and miserable. As always.

Jaci was a lot like Kate Hargrave, Dave decided. Not as beautiful. Certainly not as well educated. But just as tough and *very* good at putting a man in his place. Or trying to.

"Must have been a boring conversation," he returned, stretching his legs out under the table. "I'm not much to talk about."

"We were speculating how long it's going to take you to get up to speed."

"I'll be ready to fly when Pegasus is."

Kate arched a delicately penciled auburn eyebrow. "The first flight was originally scheduled for next week. After Bill's heart attack, Captain Westfall put it on hold."

"I talked to him late this afternoon. He's going to put the flight back on as scheduled."

The nonchalant announcement produced another startled silence. Cody Richardson broke it this time.

"Are you sure you can complete your simulator training and conduct the necessary preflight test runs by next week, Scott?"

Dave started to reply that he intended to give it

the ole college try. Just in time, he bit back the la-
conic quip. It didn't take a genius to see that this
gathering under the stars was some kind of nightly
ritual. And that Dave was still the odd man out. He'd
remain out until he proved himself. Problem was,
he'd long ago passed the point of either wanting or
needing to prove anything. His record spoke for him.

"Yeah," he answered the doc instead. "I'm sure."

The talk turned to the machine then, the one that
had brought them all to this corner of the desert.
Dave said little, preferring to listen and add to his
first impressions of the group.

There were definitely some personalities at work
here, he decided after a few moments of lively discussion. Caroline Dunn, the Coast Guard officer,
looked as if a stiff wind could blow her away, but
her small form housed a sharp mind and an iron will.
That became evident when Russ McIver made the
mistake of suggesting some modifications to the sea
trials. Dunn cut his feet right out from under him.

Then there was the site's top cop, Army Major Jill
Bradshaw. Out of uniform, she lost some of her cool,
don't-mess-with-me aura. Particularly around the
doc, Dave noted with interest. Yep, those two most
certainly had something cooking.

Which left Kissable Kate. Dave would be a long
time getting to sleep tonight. The weather scientist
did things to spandex that made a man ache to peel

off every inch of the slick, rubbery fabric. Slowly. Inch by delicious inch.

So he didn't exactly rush off when the small gathering broke up and the others drifted away, leaving him and Kate and a sky full of stars. Dave retained his comfortable slouch while she played with her diet-drink can and eyed him thoughtfully across the dented metal tabletop.

Light from the high-intensity spots mounted around the compound gave her hair a dark copper tint. She'd caught it back with a plastic clip, but enough loose tendrils escaped for Dave to weave an erotic fantasy or two before she shoved her drink can aside.

"Look, we may have gotten off to a wrong start this morning."

"Can't agree with you on that one," he countered. "Scooping a beautiful woman into my arms ten seconds after laying eyes on her constitutes one heck of a good start in my mind."

"That's exactly what I mean. I don't want you to make the mistake of thinking you'll be scooping me up again."

"Why not?"

The lazy amusement in his voice put an edge in hers.

"I made a few calls. Talked to some people who know you. Does the name Denise Hazleton strike a bell?"

"Should it?"

"No, I guess not. Denise said you never quite got around to last names and probably wouldn't remember her first. She's a lieutenant stationed at Luke Air Force Base, in Arizona. You were hitting on her girlfriend the night the two of you hooked up."

"Hmm. Hooking up with one woman while hitting on another. Not good, huh?"

"Not in my book."

Kate hadn't really expected him to show remorse or guilt. She wouldn't have believed him if he had. But neither was she prepared for the hopeful gleam that sprang into his eyes.

"Did I get lucky with either?"

Well, at least he was honest. The man didn't make any attempt to disguise his nature. He was what he was.

"Yes, you did," she answered. "Which is why..."

"What else did she say?"

"I beg your pardon?"

"Denise. What else did she tell you?"

A bunch! Interspersed with long, breathy sighs and a fervent hope that Captain Dave Scott would find his way back to Luke soon.

"Let's just say you left her with a smile on her face."

"We aim to please," Scott said solemnly, even as

the glint in his blue eyes deepened. Too late, Kate realized he'd been stringing her along.

"The point is," she said firmly, "I was married to a man a lot like you. A helluva pilot, but too handsome for his own—or anyone else's—good. It didn't work for us and I want you to know right up-front I've sworn off the type."

One sun-bleached eyebrow hooked. He studied Kate for long moments. "That flight I told you about? The one I took a year or so ago with the air force Hurricane Hunters out of Keesler?"

"Yes?"

"Your ex-husband was the pilot."

Kate's mouth twisted. Obviously she wasn't the only one who got an earful. "You don't have to tell me. I'll just assume John implied I didn't leave *him* with a smile on his face."

"Something along those lines."

She cocked her head, curious now about the workings of this man's mind. "And that didn't scare you off?"

His grin came back, swift and slashing and all male. "No, ma'am."

"It should have. As I said, it didn't work out between John and me. Just as it wouldn't work between the two of us."

"Well, I'm not looking for a deep, meaningful relationship, you understand...."

"Somehow I didn't think you were," Kate drawled.

"But that's not to say we couldn't test the waters."

"No, thanks."

She scooted off the end of the bench and rose. She'd said what needed saying. The conversation was finished.

Evidently Scott didn't agree. Uncoiling his long frame from the opposite bench, he came around to her side of the table.

"You're a scientist. You tote a Ph.D. after your name. I would think you'd want to conduct a series of empirical tests and collect some irrefutable data before you write us off."

"I've collected all the data I need."

"Denise might not agree."

There it was again. That glint of wicked laughter.

"I'm sure she wouldn't," Kate agreed.

"Then I'd say you owe it to yourself to perform at least one definitive test."

His hand came up, curled under her chin, tipped her face. Kate knew she could stop this with a single word. She hadn't reached the rank of lieutenant commander in NOAA's small commissioned-officer corps without learning how to handle herself in just about any situation.

She could only blame curiosity—and the determination to show Dave Scott she meant business—for the way she stood passive and allowed him to conduct the experiment.

Three

He knew how to kiss. Kate would give him that.

He didn't swoop. Didn't zero in hard and fast. He took things slow, easy, his mouth playing with hers, his breath a warm wash against her lips. Just tantalizing enough to stir small flickers of pleasure under her skin. Just teasing enough to make her want more.

Sternly, Kate resisted the urge to tilt her head and make her mouth more accessible. Not that Scott required her assistance. His thumb traced a slow circle on the underside of her chin and gently nudged it to a more convenient angle for his greater height. By the time the experiment ended, Kate was forced to admit the truth.

"That was nice."

"Nice, huh?"

"Very nice," she conceded. "But it didn't light any fires."

Not major ones, anyway. Just those irritating little flickers still zapping along her nerve endings.

"That was only an engine check." His thumb made another lazy circle on the underside of her chin. "Next time, we'll rev up to full throttle."

It wouldn't do any good to state bluntly there wouldn't be a next time. Dave Scott would only take that as another personal challenge.

"Tell you what." Deliberately, she eased away from his touch. "I'll let you know when I'm ready to rev my engines. Until then, we focus only on our mission while on-site. Agreed?"

"If that's what you want."

She leveled a steady look at him. Ignored the little crinkle of laugh lines at the corners of his eyes. Disregarded the way the deepening shadows cast his face into intriguing planes and angles.

"That's what I want."

Kate had almost as much trouble convincing her roommates she wanted to stick strictly to business as she had convincing Dave Scott.

Cari and Jill were both waiting when she returned to the modular unit that served as their quarters. The unit was functional at best—three cracker box–size bedrooms, an even smaller kitchen and a living area equipped with furniture more designed for utility than for comfort. The three women had added a few personal touches. Kate had tacked up some posters showing the earth's weather in all its infinite variety. Cloudbursts over the Grand Canyon. Snow dusting the peaks of the Andes. The sun blazing down on a Swiss alpine meadow. Cari had added a shelf crammed with the whodunits and thrillers she devoured like candy. Jill stuck to her army roots and had draped a green flag depicting the crossed dueling pistols of the Military Police over one bare wall. The result wouldn't win any house-beautiful awards, but the three officers had grown used to it.

They'd also grown used to each other's idiosyncrasies. No small feat for women accustomed to being on their own and in charge. Still, their close quarters made for few secrets—as Cari proceeded to demonstrate. Curled in her favorite chair, the Coast Guard officer propped the thick technical manual she'd been studying on her chest and demanded an account.

"Okay, Hargrave, *re-port*. What's with you and the latest addition to our merry band?"

"Other than the fact he drove me into the compound after my tumble this morning, nothing."

Polite disbelief skipped across Cari's heart-shaped face. Jill Bradshaw was more direct.

"Ha! Some weather officer you are. *We* all heard

the thunder rumbling around you and Scott. You sure lightning isn't about to strike?''

''I should be so lucky.''

Kate plopped down beside her on the sofa and yanked the clip out of her hair. Raking her fingers through the heavy mass, she gave the cop a rueful smile.

''I'll tell you this much. Dave isn't like Cody, Jill. You struck gold there.''

''Yeah, right,'' the blonde snorted. ''I had to put him on his face in the dirt before either of us got around to recognizing that fact. Not to mention almost arresting him for suspected sabotage.''

Kate's smile dimmed at the memory of those tense days when a mysterious virus had attacked one team member after another. As chief of security, Jill's investigation had centered on the Public Service officer—who just happened to be one of the country's foremost experts in biological agents.

''Besides which,'' Jill continued with a shrug, ''Cody and I are doing our best to play things cool until we wind up the Pegasus project.''

It was Kate's turn to snort. ''The temperature goes up a good twenty degrees Celsius whenever you two are in the same vicinity.''

Loftily, her roommate ignored the interruption. ''From where we sit,'' Jill said, including Cari in the general assessment, ''your Captain Scott doesn't look like he knows how to cool his jets.''

"First, he's not *my* Captain Scott. Second, we conducted a little experiment a few moments ago, the nature of which is highly classified," she added firmly when both women flashed interested looks. "Bottom line, the captain and I agreed to focus solely on Pegasus while on-site. As the three of us should be doing right now."

Jill took the hint and stopped probing. An intensely private person herself, she hadn't looked forward to sharing cramped quarters with two other women. After weeks with the gregarious Kate and friendly Caroline, she'd learned to open up a bit. Falling head over heels for the handsome doc assigned to the project had certainly aided in her metamorphosis.

"Speaking of Pegasus," Cari said, patting the thick three-ring binder propped on her stomach. "Captain Westfall sent over a revised test plan while you were out, uh, experimenting with Dave Scott. Our air force flyboy starts simulator training tomorrow morning."

"Yikes!" Kate's feet hit the floor with a thud. "I'd better get to work. I want to input a different weather-sequence pattern into the simulator program. Talk to you guys later."

Heading for her bedroom, she settled at the small desk wedged in a corner and flipped up the lid of a slim, titanium-cased notebook computer. The communications wizards assigned to the Pegasus project had rigged wireless high-speed satellite links for the

PCs on-site. Kate could access the National Oceanographic and Atmospheric Agency databases from just about anywhere in the compound.

The databases were treasure troves containing information collected over several centuries. Kate took pride in the fact that NOAA could trace its roots back to 1807, when President Thomas Jefferson created the U.S. Coast and Geodetic Survey, the oldest scientific agency in the federal government. Congress got involved in 1890 when it created a Weather Bureau, the forerunner of the current National Weather Service. In 1970 President Nixon combined weather and coastal surveys, along with many other departments to create NOAA.

The major component of the Department of Commerce, NOAA had responsibilities that now included all U.S. weather and climate forecasting, monitoring ocean and atmospheric data, managing marine fisheries and mammals, mapping and charting all U.S. waters and managing coastal zones. Counted among its vast resources were U.S. weather and environmental satellites, a fleet of ships and aircraft, twelve research laboratories and several supercomputers.

Civilians constituted most of NOAA's personnel, but a small cadre of uniformed officers served within all components of the agency, as well as with the military services, NASA, the Department of State and the new Department of Homeland Security. A privileged few like Kate got to fly with the Hurricane

Hunters based out of the Aviations Operations Center in Tampa.

Kate hadn't intended to join NOAA or its officer corps, had never *heard* of the agency when she started working part-time in a TV station while still in high school. Before long, she was helping analyze data and put together weather reports. She didn't seriously consider a career in weather, though, until Hurricane Andrew devastated her grandparents' retirement community just outside Miami. She spent weeks helping the heartbroken couple sort through the soggy remains of fifty-two years of marriage. The experience gave her keen insight into the way natural disasters impacted people's lives.

After that wrenching experience, weather became not just a part-time job, but a passion. Kate majored in meteorology in college, served an internship with the National Weather Service's Tornado Center in Oklahoma, went on to earn a master's and then a doctorate in environmental sciences. Now one of the senior scientists assigned to NOAA's Air Operations Center, Kate regularly devoured materials on everything from tidal waves to meteor showers.

Captain Westfall had handpicked Kate for the Pegasus project based on her expertise and her reputation within the agency for always producing results. Pegasus wasn't designed to fly or swim through hurricanes, but it was expected to operate on land, in the air and at sea. Kate had drawn on NOAA's extensive databases to design tests that would stress the vehicle's instrumentation and its crew to the max in each environment.

For the land runs, she'd simulated sandstorms, raging blizzards, flood conditions and blistering heat. For the airborne phase of the tests, she planned to subject the craft to an even more drastic assortment of natural phenomena.

Her fingers flew over the keyboard, reviewing the test parameters, adjusting weather-severity levels, adding electronic notes to herself and the senior test engineer who'd have to approve any modifications to the plan.

A final click of the mouse saved the changes. Kate sat back, a small smile on her face.

"Okay, Captain Dave Scott. This little package ought to put you through your paces. You and Pegasus both."

Still smiling, she changed into a well-washed, comfortable sleep shirt. It was early, not quite ten, but she'd have to be up by six to squeeze in her morning run.

Usually Kate zonked out within moments of hitting the sack. Tonight she couldn't seem to erase the image of a certain pilot. Or the memory of his mouth brushing hers. Damn, the man was good! Despite her every intention to the contrary, he'd certainly left her wanting more.

Okay, and what woman wouldn't? Kate rationalized. With his muscled shoulders, gleaming blue eyes and come-and-get-me grin, the man was sex on the hoof. Then there was his attitude. So damned cocky and confident. She had to admire his seemingly unshakable belief in his own abilities, even as she felt a growing urge to take him down a peg or two.

Well, he'd get a chance to show what he was made of tomorrow.

Rolling over, Kate punched her pillow.

Her inner alarm woke her well before six. The clock radio beside her bed went off just as she was lacing her running shoes. Killing the alarm, Kate put on a pot of coffee for her roommates and slipped outside to conduct her warm-up exercises. The muscles she'd pulled yesterday morning issued a sharp protest, but the ache eased within moments. Properly stretched and loose, she set out at an easy lope for the gate guarding the compound.

The MP on duty tipped her a salute. Kate returned it with a smile and lengthened her stride. The dirt road that formed the only access to the site arrowed straight ahead, a pale track in the light filtering through the peaks to the east. The steady plop of her sneakers against the dirt and the rhythm of her own breathing soon took Kate to her special, private world.

Her morning run was a sacred ritual, one she conducted whenever she didn't have a flight scheduled or a hurricane to track. The stillness of early morning cleared her head of yesterday's issues and centered her on the ones ahead. Given her penchant for pizza and greasy cheeseburgers, the long, punishing runs also kept her naturally lush curves from becoming downright generous.

After her divorce, these moments alone in the dawn had helped her regain her perspective. It had taken her a while to get past the hurt. Even longer to recognize that John's angry accusation that Kate was too driven, too ambitious, masked his own unwillingness to abandon the niche he'd carved for himself in his world. He didn't want change—or a wife who thrived on challenges.

With an impatient shake of her head, Kate put the past out of her mind. This was her quiet time, her small slice where she should be thinking about the day ahead.

So she wasn't particularly thrilled when she caught the echo of a loping tread behind her. Most of the other personnel at the test cadre fulfilled their mandatory physical fitness requirements at the site's small but well-equipped gym. Once a week Russ McIver rousted the marine contingent on station for a ten-mile run. With full backpacks, no less. Aside from that grunting, huffing squad, Kate usually had the dawn to herself.

When thuds drew closer, she threw a look over her

shoulder. Dave Scott caught her glance and jerked his chin in acknowledgment.

Well, hell!

An irritated frown creased Kate's forehead. She thought she'd made herself clear last night. Apparently Captain Scott hadn't been listening. Her mouth set, she brought her head back around and kept to her pace.

He came up alongside her a few moments later. "Mornin', Commander. You sure you should be running on that ankle?"

She ignored the question and the easy smile he aimed her way. "I thought we reached an agreement last night."

"We did."

"And this is how you intend to stick to your end of the bargain?"

"Maybe I misunderstood things." He sounded genuinely puzzled as he matched his longer stride to hers. "I thought we agreed to focus on business while on-site."

"Exactly."

"So I'm focusing. Captain Westfall made it clear he expected all military to maintain a vigorous physical-conditioning program."

"And you just happened to choose an early-morning run for your PE program?"

The sarcasm went right past the captain.

"I figured the rest of the day was going to be

pretty busy," he replied. "I also figured you might want some company. Just in case you went into a ditch and made contact with another tumbleweed."

"Sorry, cowboy, you figured wrong. Company is the last thing I want on my morning run. I use the time to clear my head and raise a little sweat."

"Not a problem," he said easily. "I like a little more kick in my stride anyway. I wouldn't want to push you."

She shook her head. As challenges went, that one was about as subtle as a bull moose pawing the ground.

"If you want a race..."

She skimmed her glance over the desert landscape now bathed in the reds and golds of morning. A half mile or so ahead, a solitary cactus raised its arms as if to welcome the new day.

"See that cactus? If I reach it first, you pick another time to run. Agreed?"

"Agr— Hey!"

She shot forward, feeding off a rush of pure adrenaline. Kate loved pushing herself to the max. In the air, surrounded by a riot of black, angry clouds and howling winds. On the playing field, whether participating or watching. In her personal life, which she had to admit had taken on an unexpected edge since Dave Scott appeared on the scene all of twenty-four hours ago.

Unfortunately, most men didn't appreciate being

left in the dust. Kate had learned that lesson the hard way from her ex. She figured now was as good a time as any to administer the same lesson to Dave Scott.

She almost succeeded. The cool desert air was stabbing into her lungs as she drew level with the cactus. At that moment, Scott drew level with her. They whizzed past the plant side by side, matching stride for stride.

Panting, Kate slowed her breakneck pace. Scott did the same, his breath coming a whole lot easier than hers.

"What do you know?" he said, that damned glint in his eye. "A tie."

"Did you hold back?" she asked sharply.

"What do you think?"

"Dammit, Scott!"

"Hey, you set the ground rules. You win, I run another time. I win, I run when and where I please. A tie…"

"A tie means we do it again," Kate snapped. She didn't like losing *or* ending matters in a draw.

"Okay by me. So how far do you plan to run this morning?"

"Another mile or so," she bit out.

"That works. I need to hit the showers and make a pass through the dining hall before I show up at test ops for my first simulator run."

Kate chewed on her lower lip. A few strides later, she offered a grudging bit of advice.

"You might want to skip the dining hall. You're going to hit some rough weather this morning. You won't impress your fellow cadre members if you up-chuck the first time you're at the controls."

He gave her a quick glance. "Taking me on a wild ride, are you?"

"Like you wouldn't believe, cowboy."

As soon as the words were out, Kate wished them back. She couldn't believe she'd let herself walk into that bit of double entendre. To her surprise, Scott didn't jump on it with wolfish glee. He looked thoughtful for a moment before nodding his thanks.

"I appreciate the warning. I'll go light on the grits and gravy."

"Good idea."

The warning surprised Dave. Given what he'd heard about Kate Hargrave's competitive personality, he would have guessed she'd take secret delight in knocking him down a peg or two. She'd certainly pulled out all the stops in their little footrace a moment ago. Dave had burned more energy than he wanted to admit trying to catch her. Once she got back up to full power she was going to give him one helluva run for his money.

A smile of pure anticipation tugged at his lips. Behind his laid-back exterior, Dave was every bit as competitive as Commander Hargrave. He suspected all fliers had that edge, that instinctive need to beat the odds every time they climbed into the cockpit. But it had been a while since he'd felt the thrill of the chase this keenly. Even longer since he'd been shot down in flames.

Kate had all but waved a red flag in front of his face last night by insisting on their so-called agreement. Dave wouldn't break his word. He'd stick to the terms—as he interpreted them. He'd also do his damnedest to convince her to renegotiate their contract.

Dave wasn't quite sure how it had happened, but the challenge represented by Kate Hargrave was starting to rank right up there with that of Pegasus.

Four

The simulator crouched like a giant blue beetle on long, pneumatic legs. The capsule's front faced huge trifold screens. Once the ride began, the screens would show vivid, dizzying projections of earth and sky. Off to one side a control booth housed the simulator's team of operators, evaluators and observers.

Anticipation simmered in Dave's veins as he climbed the metal stairs to the capsule's entrance. This was his first time at the controls of a brand-new flying, fighting vehicle. He couldn't wait to see how it handled in this simulated environment.

A technician in white overalls with the cadre's distinctive red-and-blue patch prominently displayed waited for him on the platform.

"Ready to fly, Captain?"

"Ready as I'll ever be."

The technician grinned. "I've got a six-pack riding on you. Try not to crash and burn first time up."

"I'll do my best."

Ducking through the side hatch, Dave strapped himself into the operator's seat. Pegasus had been designed for one pilot. Driver. Captain. Whatever they called the individual in the front seat, he or she had to know how to switch from land to airborne to sea mode and operate safely in all three environments. No small feat for anyone, even the highly experienced crew assembled here in the desert.

The tech checked the parachute pack built into the seat, adjusted the shoulder straps on Dave's harness and conducted a final communications check. Just before he closed the door, he offered a final bit of advice.

"Your puke 'n' go bag is right next to your left knee. In case you need it."

"Got it."

The door clanged shut, leaving Dave alone in the simulator. He'd spent most of yesterday and a good portion of last night poring over a fat technical manual, reacquainting himself with instrumentation that was familiar, studying the dials and digital displays that weren't.

He dragged out the black notebook containing the various operational checklists, propped it in the slot designed to hold it and studied the layout of the instruments. The simulator cockpit replicated the actual vehicle exactly. The same defense contractor who'd designed and built the three Pegasus prototypes had constructed the simulator.

Unfortunately, two of the three prototypes had crashed and burned during the developmental phase. Only one had survived and been delivered to the military for operational testing. The contractor was scrambling to produce additional test vehicles, but until they were delivered Dave sure as hell had better not crash the one remaining.

For that reason, these hours in the simulator were absolutely vital. Dave had to get a feel for the craft, had to learn to handle it in all possible situations, before he actually took it into the air. He took a last look around and flipped open the black notebook to the sheet containing the start-up checklist.

"Okay, team. Let's roll."

Captain Westfall's voice came through the headset. "Good luck, Scott."

"Thanks, sir."

Suddenly, the tall screens surrounding the front of the capsule came to life. Instead of dull white, they showed a desert landscape of silver greens and browns. Jagged mountains dominated the horizon. A brilliant blue sky beckoned.

Dave's gloved hand hovered over the red power switch. He dragged in a deep breath, let it out.

"Pegasus One, initiating power."

"Roger, Pegasus One."

Flicking the switch to on, Dave listened to the familiar hum of auxiliary power units feeding juice to the on-board systems. Screens lit up. Switches glowed red and green and yellow.

His gaze went to the digital display showing an outline of Pegasus. The craft was in land mode, its wings back and turboprop engines tucked away. In this mode the vehicle could race across the desert and climb mountains. Much as Dave would love to take this baby out for a run, his job was to test its wings.

"Pegasus One switching to airborne mode."

"Roger, One."

His thumb hit the center button beside the display. Right before his eyes, the shape of the vehicle outlined on the screen altered. Wings fanned out. Propeller blades were released from their tucked position. Rear stabilizers unfolded.

"Hot damn!"

"Come again, Captain?" The simulator operator's voice floated through his headset. "We didn't copy that."

"Sorry. That wasn't meant for public consumption. Pegasus One, locking into hover position."

Like the tilt-wing Osprey currently in use by the military, Pegasus incorporated Very Short Takeoff and Landing technology. With the engines in a vertical position, the craft could lift and hover like a chopper. Dave had logged several hundred hours in the Osprey and was feeling more confident by the moment.

"Pegasus One, powering up."

The familiar whine of engines revving filled his ears. The pedals shuddered under his boots. He took the craft to simulated full power and lifted off. Once airborne, he tilted the engines to horizontal. Pegasus seemed to leap to life.

They gave him a good hour to get a feel for the controls and build his confidence before the first system malfunction occurred. It was minor, a glitch in the navigational transponder. Dave corrected by switching from direct-satellite signal to relay-station signal.

A few moments later, his Doppler radar picked up some weather. A thunderstorm, racing right toward him from the west. That was Kate Hargrave's doing, Dave thought with a smile. Unless he missed his guess, he was in for a rough ride.

Sure enough, the turbulence proved too big to go around and too high to get above. Within moments, thunder crashed in his headset and lightning forked across the wide screens surrounding the capsule. Violent winds set Pegasus bucking and kicking like a wild mustang. Dave needed both hands and feet to maintain control. The wild jolting caused another malfunction. A blinking red light signaled an oil leak in engine one.

His pucker factor rising, Dave shut down the engine and fought to keep the craft in the air while diagnosing the source of the leak. He'd just narrowed it down, when a bolt of lightning slashed across the screen. Bright blue light filled the cockpit. A loud alarm sounded at the same instant another red warning light began to flash.

Hell! Number two engine took a hit. The damned thing was on fire.

Gritting his teeth, Dave flipped to the engine fire checklist. He had to restart engine one before shutting down two, though, or he'd fall right out of the sky. He got the starboard engine powered back up again, killed the other and activated the fire-suppression system.

At that point, the situation went from bad to downright ugly. The damned fire-suppression system didn't work. If anything, the fire appeared to be burning hotter, and electrical systems were shutting down faster than small-town storefronts on a Saturday night.

Too late, Dave remembered the pylons securing the engines to the wing were made of a magnesium alloy. The alloy was strong, light and flexible—all highly desirable qualities in an aircraft. But when magnesium burned, it produced its own oxygen and thus created a fire that was totally self-sustaining.

Chances were this one would eat right through the wing and hit the fuel lines.

In any other aircraft, the pilot would bail out at this point. Dave was damned if he'd punch and lose the only Pegasus prototype left, even in a simulated situation. Sweating inside his flight suit, he tried every trick in the book and a few that had never been written down to save his craft. He was still fighting when his instrument panel went dead.

"Pegasus One, your flight is terminated."

Cursing under his breath, Dave slumped back in the seat and waited for his heart to stop jackhammering against his ribs. He glanced to his right, saw a grim-faced Captain Westfall standing behind the controller in the operator's booth. Kate was next to him, her hair a bright flame in the dimly lit booth. The other officers ringed her.

His mouth set into a hard, tight line, Dave keyed his mike. "Let's conduct the postflight critique. Then we'll try this little exercise again."

In the next two days Dave battled everything from wind shears and microbursts to turbulence that almost flipped over his craft and maintenance-generated crossed wires that caused his instruments to produce faulty readings.

On one flight, he lost cabin pressurization and discovered his oxygen mask wouldn't filter the carbon monoxide he exhaled. On another, an engine stuck halfway between the vertical and horizontal position. He almost crawled out of the simulator after that particular exercise. Both arms and legs ached from using brute physical strength to wrestle with the controls of the wildly gyrating vehicle.

As a result, he wasn't in the mood for another critique of his flying skills when he joined Kate for a run the morning after that particular experience.

She'd come to accept his company with resignation if not an abundance of enthusiasm. Impatient, she paced the dirt just outside his trailer. Her hair was caught up in a ponytail, her body encased in slick-looking hot pink. Dave's stiff movements as he exited his quarters had her quirking an auburn eyebrow.

"Sure you want to run this morning?"

"Yeah."

"Better not overdo it. That last ride was a bitch."

"I was there, remember?"

His curt tone arched her eyebrow another notch. "Suit yourself."

Propping her foot on a rock, she stretched her calf muscles. The sight of all that hot pink bending and curving didn't help Dave's mood. He'd spent the past couple of nights mentally reviewing each phase of every simulated flight. When his mind wasn't churning over the effects of wing icing and emergency high-altitude landings, his thoughts had a distinct tendency to veer off in a direction that left him in even more of a sweat.

He'd replayed the kiss he and Kate had shared a dozen or more times in his mind, kicking himself each time for wimping it. He'd promised her the next one would *not* be slow and easy, and he was ready to deliver on his promise. More than ready.

Cursing himself for agreeing to her hands-off on-site policy, Dave cut his stretching exercise short.

"You ready?"

"Ready."

Kate set off at an easy pace. She'd spent enough time in this man's company by now to gauge his temper. For three days he'd been battling a machine and everything the test cadre had thrown at him. He'd won most of the battles, more than anyone had expected him to. But the ones he'd lost stuck in his craw like a fish bone.

He needed an outlet for his frustration and Kate intended to give him one. Not the one he'd no doubt prefer, she thought with a twinge of real regret. No hard, fast tussle between the sheets, muscles straining, bodies writhing, skin damp with sweat. Gulping at the image that leaped into her head, she kicked up the pace.

Dave lengthened his stride and kept up with her. He didn't indulge in his usual teasing banter. To Kate's surprise, she found she missed the give-and-take. They jogged in silence a while longer before she dropped the casual challenge.

"There's the cactus we used as a finish line the other day," she said. "We talked about a rematch. You up for it?"

He shot her a quick, hard glance. "Are you?"

In answer she merely smiled and took off in a burst of speed.

"Dammit!"

His curse was followed by the sound of his pounding footsteps. Kate didn't hold back. Fists clenched, feet pumping, heart galloping, she poured everything she had into the all-for-nothing sprint.

Mere yards from the cactus she glanced over her shoulder and debated whether to slow her pace. Her goal was to make Dave work off some of his pent-up frustration, not add to it with another defeat. The issue became moot, though, when he laid on a final burst of speed. It was all Kate could do to stay elbow-to-elbow with him as they sailed past the spiky cactus.

Grinning, she slowed her pace. "Well, what do you know," she panted. "Another tie."

"Only because you cheated. Again."

His scowl was gone, replaced by an answering grin that snatched what little air Kate had managed to draw into her already stressed lungs.

"You won't get the drop on me again," he warned.

"Think so, huh? Wait till you climb back in the simulator this morning. You're not going to know what hit you."

His groan was loud and long, but minus the surly edge. "I've already been hit with lightning, hail, ice and sandstorms. What the heck have you got left in your bag of tricks to throw at me?"

She tossed her head, laughing. "Oh, cowboy, I'm just warming up."

"I'll remember this. Trust me, I'm going to remember every jolt and lurch and sickening, thousand-foot drop."

"Ha! Threats don't scare me."

"They should." His voice dropped to a mock growl. "You're gonna pay, babe."

The promise hovered between them for an endless moment before being lost to the steady plop of their running shoes against the dirt road.

Their race might have relieved some of Dave's frustration, but it didn't help the tension that crawled up Kate's neck as the rest of the day turned into a replay of the ones that had gone before.

They put the sky jock through hell. Time and time again. Using a dial-a-disaster approach, they'd start with a minor problem like an electrical failure, then pile on problem after problem until Dave reached the point of what was politely referred to as task saturation. With six or seven major malfunctions occurring at once, he had to scramble to keep the issues sorted out and Pegasus in the air.

By the third simulated run, Kate was sweating under her flight suit and strung tight with nerves. This run would be the worst, she knew. It was an overland flight in winter weather conditions. Partway into the flight, Dave would encounter a phenomenon few pilots had ever dealt with. Swallowing, Kate glanced at the digital clock on the controller's console. Seven minutes until all hell broke loose.

Fists balled, she kept her eyes glued to the wide screens surrounding the capsule. The Alps rose in majestic splendor. Their snowcapped peaks speared into a dazzlingly blue sky. Dave was piloting his craft through a narrow valley. All systems were fully functioning.

Kate tore her gaze from the screens and watched the clock. Three minutes. Two.

She closed her eyes. Envisioned the cold, dense air mass sliding down the mountain. Picking up speed as gravity took over. Sweeping up snow. Gathering force and fury.

"What the...!"

Suddenly Dave was fighting for control in total whiteout conditions. The katabatic wind—the strongest on the planet save for tornadoes—had hit his craft with the force of a free-falling bulldozer. In the Antarctic, these dense, cold down drafts had been clocked at speeds in excess of two hundred miles per hour. In the Alps they came with the mistral, which tore down the Rhone valley through southern France and out into the Mediterranean.

Kate had intensified this particular mistral beyond what might reasonably be expected, given the simulated time of year and temperature. Now she watched with her heart in her throat as the display screens in the control booth showed a snow-blinded, out-of-control Pegasus flying straight at a towering peak.

Pull up! The silent prayer intensified to a near shriek inside her head. *Pull up!*

For a heart-stopping moment, she thought he'd make it. He yanked on the stick, got the craft's nose up, almost—*almost!*—maneuvered around the towering wall of snow and rock.

A second later, the displays went flat. The controller blew out a long, ragged breath and keyed his mike.

"Pegasus One, your flight is terminated."

A stark silence descended over the control booth. Russ McIver finally broke it. "That's twice Scott has augered in now."

His eyes flinty, Captain Westfall nodded. "I'm aware of that, Major."

"I don't think we can blame this one on pilot error or unfamiliarity with the systems," Kate said carefully. "I may have made the weather conditions too extreme for this scenario."

Russ set his jaw. "Extreme or not, if this had been

a real mission we'd be calling for body bags right now.''

As frustrated as everyone else in the booth, Cari Dunn dragged off her ball cap and raked a hand through her hair. ''Why don't you wait for the debrief before you start burying the dead, McIver.''

The marine stiffened up. ''Are you addressing me, *Lieutenant?*''

''Yes, *Major,*'' she snapped. ''I am.''

Dave's voice came over the intercom, cutting through the tension with the precision of a blade.

''Russ is right. I blew it. Let's run this one again.''

Captain Westfall leaned into the mike. ''You've been at this twelve solid hours. Why don't you take a break and we'll run it tomorrow.''

''I'm okay, sir. I'll take another stab at it. What the hell hit me, anyway?''

All eyes in the booth turned to Kate. She stepped up to the mike.

''It's called a katabatic wind, after the Greek word *kata,* meaning downward. It forms when a cold, dense mass of air slides down a mountainside, picks up speed and plunges to the valley below. This type of wind occurs everywhere on the planet but, uh, not usually with this much force.''

She half expected him to mutter an angry curse. Kate knew she wouldn't be feeling too friendly if someone had just put her through that particular experience. To her surprise, a chuckle floated across the speakers.

"Don't forget, Hargrave. I'm keeping score. Every lurch. Every jolt. Every damned kata-whatever. Okay, team, let's power this baby up and see if I can get Pegasus to ride on the wind this time."

Five

The officers didn't gather at the picnic tables that night. Or the next. Dave kept them at the simulator, conducting run after run, analyzing the system failures, admitting his own with brutal honesty.

By Friday the entire test cadre was worn to the bone, but both Dave and Pegasus had proved their stuff. In simulated environments, anyway. The real test would come with the first actual flight on Monday morning.

Dave had planned to spend the weekend prepping for the flight, but Captain Westfall gathered his officers and senior civilians early Saturday to declare a stand-down.

"I received a request from the Joint Chiefs for a briefing on our progress to date. I'm flying to Washington this morning and will return Sunday evening. We'll resume test operations on Monday."

His glance roamed from one to another of his senior officers and civilians. The strain of the past weeks showed clearly in their faces.

"Use this downtime to give your troops a break. You folks take one, too. I want everyone rested, relaxed and ready to launch Pegasus into the sky by oh-seven-hundred Monday morning."

He didn't get any arguments. Dave noted how Doc Richardson's glance skipped immediately to Jill Bradshaw. The blonde kept her expression deliberately neutral, but a slight flush rose in her cheeks. Dave would bet his last buck those two would have headed for the nearest motel as soon as this meeting broke up if not for the fact that Richardson stood next in order of rank.

"Commander Richardson has the stick until I return," Westfall said, confirming the doc's seniority. "He'll have to remain on-site during my absence, but the rest of you are free to take off."

"I haven't been off-site since I arrived," Russ McIver commented as the small group walked out into the bright morning sunlight. "I'll have to figure out what to do with myself."

"How about we hit the links?" Dave suggested.

"I've got my golf clubs stashed in my truck. I hear Fort Bliss has a great course."

"Sorry, never had time to learn the game."

Cari couldn't resist. "Too busy polishing your combat boots?"

Mac's eyes narrowed. "My boots aren't the only articles that need polishing around here, Lieutenant. Your attitude could use a little work."

"Is that right?" The Coast Guard officer smiled politely. "Are you going to put me in a brace and work on my military manners?"

The marine gave her a long, considering look. "If I put you in a brace," he said finally, "your manners wouldn't be all we worked on."

Cari's smile slipped. Before she could decide just how to respond, Mac tipped two fingers in a casual salute and strode off. Frowning, the brunette watched him disappear around a corner before she spun on her heel and headed in the opposite direction.

"Well," Kate murmured when the dust settled. "That was interesting."

"Very," Jill Bradshaw agreed. The cop slanted a glance at Cody Richardson, and Dave guessed it wouldn't be long before the two of them disappeared as well. The doc couldn't leave the site, but this was a *big* site, with lots of long, empty stretches of road.

Dave guessed right. Not ten seconds later Jill said she needed to run a perimeter check and Cody volunteered to run it with her. That left Kate, who surprised Dave by falling in with his original suggestion.

"I've knocked around a few white balls in my time. I wouldn't mind getting off-site for a few hours to find out if I've still got my swing."

She still had it. It was right there, in every long-legged stride. Dave could vouch for that.

"What kind of handicap do you carry?" he asked, wondering if she was as good at golf as she seemed to be at everything else.

"Seven."

Well, that answered that.

"What's yours?"

"Twelve."

Her mouth curved in a smug smile. "Looks like I'll have to give you some strokes, cowboy."

With a silent groan, Dave passed on that one.

"Of course," she continued, her competitive batteries already charging, "we'll have to adjust for the fact that you'll be using your own clubs and I'll have to make do with rentals."

"Of course."

"And I'll be in sneakers instead of golf shoes."

"Mine are soft spiked," Dave protested.

"Doesn't matter. They still give you a better grip on the turf."

"All right, already. We'll negotiate the handicaps when we get there. I'll pick you up in twenty minutes."

Thinking that this week from hell just might end a whole lot more enjoyably than he would have imagined a few hours ago, Dave peeled off and headed for his trailer to change out of his uniform and into civvies.

Kate couldn't believe the weight that rolled off her shoulders as Dave's battered pickup passed through the perimeter checkpoint. She loved working on the Pegasus project, was thrilled to have been chosen as the NOAA rep. Still, she hadn't realized how the weeks of excitement and pressure had accumulated until the pickup hit the county road. With that transition from packed dirt to pavement, she felt as though she was reentering the world.

Sighing, Kate slouched down in her seat. Desert landscape rolled by outside the pickup. Inside, the lively strains of Trisha Yearwood's latest hit rolled from the radio.

"Captain Westfall was right," she commented as the song ended. "We needed to stand down and give folks a break. I can't believe how good it feels to get off-site for a few hours."

Dave nodded, but didn't comment. As the newest member of the group, Kate supposed he could hardly complain about the stress. Not that the entire cadre hadn't done their best to pile it on him this week.

If all those hours in the simulator had gotten to him, it didn't show in his face or lazy slouch. Like

Kate, he'd changed into comfortable slacks and a knit shirt. The short-sleeved shirt was collared, as required by many golf courses, and looked as though Ralph Lauren had designed it with him in mind. The cobalt color deepened the blue of his eyes and contrasted vividly with his tanned skin and tawny hair. Kate was still secretly admiring the way the knit stretched across his muscled shoulders when they passed through the small town of Chorro.

A few miles beyond the town, Dave pulled up at an intersection. The two-lane county road they were traveling wound through the desert. To the west, it led to Las Cruces. To the east, to El Paso and the army post at Fort Bliss. The road intersecting it ran north toward Alamogordo and south to God knew where in Mexico.

Dave hooked his wrists over the steering wheel and angled Kate a considering glance. She couldn't tell what he was thinking, but it was clear he had some change of plan in mind.

"Why the stop?" she asked.

"I'm thinking we might extend this excursion for more than a few hours."

"Extend it how?"

"I hear there's a great course up by Ruidoso, at the Inn of the Mountain Gods. The fairways wind through the mountains and the tee boxes are at some of the highest elevation in the country. You hit a golf ball at seven thousand feet," he offered as added inducement, "and it'll fly almost to the next county."

"You take a swing at seven thousand feet," Kate retorted, "and it's all you can do to suck in enough air for another."

Rueful laughter filled his eyes. "I've been sucking in a whole *bunch* of air this week. I can manage more than one swing if you can."

It was the laughter that snagged her, not the challenge. Kate had had a front-row seat this past week. She'd witnessed Dave's frustration, watched him push himself twice as hard as the team had pushed him. The fact that he could laugh at his failures—and had yet to brag about his successes—went a long way to altering her initial perception of him as just another hotshot sky jock.

She glanced at the narrow road winding toward the distant mountains. "Isn't Ruidoso a good hundred miles from here?"

"More or less."

"It'll take us all day to drive up there and squeeze in eighteen holes. We'll be driving back through the mountains at night."

"Unless we decide to stay over."

"Stay over? I didn't bring so much as a toothbrush with me. I don't usually need one to play golf," she tacked on with a touch of sarcasm.

"Ever hear of drugstores?"

Kate started to enumerate all the reasons why spinning a simple round of golf into a weekend expedition wasn't a good idea. Number one on her list was the fact that their agreement to focus strictly on Pegasus applied while on-site. How they handled matters off-site had yet to be negotiated.

To her disgust, Kate found that also topped her list of reasons to head for Ruidoso. She wasn't stupid or into self-denial. This man turned her on. She thought she'd been inoculated against handsome charmers like Dave Scott. Obviously, the inoculation had worn off.

He'd shown what he was made of this week. Maybe she should see what he was like away from their work environment. Discover if there was more to the man than that sexy body and his awesome skills as an aviator.

"Why don't we play this by ear?" she suggested. "See how long it takes to get there. And how we feel after eighteen holes."

"Sounds like a plan to me. Let me call and make sure we can get on the course this afternoon."

A quick call to information on his cell phone produced the number for the Inn of the Mountain Gods. The gods must have been smiling, because Dave managed to snag a 1:20 tee time that someone had just canceled. With a satisfied smile, he pocketed his cell phone, hooked an elbow on the window frame and aimed his pickup north.

* * *

Kate fell instantly in love with Ruidoso.

A onetime hideout of Billy the Kid, the old mining town was nestled high in the Sierra Blanca Mountains and surrounded by the Lincoln National Forest. Ski resorts, casinos, a racetrack, art galleries, boutiques and the many nearby lakes gave evidence that Ruidoso offered year-round fun for all ages and tastes.

Kate could envision the town blanketed in fresh white powder. Imagine it in summer, swarming with tourists eager to escape the blistering heat at lower elevations. Almost see the profusion of wildflowers that must carpet the high meadows in spring.

But she was sure fall *had* to be the most perfect time to visit. Tall green pines and blue spruce spilled down the slopes surrounding the town, interspersed with stands of oak, maple and aspen that added breathtaking splashes of color. Kate's delighted gaze drank in flaming reds, shimmering golds, impossibly bright oranges.

"Oh, boy. I hope this golf course of yours has scenery like this!"

It did. Owned and operated by the Mescalero Apaches, the resort was located on their reservation some miles out of Ruidoso. Mountains blazing with color surrounded the brand-new hotel and casino. Shimmering lake waters lapped at pebbled shores and reflected both the resort and the mountain peaks. The

golf course, Kate saw as Dave parked in the lot behind a clubhouse constructed of pine and soaring
glass, wasn't for the faint of heart.

The first hole—the very first!—required a clean
shot over a stretch of clear blue lake to a small island.
The second shot had to carry over water again to a
raised green. Low bridges constructed of pine linked
the island to shore and allowed access by cart.

"Forget handicaps!" Kate exclaimed. "We'll be
lucky if we don't lose all our balls on the first hole."

Grinning, Dave hefted his bag. "Oh, no! You're
not going to wiggle out of giving me strokes. I'm not
handing you any advantage this time, Commander."

With another look at that killer first hole, Kate
headed for the pro shop. Dave propped his bag on
the rack by the door and followed her inside. His
clubs, Kate noted, were well used and the finest that
money could buy. Evidently the man took his golf as
seriously as he did his flying.

The pro fixed her up with a decent rental set and
they just had time to grab a lunch of Indian tacos
washed down with ice-cold beer. Then Kate dragged
a visor down low on her forehead to block the glare
off the lake and teed up. After a few practice swings
with a four iron, she sent her ball sailing across the
water. It landed smack in the center of the small
green island.

Dave gave a low whistle. "Nice shot."

"Thanks."

She couldn't help sashaying a bit as she strolled to the back of the tee box to help track his ball in flight. Not that it needed tracking. The little white sphere soared in a high, sweet arc and plopped down not two feet from hers.

When he turned to her with a smug grin, Kate knew the battle was on.

The war raged for seventeen holes.

Grudgingly, Kate gave him the strokes he demanded to even their games. She also voiced strong doubts about the twelve he supposedly carried as a handicap. Dave ignored her grousing and whacked ball after ball through the thin mountain air.

Kate had to pull out all the stops to stay even on the front nine, and led by two strokes as they approached number seventeen. It was a par three, only about a hundred and twenty yards from tee to green. In between was a sheer drop of a thousand feet or more!

Of course, she shanked her ball and lost it in the dense undergrowth at the bottom of the gully. That cost her two strokes, putting them even for number eighteen. They both made the green in regulation and the game boiled down to the final putt.

Dave was closer to the pin, so Kate putted first. It took her two tries to sink her ball. Not bad, considering how far out she'd been, but she held her breath while Dave lined up his shot. If he made this putt, he'd win.

He stroked the ball gently. His putter made its distinctive little *ping*. The ball rolled right for the cup—and stopped an inch short. Shaking his head, he walked up and dropped it in. His eyes held a glint of pure devilry when he retrieved his ball.

"How do you like that? Another tie."

Kate eyed him suspiciously. "Did you short that putt on purpose?"

"What do you think?"

It was the same answer he'd given her the first time they raced, and she didn't like it any better this time than she had then.

"Get this straight, Scott. When I play, I play to win."

He tossed his ball a few times, catching it in his palm. "Could be we're just well matched."

Belatedly, she remembered her ex had given him an earful. "And it could be," she said carefully, fighting the memory of old hurts and recriminations, "you think I'll get all bent out of shape if I lose."

"Win or lose, Hargrave, you couldn't get bent out of shape if you tried."

"I'm serious about this. I don't like the idea you're toying with me."

His fist closed around the ball. He fingered the dimples for a few moments before answering. "I like

to win as much as you do. What I don't like is when
healthy competition turns mean.''

Kate stiffened. ''As I'm sure my former husband
told you happened in our marriage.''

''He implied something of the sort,'' Dave admitted with a shrug, ''but I wasn't thinking of your marriage when I said that.''

''Whose were you thinking of, then?''

''My brother's.'' His forehead creasing, Dave
frowned at the ball still clutched in his hand. ''My
sister-in-law is on his case all the time. About money.
About the kids. Who's doing a better job with both.
Ryan takes it, but it's eating him alive.''

''Why doesn't he walk?''

His gaze lifted and locked with hers. ''He says he
loves her.''

''Funny thing about love.'' Kate managed to swallow the lump that suddenly formed in her throat.
''Sometimes it just plain hurts.''

''Well, I can't say I'm an expert on the subject,
but I'll tell you this. I wouldn't walk, either, if I loved
a woman as much as Ryan loves Jaci.''

''What would you do?''

''Find some way to call it a draw, I suppose.''

''Like this round of golf?''

His grin slipped out, quick and slashing. ''Like this
round of golf.''

Kate wasn't sure, but she thought her heart did a
funny little flip-flop at that point. How the heck could

the man look so damned sexy with his cheeks singed red from the sun and his hair matted down from the ball cap he'd tugged on halfway through the game? Dragging her gaze from the tawny gold, she forced herself to concentrate as Dave offered a suggestion.

"Why don't we officially declare this game a tie and duke it out with another round tomorrow? If we arrange an early tee time, we can still make it back to the base by evening."

She breathed in the cool, clean air. Swept a glance at the riot of colors spilling down the mountain slopes. Brought her gaze back to the man who, despite her best efforts to hold him off, had somehow breached her barriers.

"You're on."

Dave had figured she couldn't resist the challenge. Hiding a smile, he dropped his putter back in his bag and waited for her to settle in the golf cart beside him.

His conscience didn't so much as ping at him for dangling the bait of another match. Golf was the last thing on his mind at this point. That was occupied with schemes to finesse Lieutenant Commander Kate Hargrave into bed.

Tonight. Right after dinner. Or before, if he could manage it.

God, he wanted her! Their morning runs had been enough to tie him in knots. Kate Hargrave in stretchy tights could tie *any* man in knots. Yet working with her this past week had added an entirely different dimension to his craving.

Dave had dated his share of beautiful women. He'd also worked alongside a good number of smart, dedicated ones. But Kate's particular combination of gorgeous and intelligent and dedicated was fast pushing the memory of all other females right out of his head.

He was still trying to lay out his game plan for the rest of the evening when they entered the two-story lobby of the resort. The pride the Mescalero Apaches took in their heritage showed in the soaring pine beams, the massive circular stone fireplace and the artistry of the woven rugs and baskets decorating the walls.

If the woman at the front desk took note of the fact that neither Kate nor Dave carried any luggage, she was too well-trained to show it. Her black eyes warm, she greeted them courteously.

"Welcome to the Inn of the Mountain Gods. May I help you?"

Dave returned her friendly smile. "We don't have a reservation, but would like to stay tonight. Do you have any vacancies?"

"Yes, sir, we do." Her fingers flew over a keyboard. "I can offer you a choice of views. Rooms with lake views are a little higher priced than those that look toward the mountains, but you'll consider the extra twenty dollars well worth the cost when you see the sunset.''

"A lake view it is then.''

"Will that be one room or two?''

Dave turned to Kate. She chewed on her lower lip, and he decided he wouldn't rush her. Not until after supper. He turned back to the clerk, intending to inform her they'd need two rooms, when Kate preempted him.

"One room, please.''

Just in time, Dave choked back his words.

"Yes, ma'am,'' the clerk replied, unaware the earth had just rocked under his feet. "Would you prefer smoking or nonsmoking?''

"Nonsmoking.''

"Two queen beds or one king?''

Dave sent a swift, silent prayer to the mountain gods.

They answered his prayer. Or rather, Kate did. With a small, private smile, she said the magic words.

"One king.''

Short moments later, they headed for the elevator. Dave's blood was already drumming in his veins, but he had Kate wait for him at the elevators while he made a quick detour to the gift shop. He returned with a small paper sack bearing the inn's distinctive logo. Grinning, he responded to her look of inquiry.

"You said you needed a toothbrush.''

He'd purchased one for himself, too. Along with a box of condoms. With luck, stamina and a little ingenuity, he and Kate would run through the entire dozen before they had to return to the site tomorrow.

Six

Dave put both his ingenuity and his stamina to the test the moment the door to their minisuite thudded shut. He got a brief glimpse through the floor-to-ceiling windows of the still, silver lake and the neon eagle soaring above the casino. Ignoring both, he tossed the paper sack on a chair and snagged Kate's wrist.

A single tug spun her around. One step and he had her backed against the wall. Her head came up. Surprise flitted across her face.

"I warned you," Dave reminded her gruffly. "After our last kiss. No 'nice' this time."

Laughter leaped into her green eyes. "That still stings, does it?"

"Like you wouldn't believe."

"Seems I recall another part of the conversation. Didn't I say I'd give the signal when I was ready for you to conduct another test?"

"You already gave the signal. Downstairs. When you opted for one king."

"You're right. I did. Okay, flyboy, you have my permission to rev up to full throttle."

He was already there, Kate discovered when she slid her hands up his chest to his shoulders. The hard, roped muscles under her palms thrilled her. The rock-solid wall of his body against hers sent an arrow of pure sensation straight to her belly.

And when his mouth covered hers, Kate knew instantly nice was the last thing she wanted. She craved this heat, needed this hunger. The raw sensuality of her emotions stripped away any need for pretense. Every bit as greedy as Dave, Kate locked her arms around his neck and arched her body into his.

She was lost in his kiss, feeling its punch in every corner of her body, when he dragged his head up. Red singed his cheekbones. His breath came fast and hard. She thought he was going to gentle his touch, slow things down, and had to swallow a groan.

She thought wrong. With a skill that had to have come from plenty of experience, he tugged her knit shirt over her head, popped the snap on her slacks and stripped her down to her bra and panties. To

Kate's intense satisfaction, though, he was the one who groaned.

"Oh, baby." A callused palm shaped her breast, cradling its weight and fullness. "You couldn't count the hours I've spent imagining this moment."

She pretended to give the matter serious thought. Not an easy task with his thumb creating a delicious friction as it grazed over her nylon-covered nipple.

"Let's see. You've been on-site all of six days. Spent at least ten hours a day in the simulator, another five to six poring over tech manuals. If we subtract two for eating and six for sleeping, that doesn't leave much time for— Oh!"

She broke off, gulping, as he bent and replaced his hand with his mouth. His breath came hot and damp through the thin fabric of her bra, his tongue felt raspy on her now-engorged nipple. Her gulp turned to a swift, indrawn hiss when his teeth took over from his tongue.

"That left," he growled between nibbles, "plenty of time. To imagine this. And this."

Keeping one arm wrapped tight around her waist, he planed his other hand down the curve of her belly. His palm was hot against her skin, his fingers sure and strong when they cupped her mound. Within moments, Kate was a puddle of want.

She wasn't the kind to take and not give, though. Somehow, she managed to find the strength to put a few inches between them and drag his shirt free of his jeans.

"My turn, cowboy."

Dave ducked his head, more than willing to let her take the reins. His entire body ached with wanting her and he wasn't sure he could stand straight for much longer, but the glide of Kate's hands and mouth and tongue over his skin was worth the agony.

When she unsnapped his jeans and slid her palm inside, though, he came too damned close to losing it to remain standing. Scooping her into his arms, he headed for the bedroom. The sand-colored walls, prints of Apaches mounted on tough little mustangs, and incredible vista of lake and mountains alive with color imprinted on a small corner of his mind. A *very* small corner! The rest was filled with Kate. Gorgeous, sensuous, Kissable Kate.

She stretched like a cat on the luxurious down comforter. Her smooth, sexy curves made Dave's throat go tight. While he peeled off the rest of his clothes, she wiggled out of her bra and panties. Her glance measured his length, smiling at first, then with a greedy hunger that fed Dave's own. Rock hard and aching, he joined her on the bed and gathered her under him. His knee had wedged between hers before he remembered the damned sack.

"Hell!" He rolled off the bed in one lithe movement. "I'll be right back. Don't move."

Yeah, right! Kate thought wryly. As if she could!

Her heart hammered so hard against her chest she could hardly breathe, and everything from her waist down felt hot and liquid. She had a moment, only a moment, to wonder if she was crazy for tumbling into bed with a man who'd told her straight out he wasn't interested in any long-term relationships, before Dave was back with a full box of condoms. Kate's doubts disappeared on a gurgle of laughter.

"You don't really think we're going to need all those, do you?"

"A guy can only hope."

Opening the box, he dumped the contents on the bedside table. She was still chuckling when he rejoined her in bed. She welcomed him into her arms eagerly, hungrily, and into her body with a gasp of sheer delight.

Kate wasn't prepared for the intensity of the fire he stoked within her. He used his teeth and tongue and hard, driving body with a skill that soon had her writhing. The sensations piled one on top of each other, tight, hot, swirling. They came so fast and hard, Kate groaned out a warning.

"Dave! I can't...hold on!"

"So don't."

He flexed his thighs. His muscles in his back and butt went tight under her frantic fingers. Gasping, Kate tried to contain the wild sensations.

"I don't...want it to end...yet."

He lifted his head. His blue eyes held a wicked

glint. "Oh, sweetheart, it's just beginning. I swore I'd pay you back for every jolt and sickening drop you put me through, remember? This is just payback number one."

He flexed again, the sensations exploded, and Kate lurched almost out of her skin.

After that first frenetic coupling and several more not quite as fast but just as furious, they came up for air long enough to order a late dinner from room service.

Dave hit the showers while waiting for the delivery. Kate took her turn next and made good use of the toothbrush he'd purchased for her. Luckily, she had a comb in her purse to drag through her tangled hair. Wrapped in one of the inn's luxurious terry-cloth robes, she joined Dave at the table beside the tall windows for a feast of crusty bread, crisp salad and mountain trout crusted with piñon nuts. A million stars glittered in the black-velvet sky outside, but Kate's mind wasn't on the spectacular nightscape. It was focused completely on the man across the table.

"Tell me more about your family," she asked him between bites. "Do you have any sisters or brothers besides the one you told me about?"

"Nope. There's just Ryan and me. Our folks died some years ago. How about you?"

"Both parents and three grandparents alive and well, along with three brothers, one sister."

"Are they all as good at what they do as you are?"

"Better," she said with a smile, thinking of all the support and encouragement her large, gregarious family gave each other. "My grandmother breeds and shows champion collies. My sister Dawn won a bronze in the Pan-American Games as a marathon runner and now coordinates the Special Olympics for a five-state region. One of my brothers is a fireman, another is on the pro tennis circuit. Josh, the baby of the family, is still in college. On a golf scholarship, I might add. I haven't beat him since his junior-high days, the stinker."

"So that's where you get it."

"Get what?"

"That mile-wide competitive streak. It's in your genes."

"Yes, it is."

She hesitated, reluctant to admit even now how much her inbred competitive spirit had played in the demise of her marriage.

"I tried to change," she confessed after a moment. "John—my former husband—interpreted my ambition and desire to excel as some sort of challenge to his masculinity. But the more I tried to hold back and suppress my natural instincts, the more I began to resent him for *wanting* me to hold back. There were other factors involved, of course."

Like a nineteen-year-old blonde, Kate thought sardonically.

"But the bottom line was he just didn't like being beat," Dave finished for her.

"That's about it." Kate laid down her fork. "Neither do you, or so you say. Yet every contest we've had so far has ended in a tie. Was that by chance or design?"

"You want the truth?"

"I asked, didn't I?"

"When we raced that first morning, I held back a little. *Only* because I was worried about your ankle," he added when Kate bristled. "I just about bust a gut trying to catch up to you the second time we raced."

That made her feel a little better.

"What about the putt you missed today?"

His mouth curved. "You didn't hear the four-letter words bouncing around inside my head after that stroke."

She tapped her fork against her plate, wanting to believe him. After her experience with John, she *needed* to believe him. There was no way she could change her basic personality and it was becoming increasingly important Dave know that right up front.

She was pushing a last, slippery little piñon seed around her plate when it occurred to her Dave couldn't change his basic personality, either. With a suddenly sinking feeling, she remembered her conversation with the weather officer at Luke.

"What about that?" she asked him, waving her fork at the rumpled bed. "How much of what just happened here is a game to you? One with tactical and strategic moves?''

"Oh, babe! All of it.''

Grinning, he pushed out of his chair and came around the table. A tug on the knotted tie of her robe brought Kate to her feet.

"I started scheming ways to finesse you into bed three and a half seconds after I spotted that turquoise spandex coming at me out of the dawn.''

"Why am I not surprised?'' Kate drawled.

"You shouldn't be.'' Unrepentant, he dropped a kiss in the warm V between her neck and shoulder. "You, Lieutenant Commander Hargrave, are eminently finessable.''

"Is that supposed to be a compliment?''

"Of the highest order,'' Dave assured her solemnly, his fingers busy with the knot at her waist. The ties gave, and he slid his hands inside the folds to stroke the long, smooth curve from ribs to hips.

"Now, about dessert...''

"Yes?''

"I was thinking of something hot and sweet.''

Very hot and very sweet, he thought, his gut tightening as he slid his hand to the fiery curls at the juncture of her thighs. Slowly, he went down on one knee.

Kate woke to dazzling sunlight and the sound of running water. She rolled onto her side and watched

Dave slide a plastic razor through the lather covering his cheeks with sure, clean strokes.

He must have taken another shower. The tawny gold of his hair was still damp and water drops glistened on his bare back above the waistband of his jeans. Kate swallowed a sigh as her glance lingered on his perfect symmetry. Broad, muscled shoulders. A nice lean waist. That tight butt.

No doubt about it. The man was beautiful.

He was also, she reminded herself, taking a new vehicle into the sky for the first time tomorrow. A shadow seemed to cloud the sun as she thought about the two Pegasus prototypes that had crashed and burned. The pilot had been killed in the first one. The crew had survived the second, but sustained severe burns.

Kate had lost friends and associates to the vicious weather they routinely flew into. In her line of business, the risks were as great as the rewards. Yet the thought of Dave battling a violent wind shear or an engine stuck in half-tilt position made her feel sick.

She managed a smile, though, when he caught her watching in the mirror. You didn't talk about the odds. You just lived with them. Toweling his face, he strolled into the bedroom.

"We slept right through our tee time this morning."

"Did we?"

Kate couldn't get excited about missing a rematch

on the links. She'd stretched every muscle and tendon in her body last night, and then some. In fact, she wasn't sure she had enough strength to make it to the bathroom.

"We did," he confirmed, hitching a hip onto the side of the bed. "We also missed breakfast and lunch."

"Lunch?" Struggling up, Kate pushed the hair from her eyes. "What time is it?"

"Almost one."

"One?" she echoed incredulously. "As in p.m.?"

"As in p.m."

"Good grief!"

"Not to worry. I called down and arranged a late check-out." He waggled his eyebrows in an exaggerated leer. "So what do you want to do until two?"

"Well…"

By the time they finally abandoned their room and grabbed a late lunch in the hotel's dining room, it was after three. Yet Dave didn't seem any more anxious to end their stolen hours of freedom than Kate.

She'd checked in with her roommates by cell phone. Twice. Jill had already pinpointed their location via the tracking devices embedded in the IDs issued to both Kate and Dave, so there wasn't any use trying to deny they'd spent the night together. Promising to fill her and Caroline in later, Kate confirmed Captain Westfall hadn't returned from D.C. yet and hung up.

With no briefings or meetings pulling at them, she and Dave decided to take the slow way back to the site. From Ruidoso they headed south toward Cloudcroft. En route, the road meandered through the high mountain ridges and produced spectacular color at every turn. To Kate's delight, it also produced a turn-off for Sunspot.

"Who or what is Sunspot?" Dave asked.

"It's the home of the National Solar Observatory. *The* premier research facility for solar phenomena in the country. I've been wanting to visit for years."

She took a quick look at her watch, another at the mile indicator on the signpost, and calculated they could squeeze in a quick visit.

"Think they're open this late on a Sunday afternoon?"

"Not to the general public, maybe. But I've done some work with the observatory's director. If I drop his name a few times, maybe they'll let us poke around."

The sixteen-mile drive up to the observatory took a half hour and climbed over four thousand feet. Considering they were already at five thousand, Kate felt as though they'd reached the top of the world when they arrived at the cluster of buildings that constituted Sunspot, New Mexico. There was no restaurant, no grocery store, no services of any kind, so she could only hope the pickup had enough gas in it to get them back down the winding twists and turns.

What Sunspot did have, though, was a searingly blue New Mexico sky known for its clarity and transparency. For this reason, the U.S. Air Force had asked Harvard University to design a geophysics center on the site back in 1948 to observe solar activity. They started with a six-inch telescope housed in a metal grain bin ordered from Sears Roebuck. The site had since developed into a complex that included two forty-centimeter coronagraphs, high-tech spectrographs to measure light wavelengths and the Richard B. Dunn Solar Telescope—an instrument that was thirty stories tall and weighed some two hundred and fifty tons.

Kate couldn't wait to see it. Being able to show Dave some of her world was an added excitement.

"Park there by the gate," she instructed. "Let's go name-drop."

As it turned out, the only name Kate had to drop was her own. The director wasn't available, but his deputy happened to be on-site and came personally to escort her. Fence-pole thin and tanned to leather by the high altitude and thin air, the scientist pumped her hand.

"Dr. Hargrave! I'm Stu Petrie. This is an unexpected pleasure. I read your paper on the effects of ionization on water droplets spun up into the atmosphere by hurricane-force winds. *Most* impressive."

"Thank you. This is Captain Dave Scott, United States Air Force."

The deputy greeted Dave with a polite nod, but it was clear his interest was in Kate. So was Dave's, for that matter.

"Are you here on business? I didn't see a request from NOAA to use the facilities, but maybe it hasn't reached my desk yet. Sometimes the paperwork takes weeks to process."

"No, this is strictly spur of the moment. Dave and I were driving down from Ruidoso and saw the sign for the observatory. I couldn't resist taking a quick peek."

"We can do better than a peek. Please, let me give you a guided tour."

Dave's travels had afforded him the opportunity to view a good number of the world's marvels, both ancient and modern. The Dunn Telescope certainly qualified as the latter. The telescope's upper portion was housed in a tall, white tower that rose some thirteen stories into the air. The lower portion lay underground. The entire instrument was suspended from the top of the tower by a mercury-float bearing. The bearing in turn hung by three bolts, each only a couple of inches in diameter. Thinking about those nine meager inches didn't make Dave feel exactly comfortable when he followed the two scientists out onto the observing platform.

"The telescope is set to look at the quiet side of

the sun right now," Petrie said apologetically as Kate peered through its viewer. Dave took a turn and saw a dull gray ball.

"We use a monochrome camera to record the video image," Petrie explained. "This one is being taken in hydrogen alpha light, at about sixty-five hundred angstroms."

"Right."

Thankfully, Kate drew the scientist's attention with a comment. "You must use an electronic CCD to record the color images captured by your spectrographs."

"We do. With the Echelle Spectrograph we can measure two or more wavelengths simultaneously, even if they're far apart on the spectrum. We can also conduct near-ultraviolet and near-infrared observations."

Like most pilots, Dave had studied enough astrophysics to follow the conversation for the first few minutes. He knew near-ultraviolet and near-infrared light were just outside the visible range. After that, the two scientists left him in a cloud of dust.

He trailed along behind them, as fascinated by Kate's excitement and animated gestures as by her seemingly inexhaustible knowledge. She wasn't wearing a trace of makeup. She'd caught her hair back with a rubber band she'd snagged from the reservations clerk on the way out. Her knit shirt showed more than a few wrinkles from lying where Dave had tossed it the night before. She looked nothing like the spit-and-polish officer he'd worked with at the site. Even less like the runner in tight spandex.

Strange. Dave wouldn't have imagined she could replace either image in his mind, but her lively questions and the impatient way she tucked a loose strand behind her ear gave him a kick to the gut. Not as big a kick as Kate all naked and flushed from his love-making, of course. But close.

Busy studying her profile, Dave missed the comment that drew her auburn eyebrows into a quick, slashing frown.

"How much activity?" she asked Petrie.

They were talking about sunspots, Dave realized after a moment. The real thing, not the town. Evidently the folks at the observatory had recorded a buildup of energy in the sun's magnetic fields.

"There's definitely potential for eruptive phenomena."

That sounded serious enough for Dave to display his ignorance. "What's going to erupt where?"

Stu Petrie gave him the high school version. "Sunspots occur when the magnetic fields on the sun start to twist and turn. This movement generates tremendous energy, which is often released in a sudden solar flare."

"How much energy are we talking about?"

"Roughly the equivalent of a million hundred-megaton hydrogen bombs all exploding at once. The radiation is emitted across virtually the entire electro-magnetic spectrum, from radio waves at the long-wavelength end to optical omissions to X ray and gamma rays at the short-wavelength end. Given their tremendous speed, these waves can reach the earth in as little as eight minutes after a major flare and produce some very spectacular results.''

"Like the lights of the aurora borealis," Dave finished, feeling somewhat redeemed. Maybe he hadn't forgotten everything he'd learned about astrophysics after all.

"Solar flares can cause more than just lights in the sky," Kate put in, giving him a severe reality check. "They can knock out power and fry electronics. In 1985, a flare blacked out Quebec. Another flare in 1998 knocked out the Galaxy 4 satellite and interrupted telephone pager service to some forty-five million customers."

That caught Dave's attention. He was only hours away from going up in an aircraft crammed with the most sophisticated electronic circuitry yet devised. He wasn't real anxious for it to get fried while he was in the air.

"So, Doc," he asked Stu. "What's the prognosis on this activity you're talking about?"

"We don't feel there's any cause for alarm at this point, but we're watching the energy buildup. Closely."

"So will I," Kate muttered under her breath.

* * *

She left the National Solar Observatory considerably less relaxed than when she'd arrived. Her day didn't totally turn to crap, however, until Dave stopped to gas up in Chorro.

Seven

"**B**e right back," Kate said as Dave inserted his credit card into a gas pump. "I need to hit the ladies' room."

Busy squinting at the buttons in the dim glow cast by the moth-speckled overhead light, Dave nodded. Dusk had fallen while they were still on the narrow winding road down from the observatory, followed by one of New Mexico's clear, star-studded nights.

A glimpse of the gas station's single, dingy rest room had Kate opting for the restaurant across the street. As she pushed through the doors of the Cactus Café, Bar and Superette, she was still mulling over her conversation with Stu Petrie. Solar flares were a common enough occurrence. Nothing to become unduly alarmed about unless they gathered intensity and erupted with enough force to send huge pulses of energy hurtling through space. Then it was anyone's guess how much, if any, havoc the flares could wreak.

She'd stay in close contact with the National Solar Observatory over the next few days, Kate decided as she wove a path through the tables. Check their Web site regularly, just to see what was happening with those flares. That way she could...

"Hey!"

Jerked out of her thoughts, Kate turned to face a woman in tight black jeans, a puckered chambray top that left most of her midriff bare and dangling silver earrings. She held a plastic pitcher of iced tea in one fist. The other was planted on her hip.

"Did you just climb out of the pickup across the street?" the waitress asked Kate.

"Yes, I did. Why?"

The woman's glance flicked to Kate's left hand, noted the lack of rings, then shifted to the café's front window. It gave a clear view of the man at the pumps.

"I, uh, know the driver."

"Do you?"

"He stopped by the café a week or so ago. We hit it off, if you know what I mean."

Kate felt her limbs stiffen one by one. "I'm getting the picture."

"He had to leave early the next morning, said he was late for some business meeting. He promised he'd call me. Never did, though." She shook her head, smiling despite her obvious disappointment that Dave hadn't followed through. "That was some night, I can tell you."

"Yes, I'm sure it was."

The waitress—Alma according to her name tag—heaved a long sigh. "Oh, well, maybe you'll have more luck with him than I did. The handsome ones are always the hardest to bring to heel."

"That's what I hear. Where's the ladies' room?"

"Back of the café and to your left."

"Thanks."

Kate kept a tight smile on her face until she gained the privacy of the one-stall rest room. Slamming the bolt, she propped both hands on the chipped porcelain sink and let the idiot in the mirror have it.

"You dope! You almost fell for the guy. Him and his macho, do-it-till-we-get-it-right attitude in the simulator. And those morning runs! You let him invade your space, your solitude and your head."

The eyes staring back at her from the mirror blazed with scorn.

"You are *so* pathetic, Hargrave. He told you right up front he wasn't interested in long-term commitments. Hell, last night he admitted that he'd been scheming to get you into bed since day one, that it's all a game to him.''

He couldn't have laid things out any plainer! Yet just this morning Kate had gotten all warm and gooey inside and started thinking maybe, just maybe, she might have something going here.

''For a supposedly intelligent woman,'' she said in total disgust, ''you sure don't display many smarts when it comes to men.''

Furious with herself, Kate twisted the cold tap to full blast and splashed her face. The shock of the icy water and a thorough drying with rough paper towels went a long way to restoring her equilibrium. Forcing herself to get a grip, she leaned on the sink once more and lectured the face in the mirror.

''What the heck are you so mad about, anyway? You got off-site for a couple days. Shot a great round of golf. Indulged in some world-class sex. No promises of undying devotion were given or received, so there's no harm, no foul. On either side,'' she said sternly. ''Now it's back to business. Strictly business. Got that?''

Okay! All right! She got it.

She jerked the bolt and started to march out, but remembered her original purpose for exiting the pickup. Locking the door again, she hit the stall.

Alma was behind the counter in the café when Kate sailed through. The waitress popped her gum and flashed a rueful grin.

"Good luck, honey."

Kate didn't need luck. She had her head back on straight. But she returned the smile.

"Thanks. How about two cups of coffee to go?"

"You got 'em."

Dave was just finishing at the pump when she stepped outside.

"I brought you some coffee," Kate said, proud of her nonchalance

"Thanks." He took the cup she offered and downed a cautious sip. "Sure you don't want to grab something to eat?"

And have Alma wait on them? Hardly!

"We'd better get back to the site. Last time I talked to Jill, they had an ETA of twenty-one-hundred for Captain Westfall. If we push it, we can beat him back."

Taking care not to splash the hot coffee, Kate reclaimed her seat. Dave did the same.

"Jill didn't indicate the old man wanted to brief us tonight, did she?"

"No."

"Then what's the hurry? We've still got our toothbrushes and a few emergency supplies."

The crooked grin didn't work this time. If anything, it grated on Kate's nerves like fingernails scraping down a blackboard.

"There's a motel down the road a bit," Dave added while she fought to hang on to her temper.

"Nothing special like the Inn of the Mountain Gods, but clean and handy."

She just bet it was. No doubt Dave and Alma had made good use of it. Somehow, Kate managed to infuse her voice with just the right touch of amusement.

"Look, cowboy. This was fun, but playtime is over. It's time to get back to work."

"Fun?"

"Hey," she tossed off with a shrug, "fun is a big step up from nice. Let's go, Scott. It's getting late, I'm tired, and we both need to log in a good night's sleep before the flight tomorrow."

His eyes narrowed, but Kate was past caring. Her nonchalance meter had pegged out. Thankfully, he dropped the sexy, bantering tone and shoved the key in the ignition.

"Yes, *ma'am.*"

She wasn't up for any more talk. Reaching out, she flicked the switch on the CD player.

They passed through the last checkpoint a little before 9:00 p.m. Kate shoved her ID back in her pocket and waited impatiently until Dave pulled up outside her quarters. The squat, square modular unit had never looked so good. She reached for the handle and was out of the pickup before Dave had killed the engine.

"I'll see you tomorrow," she said. "Thanks for...for everything."

That was lame. Really lame. But the best she could do at the moment.

Evidently Dave shared the same opinion. His door slammed shut a half second after hers. Stalking around the front of the truck, he intercepted her straight path to her quarters.

"What the hell's going on here?"

She had her answer ready. She'd been working on it all the way in from Chorro.

"Nothing's going on here. Nothing *will* go on here. We're back on-site. We declared this a no-fly zone, remember?"

"Sure felt like we made some changes to the rules last night."

"Last night we were off base," Kate said stubbornly. "We'd been ordered to relax, relieve some stress. We're back now and—"

"Relieve some stress!" he interrupted, his eyebrows snapping into a scowl. "Is that what you thought we were doing?"

His apparent anger surprised her. She would have guessed Dave Scott would be the first to argue that sex was the perfect antidote for everything. She couldn't resist getting a little of her own back.

"Come on, Scott. You have to admit you're a whole lot looser than when you left yesterday."

"I was," he retorted. "That looseness seems to have dissipated in the last half hour or so."

Feeling considerably better than when she'd walked out of the Cactus Café, Kate smiled. "Sounds like you've got a problem, cowboy. See you tomorrow."

Dave had a problem, all right. It was sashaying away from him at the moment. Folding his arms, he propped his hips against the fender of his pickup and tried to figure out what the heck just happened.

Kate couldn't be serious about this "not-on-site" stuff. Not after last night. Not to mention this morning. The mere memory of her smooth, slick skin and smoky taste had his throat going tight.

He was as serious about the mission as the next guy. More so. He was the one who'd put his life on the line when Pegasus lifted off, for Pete's sake. So where did Kate get off suggesting he was such a jerk he couldn't concentrate on her *and* on the mission at the same time?

And why did he want to?

That last thought brought him up short. Frowning, he stared at the door Kate had just disappeared through. Okay, they'd had some great sex. Better than great. He got a hitch in his breath just thinking about it. But the lady had made her druthers clear and Dave didn't usually push so hard or so long after being waved off.

Still frowning, he shoved away from the fender and headed for his own quarters.

"Please tell me it was awful," Cari begged as Kate dropped onto the sofa. "I've already wormed a report out of Jill and I'm not sure I can take being the only sex-starved female officer on-site. Tell me Scott's only so-so in bed."

"Scott is excellent in bed. He's also a total jerk. No, that's not right. I'm the jerk."

Obviously that wasn't the answer Cari expected. Blinking, the Coast Guard officer laid aside her dog-eared paperback. "What happened?"

Kate blew out a long breath. "We drove up to Ruidoso, played some golf, hit the sack."

"And the problem with that sequence of events is…?"

"There wasn't any problem," Kate admitted wryly, "until we stopped for gas on the way back and I bumped into Dave's little bit of 'personal business.' The one who caused him to call in and delay his arrival on-site," she added at Cari's puzzled look.

"Uh-oh."

"Right. Uh-oh."

The brunette bit her lip. She knew Kate had good reason to be wary of too-handsome, love-'em-and-leave-'em types like Dave Scott. Still, anyone standing within fifty yards of the weather officer and the sky jock had felt the heat from the sparks they'd been striking off each other since the first day Scott appeared on the scene.

"In all fairness," she pointed out, "Dave obviously met that little bit of personal business, as you term her, before he met you."

"True."

"And he hasn't been off-site since he got here—except with you."

"Also true."

"So why do you think you're a jerk for having a nice steamy weekend fling with the guy?"

When her roommate didn't answer right away, Cari's eyes widened. "We *are* talking just a weekend fling, aren't we?"

"Of course we are. I guess."

"Kate!"

"I know, I know! It's just... Well, for a crazy moment or two I was starting to think it might be something more. Stupid, huh?"

"Not necessarily," Cari countered, recovering from her surprise.

"Yes, it was. *Very* stupid. We'll only be here for another month at most, after which we'll all return to our respective units."

"So you go back to MacDill and Dave returns to Hurlburt. The two bases are both in the Florida panhandle, not more than a hundred or so miles apart."

"A hundred miles is a hundred miles," Kate said doggedly. "I learned the hard way that long-distance relationships don't work. Not for me, anyway. Besides which," she added with a shrug, "Dave made it clear his first or second day on-site he's not in the market for anything long term."

"He did?"

"He did."

Kate's ready sense of humor inched its way through the funk that had gripped her since her encounter with Alma.

"We got in one heck of a round of golf, though. I have to admit the man has a great swing."

"I'll bet."

"Oh, and we stopped at the National Solar Observatory on the way back."

"Golf, sex *and* the National Solar Observatory." Cari rolled her eyes. "What more could a girl ask for?"

Her amusement disappeared when Kate related the news about possible solar-flare activity. Having spent most of her career on the water, the Coast Guard officer had learned to pay serious attention to any unusual weather activity.

They were still discussing the potential impact on the Pegasus test program when Jill returned from one of the perimeter checks she ran at random times.

"Hey, you finally made it back," she said to Kate. "How was your, uh, golf game?"

"Terrific. How was yours?"

"Terrific," Jill replied, laughing. Tossing aside her

fatigue cap, she raked her fingers through her blunt-cut collar-length hair. "So? What's the scoop? Is Dave Scott as good with his hands out of the simulator as he is in it?"

"Better. As I was just telling Cari."

Kate lifted her arms in a lazy stretch. She was fine now, over her brief spate of lunacy. She'd let down her guard for a few hours and Alma had jerked it back up. She owed the woman for that.

"And as I told Dave a few minutes ago," she continued, "the weekend was fun. But now it's over and we both need to concentrate on more important matters."

Jill's eyebrows soared. "Fun? You told him it was fun? How did our hotshot pilot take that?"

Not as well as Kate had expected, surprisingly. She supposed she could have phrased things a little more politely, but she'd been in no mood to stroke the man's ego at that point.

"He took it," she said dismissively, and deliberately changed the subject. "Did Captain Westfall get back?"

"He's twenty minutes out," Jill confirmed. "Rattlesnake Control just notified me. They also relayed a message from the boss. He wants the senior test-cadre personnel to convene at his quarters as soon as he touches down."

"Any idea why?"

"Not a clue. I've already notified Russ McIver.

He'll pass the word to Dave. Consider this your official notification.''

Kate surged off the couch. ''I better scrub away some of this road dust and get into my uniform.''

Cari was right behind her. They took turns in the tiny, closet-size bathroom and bumped elbows squeezing past each other in the narrow hall. Brushed, buffed and uniformed, they were ready when Rattlesnake Control confirmed the captain had returned to the site.

The three women walked the short distance to the captain's quarters. Dave and Russ were already there, along with the senior civilian test engineers. Kate gave the men a friendly smile, Dave included. He returned it, but a crease formed between his eyebrows and stayed there until Captain Westfall called the impromptu meeting to order.

''The good news is that the Joint Chiefs are pleased with the way we've gotten the Pegasus test schedule back on track. I told General Bates that was due in large part to your skill, Captain Scott.''

Dave took the news that Captain Westfall and the air force's top-ranking four-star general had discussed his abilities with a nod.

''General Bates suggested our progress probably had more to do with your tenacity than your expertise,'' Westfall added, his gray eyes glinting. ''He

had a few words to say about your insistence on doing a task again and again until it gets done right.''

"I was in the left seat when he took the Osprey
up for the first time,'' Dave explained with a grin.
"I failed him—on that check ride and the next.''

"So he indicated.''

Sobering, Westfall glanced around the group.
They'd formed a tight bond, officers and civilians
alike. Some tighter than others, he suspected. Normally he wouldn't tolerate fraternization within the
ranks, but this small test cadre represented a unique
set of circumstances. Although the six uniformed officers had chopped to him for the duration of the
Pegasus project, they still reported to their respective
services. More to the point, they were all experts in
their fields. Each of them was vital to a project that
had just jumped the tracks from fast to urgent.

"The bad news is that all hell is about to break
loose in Caribe.''

"Again?'' Russ McIver shook his head. "The island has gone through three coups in two years, each
one bloodier than the last. I thought the U.S. had
poured enough money and troops into the area to
keep this president in office for more than a few
months.''

"That's the problem. We poured in too many
troops, some of whom are now needed on the other
side of the globe. The Pentagon intends to withdraw
elements of the 101st and the 2nd Marine MAF. They

also want to speed up the air and sea trials of Pegasus. The thinking is that Pegasus would make a perfect insertion vehicle if it becomes necessary to go back into Caribe in a hurry.''

"No problem with the sea trials, sir,'' Caroline said firmly. "I'll take a look at the test schedule and see what runs we can shave off.''

"Good. Captain Scott?''

"Pegasus is ready to fly, sir. So am I. We'll test our wings tomorrow.''

Eight

Pegasus took to the sky like the mythical winged steed it was named for.

Two chase vehicles accompanied it. The first was the site's helo. Painted in desert colors, the chopper hovered like an anxious brown hen while Pegasus rose slowly from the desert floor. Russ McIver viewed the prototype's ascent from the chopper's cockpit.

"We've got you at fifty feet, Pegasus One. Seventy. One hundred."

"Confirming one hundred feet, Chase One."

His hands and feet working the controls, Dave held the hover. Sand blew up from the rotors' downwash and obliterated any view outside the cockpit windows, but he kept his gaze locked on the instruments and ignored the whirlwind.

Like the tilt-winged Osprey that was its predecessor, Pegasus was designed to lift off from small, unimproved patches of dirt, fly long and hard, and drop down in another small patch. Dave maintained the hover for a good ten minutes before taking the craft back down. Foot by foot, inch by inch, with the desert sand whirling in a mad vortex until the wide track tires just kissed the dirt.

After three more touch and go's, he was ready to switch to cruise mode. He brought the vehicle back up to a hundred feet, retracted the wheels into the belly of the craft, and ran through a mental checklist before sucking in a deep breath.

"Pegasus One, preparing to tilt rotors."

"Roger, One."

At ten degrees tilt, the test vehicle still handled like a helicopter. Dave nosed it forward, added speed and increased the tilt. The craft bucked a bit at thirty degrees, then the blades on the two engines began slicing air horizontally instead of vertically. Dave pushed the throttles forward and Pegasus took the bit. Within moments he had gained both altitude and airspeed.

Chase One kept up with them for the first few miles. Chase Two took over as the chopper fell behind.

"Pegasus One, this is Chase Two. We've got you in sight. You're lookin' good."

The C–130 Hercules and its crew were detached from the 46th Test Operations Group at Holloman AFB, New Mexico. The highly instrumented aircraft had been designed for just this purpose—observing and testing the latest in sophisticated weaponry. Kate and a team of evaluators were on board to serve as observers for the long-distance portion of the flight. Straining against her shoulder harness, she peered over the flight engineer's shoulder at the sleek white vehicle streaking through the sky. The Herc's pilot kept Pegasus just off his left wing.

"Look at that baby move," she heard him comment to his copilot. "He's approaching a hundred and fifty knots and still piling on the airspeed."

Kate's heart stayed firmly lodged in her throat as Dave pushed Pegasus to perform at maximum capacity. Both the test vehicle and its chase plane reached two hundred knots, with the desert sliding by below them in a blur of silver and tan. Two-twenty. Two-thirty.

"Control, this is Pegasus One."

Dave's voice came through Kate's headset, cool and calm above the background static.

"I'm feeling a vibration in the right aft stabilizer area."

Test Control came on immediately. "Are you showing any system malfunction or warning lights?"

"Negative, Control."

"Is the vibration such that it could affect the structural integrity of the tail section?"

Kate held her breath. That was a judgment call, pure and simple. An educated guess based on the pilot's expertise and familiarity with his craft. A sick feeling gripped her as she remembered that one of the first two prototypes had gone down after a structural stress fracture almost took off a wing. She could hardly hear Dave's reply through the pounding of her heart.

"Negative, Control. He's giving me a bumpy ride, but not trying to buck me off."

"Copy that, Pegasus One. We recommend you decrease your airspeed to two hundred knots. Let us know if the vibration continues."

"Roger."

Kate strained forward. Her harness straps cut into her shoulders. A vein throbbed in her left temple. She counted the seconds until Dave came on again.

"Airspeed now at two hundred knots and I'm not feeling the tail shudder."

The controller didn't try to disguise his relief. "Roger that, Pegasus One. Recommend you keep the airspeed below two hundred for the duration of this flight."

"Will do."

Gulping, Kate tore her gaze from the vehicle across a stretch of blue sky and checked the Doppler radar screen. It showed clear, no sign of weather within the projected flight pattern, but she used the satellite frequency assigned to her to call for regular updates throughout Pegasus's first flight.

It lasted for one hour and seventeen seconds. Dave took the craft in a wide circle over the New Mexico desert, testing the flight-control systems at various altitudes. By the time he slowed the vehicle, rotated the engines from horizontal to vertical and set down in the same patch of dirt he'd lifted off from, Kate was a puddle of sweat inside her flight suit.

The C–130 landed at an airstrip bulldozed out of the desert specifically for the Pegasus tests. The crew piled out as soon as the pilot shut down his craft, then boarded the waiting shuttle to take them back to Test Operations for the mission debrief. There they congratulated a sweaty, grinning Dave Scott.

"Good ride, Captain." The C–130's pilot pumped his hand. "You really put that baby through his paces."

The navigator, who had evidently flown with Dave before, pounded him on the back. "Sierra Hotel, Scott."

Kate hid a smile at the aviators' universal short-hand for shit hot, but her congratulations were every bit as sincere.

"You did good, Captain."

"Thanks, Commander." The tanned skin beside

his eyes crinkled. The glint in their blue depths was intended for her alone. "How about we get together later this evening and review the flight-test data?"

With the thrill of success still singing in her veins, Kate had to force herself to remember Alma. And Denise. And who knew how many other women this man had charmed with that same wicked glint. Keeping an easy smile on her face, she sidestepped the invitation.

"I have a feeling Captain Westfall will want to pore over every bit of data right here, right now."

She was right. They spent the next three hours reviewing every phase of the flight and analyzing instrument readings. Captain Westfall was particularly concerned about the vibration and asked the engineers to examine every inch of the tail section before the next flight, scheduled for the following Thursday.

That was only four days away. Barely enough time to make any changes or corrections in either the instrumentation or the body of the vehicle itself if necessary. Chewing on her lower lip, Kate gathered her stack of computer analyses and stuffed them in her three-ring binder for additional review tomorrow. From her experience during the land phase of testing, she knew the euphoria from the flight would have subsided by then and reality would set in with a vengeance.

Dave and Russ were the first to arrive at the picnic table later that evening. Jill Bradshaw soon joined them. She'd spent the day racing across the desert in a souped-up Humvee, directing ground security for the flight. If Pegasus had gone down, she and her troops would have had to secure the crash site immediately. She was still in uniform and her cheeks showed a flush of red sun and windburn below the white patches made by her goggles.

"You look like you could use a cool one," Russ commented, pulling a beer from the ice chest.

"I could. A *long* cool one." She took the dripping can, popped the top and clinked it against Dave's. "In all the hubbub this afternoon, I didn't get to offer my congrats. Good flight, Scott."

"Thanks."

Caroline Dunn joined the group a few moments later, followed in short order by Doc Richardson and Captain Westfall. Isolated by the responsibility of command, Westfall didn't often unbend enough to gather with his subordinates. Tonight marked a definite exception.

Gradually, the tension that had held Dave in its grip since early morning slid off his shoulders. Just as gradually, a different kind of tension took hold.

"Where's Kate?" he asked Cari during a lull in the conversation.

"At her computer. She said she wanted to review the latest reports from the solar observatory."

Dave nodded and tipped his beer, but it didn't go

down with quite the same gusto as it had before. Nor could he shake the urge to slip away from the crowd, rap on Kate's door, and sweet-talk her into a private little victory celebration. He could almost feel her curves and valleys against his body. Taste her on his tongue. He didn't realize his fist had tightened around the beer until the can crumpled and slopped cold liquid over his hand.

"Damn!"

Laughing, Cari passed him a paper napkin. "Good thing your hand was steadier this morning."

He gave the Coast Guard officer a sheepish grin and was about to reply, when her cell phone buzzed. Everyone on-site had been issued special instruments that picked up the signals from their personal phones and relayed them through a series of secure networks to the test site. Friends and relatives could still keep in touch, but no one would find any record of calls made to or from this particular corner of New Mexico.

Flipping open the phone, Cari put it to her ear. "Lieutenant Dunn. Oh, hi, Jerry."

She listened a moment and a smile come into her eyes. "No kidding? I bet that was something to see."

Holding her hand over the mouthpiece, she excused herself from the group and walked a little way away.

"Jerry again," Jill muttered to Cody. "I wish the man would get a life."

Cody nodded. Russ McIver frowned into his beer. Obviously the only one in the dark, Dave voiced a question.

"Who's Jerry?"

"A navy JAG," Jill answered. "He calls Cari every few days."

Dave lifted an eyebrow. "Sounds serious."

"He'd like it to be."

"But?"

Jill hesitated, obviously reluctant to discuss her friend's personal life. Once again, Dave sensed he was still an outsider, that the rest of the group had yet to fully accept him into their tight little circle. It was left to Doc Richardson to fill in the gaps.

"Commander Wharton has three kids by an ex-wife. Evidently he has some reservations about starting another family while he's still on active duty."

Dave could understand that. He'd seen how tough it was for air force couples to juggle assignments and child care. Throwing long sea tours into the equation would make it even tougher.

Russ McIver voiced the same reservations. "The guy has a point. Be hard to raise kids with one parent at sea and the other deployed to a forward area."

"I've seen it done," Captain Westfall said calmly. "It takes a lot of compromise and a couple as devoted as they are determined."

Mac was too well trained to contradict his superior,

but his disagreement showed on his face as he eyed the small, neat figure some yards away.

The gathering broke up soon after that. Still too hyped from his flight, Dave wasn't ready to hit the sack. The urge to rap on Kate's door and coax her out into the night was still with him. He managed to contain it with the knowledge he'd have her to himself tomorrow morning when they went for their run.

She didn't show.

Dave waited in the chilly dawn while reds and golds and pinks pinwheeled across the sky. Arms folded, hips propped against the fender of his pickup, he watched the glorious colors fade in the slowly brightening sun. They seemed to burn brighter and take longer to dissipate, just as the minutes seemed to drag by. Finally he shoved back the sleeve of his sweatshirt and checked his watch. If he pushed it, he'd have time to get in a quick five miles before breakfast and the round of postflight briefings scheduled for 0800.

He worked up a solid sweat and a fierce hunger on the punishing run. A dark V patch arrowed down the front of his shirt. His drawstring sweatpants felt damp at the small of his back. Swiping his forearm over his face, Dave made for the dining hall. He'd scarf up some of the cook's spicy Mexican scramble, hit the showers and track Kate down before the meeting to find out why she'd missed her run.

He didn't have to track far. She came out of the dining hall just as Dave was going in. He stopped, frowning as he took in the towel draped around the neck of her warm-up suit and the perspiration glistening on her cheeks and temples.

"What's going on? Did you change your exercise routine?"

"It's getting a little too cool in the mornings for me. I decided to use the treadmill in the gym instead."

"You could have told me about the change in plans. I waited a half hour for you."

"Sorry."

She looked anything but. Dave's jaw tightened. He had received his share of brush-offs, but none of them had left him both angry and frustrated. Kate was doing a helluva job at both.

"We need to talk about the other night," he told her brusquely.

"No, we don't."

"C'mon, Kate. I'm not buying this on-site, hands-off crap. What's the problem here?"

She opened her mouth, shut it, then tried again.

"The problem is me. I've discovered I can't combine fun and work without one slopping over into the other. So one has to give."

"When did you make this big discovery?"

"After talking to Alma."

"Who?"

She stared at him for long moments. "Never mind. She's not important. What's important is Pegasus. That's why we're here, Dave. And that's why the on-site, hands-off rule will stay in effect."

She issued the edict as if expecting him to snap to, whip up a salute and bark "Yes, *ma'am!*"

Dave wasn't about to bark anything. Cocking his head, he weighed his options and chose the one he suspected she would least expect.

"You don't have to cut out your morning run. I'll take mine in the evenings. In exchange, you stop treating me as though I'm some plebe at the academy who needs to be reminded of his purpose in life every hour on the hour."

Her startled expression had him shaking his head.

"It's called compromise, Hargrave. I give a little. You give a little. Before you know it, we've found a satisfactory solution to this problem we appear to have."

He left her at the door, feeling pretty smug. It was good to see *her* knocked off balance for a change. She'd sure as heck kept Dave flying a broken pattern almost from the day he'd arrived.

He didn't realize how broken until two nights later.

The compromise he'd proposed wasn't working. Not for him, anyway. He missed his early-morning runs with Kate and her collection of spandex. He even missed her officious tone when she'd tried to pull rank or put him in his place. All he got from the woman now were cool smiles and polite nods that left him edgy and frustrated and hungering for the fire he knew smoldered inside her.

It took a call from his brother to open his eyes to the truth. Like Caroline's JAG, Ryan was patched through a series of relay stations that gave him no clue where Dave was. Not that Ryan particularly cared. He was too used to his brother's nomadic life-style—and on this particular occasion too drunk—to question his whereabouts.

"Hey, bro," he got out, the slur thick and heavy. "I thought I'd better call you and give you the news."

Dave propped himself up on an elbow and squinted at the bedside clock: 2:30 a.m. New Mexico time. Four-thirty back in Pennsylvania. Alarm skittered along his nerves. Ryan drunk was a rare occurrence. Ryan drunk and out all night had never happened before. Not to Dave's knowledge.

"What news, Ry?"

"Jaci and me. We're calling it quits."

"Aw, hell!"

"That's what I said. Right before I walked out."

Ryan burped, thunked the phone against something and cursed.

"I couldn't take it anymore," he said a moment later. "I tried. The Lord knows, I tried."

"Yeah, you did. Where are you now?"

"I'm at my office."

It figured. Over the years Ryan's office had become more than a workplace or source of income. It had become his refuge, his retreat when the arguments got too heated and too hurtful. Struggling upright, Dave punched the pillow behind him and tried not to wince when a pitying whine crept into his brother's voice.

"I still love her. That's the rotten part. I can't imagine life without Jaci and the kids."

"So don't imagine it."

"Huh?"

"You're drunk, Ry. You need to sleep this off, then go home and talk to your wife. See if you can't work a compromise."

"What kind of compromise?"

"Hell, I don't know. Maybe if you spend a little less time at the office and a little more with Jaci and the kids, she'll get off your back some."

"Thass what she says."

Another morose silence descended, interspersed with some heavy breathing.

"Dave?"

"I'm here."

"I'm drunk. I'm going to sleep it off."

"Good idea."

"Dave?"

"What?"

"Have you ever wanted a woman so bad you ached with it?"

All the time, bro.

His brain formed the flip reply, but the words stuck in his throat. The truth came out of the darkness and hit him smack in the gut.

"As a matter of fact, Ry, I'm kind of in that situation now."

He waited for a response. All that came over the phone was a loud snore.

"Ry! Hey, Ryan!"

"Huh?"

"Hang up the phone, man. Then get some sleep and talk with Jaci in the morning."

"Yeah."

The receiver banged down. Wincing, Dave flipped his cell phone shut and dropped it on the bedside table. He took a long time going back to sleep. Worry for his brother was a habit that went deep. Ryan and Jaci had been going at each other for a long time. Dave only hoped they'd find a way to patch things up.

In the meantime, he had another problem to keep him awake. One that came packaged with flaming copper hair, a mouth made for kissing and a bone-deep stubborn streak.

Here, alone in the dark, Dave could admit the truth. He ached for Kate. Physically *and* mentally. The feeling was as unsettling as it was unfamiliar.

Hooking his hands behind his head, he stared up at the ceiling and tried to figure out when lust had slipped over into something deeper, something he wasn't quite ready to put a name to yet.

He couldn't pinpoint the exact moment, but to his surprise he suspected it had happened well before their weekend in Ruidoso. He'd wanted Kate in his bed, sure. He *still* wanted her in his bed. Looking back, though, he realized he'd come to crave her laughter and her company as much as her seriously gorgeous body.

The realization had him scowling up into the darkness. Okay, he wanted Kate. All of her. Like he'd never wanted another woman. The problem now was what the hell to do about it.

Nine

Dave made his move the next evening.

The timing was iffy. The entire test cadre had been going full out for three days to analyze the data from the first flight and prepare for the second. The engineers hadn't been able to pinpoint what caused the vibration in the tail section. With the second flight scheduled for tomorrow afternoon, Dave had insisted on more hours in the simulator to practice emergency responses to possible structural failures. By the time he climbed out around six that evening, he felt as though he'd been ridden hard and put away wet.

A long shower and a hearty meal of steak and home fries revived him. So did the prospect of getting

Kate alone for an hour. He caught her on her way back to Test Operations. Unlike Dave, she was still in uniform. The sky blue of her zippered flight suit formed a perfect foil for the fire of her hair.

"I thought we were done for the day," he commented, falling in beside her.

"I thought so, too. But tomorrow's flight is going to take you into the mountains and I want to review the wind patterns one more time. I wouldn't want you to run into another katabatic wind," she added, her lips curving.

It was the first real smile Dave had received from her in days. He felt like a kid who'd just been handed a fistful of penny candy.

"Trust me, I have no desire to get hit with another whammy like that one. Think it's possible?"

"Highly unlikely. The air temperatures at the higher altitudes are dropping significantly, but there's no snow on the peaks yet. You could experience some severe downdrafts, though."

"I'm wondering if that's all I'll experience. Did you notice a greenish glow in the sky when you were running this morning?"

She threw him a sharp look. "No."

"I saw it last night while I was running along the perimeter road. It was hanging low in the northern sky. I just caught a glimpse of it through the peaks."

"What time was that?"

"About eight-forty."

Her eyebrows drew into a frown. "I didn't see any reports of unusual light patterns on the weather sites this morning."

"The glow only lasted for a short while, maybe two or three minutes."

Dave wasn't lying. Not exactly. He *had* noticed a dim glow, but it was more smoky than green. Anything could have caused it. A dust cloud thrown up by a passing vehicle. A low-hanging storm cloud scudding across the sky, lit from within by the moon. Given the recent reports of possible solar-flare activity, though, he'd figured Kate would want to check it out.

Sure enough, she took the bait. Still frowning, she checked her watch. "It's eight-fifteen now. Can you show me where you spotted this glow?"

"I'll get my truck and drive you out there. We should just make it."

The pickup jounced along the unmarked dirt track that served as the site's perimeter road. Dave checked the odometer, squinted at the dark shapes to the north and pulled over.

"This is about where I spotted the lights." Leaning across Kate, he pointed to the jagged ridgeline. "Over there, through those peaks."

She reached for the door handle, but Dave stilled her with a quick warning. "We'd better notify Security before we climb out. We're right on the perimeter. Their sensors are probably already flashing red alert.''

All it took was a quick press of one key on his specially configured cell phone to connect him with Security Control.

"This is Captain Scott. I'm out along the perimeter road, 3.2 miles into the northwest quadrant.''

"We've got you on the screen, Captain Scott.''

"Commander Hargrave is with me. We're going to step out of our vehicle.''

"We'll track you. Watch where you walk. You don't want to put your boot down in a nest of diamondbacks.''

Dave didn't take the warning lightly. He'd heard that one of Jill Bradshaw's cops had done exactly that before he'd arrived on-site.

Kate was doubly cautious. "I listened in via the radio net with the rest of the test cadre that night when Jill and Doc Richardson jumped a chopper and raced to the injured cop. That wasn't an experience I'd want to see repeated. We'd better not stray too far from the truck.''

That suited Dave just fine.

"No problem. I'll just back it around and let down the tailgate. We can perch there while we wait for the show.''

With the truck in position, he and Kate climbed out. They couldn't have asked for a better night for star watching. Above the black mass of the mountains, the sky was deep and dark. A couple of million stars shone with the brilliance only visible at these high altitudes. The nip in the night air had Dave reaching into the back seat for a worn leather bomber jacket. When he offered it to Kate, she declined.

"You'd better put it on. My flight suit will keep me warm."

When Dave lowered the tailgate, Kate propped her hips on the edge. He opted to stand and watch the northern sky for signs of unusual activity. The moments slid by with only the still, dark night around them. Kate checked her watch a couple of times. Dave couldn't tell from her expression whether she was relieved or disappointed that nothing happened.

"I got a call from my brother last night," he said after a while.

She angled her head around. "The one having problems with his marriage?"

"That's the one. Ryan said he and Jaci are calling it quits."

"Ouch." Her face softened in sympathy. "Been there, done that. It's not fun."

"Didn't sound like it from Ryan's perspective."

"What made him finally decide to walk?"

"I'm not sure. He was pretty drunk when he called. I couldn't get much out of him."

"You said they love each other despite their problems. Maybe they'll patch it up."

"Maybe." He hadn't forgotten her remark that

love can sometimes hurt. "What about you? What made you decide to walk?"

Her mouth twisted into a rueful grimace. "A nineteen-year-old blonde. Evidently she was just what my ex needed to stroke his ego after the way I'd pounded it into the dust. His phrasing, not mine, by the way."

"In other words, he couldn't keep up with you on the golf course."

"Or off it." Her shoulders lifted under the blue Nomex of her flight suit. "Took me a while to stop feeling guilty about that."

"Is that why you skittered away from me after we got back from Ruidoso? You were afraid I couldn't keep up with you on or off the course?"

"I didn't skitter away. I merely redrew the lines we had already established."

"The lines *you* had established. I've been thinking about those."

He pushed away from the fender. A single step placed him in front of her. His hands slid up her arms, gliding over the smooth fabric of her flight suit. With a gentle tug, he pulled her to her feet.

"Dave, we agreed. Not on-site."

"Well, technically we're off-site. I angled the truck around. The tail end is sticking clear over the perimeter road."

Anger flared hot and quick in her eyes. Planting her palms flat on his chest, she stiff-armed him. "So this was all a ploy? A ruse to get me out here?"

"Partly. I did see a strange glow last night. I also wanted to get you back on neutral ground, so we can rekindle the fires we lit last weekend."

"We can't." Jerking free of his loose grip, she folded her arms. "And even if we could, I don't want to compete with Denise and Alma."

"Denise I remember," Dave said, exasperated, "but only because you keep bringing her into the conversation. Who the heck is Alma?"

"She's a waitress at the Cactus Café. About five-five. Brown hair. Lots of mascara. Remember her?"

"Now I do," he replied with a sheepish grin.

Talk about ironic. Dave had been sure he'd never forget that wild night. Since tangling with Kate, though, he could barely remember his name at times, let alone his carefree days before he arrived on-site.

"Let me guess," he said wryly. "You bumped into Alma when we stopped to gas up in Chorro."

"Bingo."

"And she's the reason you've been giving me the deep freeze all week?"

Arms still folded, she tapped a foot and considered her answer. Dave had spent enough time with her by now to know she wouldn't dodge the issue.

"Alma is part of the reason," Kate admitted at last. "Only because she made me face up to hard, cold reality. The problem is it's impossible to keep personal feelings from slopping over into our professional situation. For me, anyway. The thought of be-

ing the latest in your string of weekend flings made me furious until—''

''I'm not keeping score,'' Dave interrupted dryly. ''You can check my bedpost. You won't find any notches carved there.''

''Until I realized I had no right to be angry,'' she finished firmly. ''We had some fun, that's all. Neither one of us made any promises. I had no reason to feel hurt or jealous. More to the point, I don't *want* to feel hurt or jealous. Not again.''

''I can't change the past, Kate. Nor am I going to apologize for it. But did it ever occur to you I might just be looking for the right woman?''

''You have my permission to keep looking, cowboy.''

''Funny,'' Dave mused, ''I wouldn't have pegged you as a coward.''

Stiffening, she lifted her chin. Before she could lash out at him, he offered his own take on the situation.

''I don't think you're afraid of feeling hurt or jealous. You're afraid of failing. You like to win, Kate. You want to be the absolute best you can be at everything. Golf. Work. Marriage.''

''And that's bad?''

''No. That's good. Very good. You go into everything heart first.''

She was still stiff, still a little torqued at being

called a coward. Smiling, Dave brushed a knuckle down her cheek.

"The problem is, there are no guarantees when it comes to this love business. Not for Ryan and Jaci. Not for us."

"Who's talking about love?"

"I am. I think."

At her look of astonishment, his smile took a lop-sided tilt.

"I know. Half the time I'm convinced it's only plain old-fashioned lust. All I have to do is picture you in turquoise spandex and my throat goes bone dry. Then I watch you at work, see the sweat and long hours you put into this project, and lust gets all mixed up with admiration and respect and something I've had a hard time putting a name to."

"Dave, this is crazy. You can't... You don't..."

She stopped, drew in a slow breath, and adopted the gentle tone of a nurse addressing a seriously ill patient.

"Respect and admiration I appreciate. Lust I understand. I've felt more than a few twinges of all three myself where you're concerned. But love... Well..."

She glanced to the side, as if expecting the right words to materialize on the cool, crisp air.

"It's okay." A grin stole into his voice. "The idea kind of gives me goose bumps, too."

It gave Kate more than goose bumps. It shook her

right down to her boot tops. She'd worked so hard at convincing herself she was just another trophy in his collection, that one torrid weekend defined the parameters of their relationship. It stunned her to hear his feelings went deeper. And that they had confused him as much as Kate's had confused her.

But love...

Her face must have expressed her welter of uncertainty, doubt and wariness. Chuckling, Dave stroked her cheek again with the back of a knuckle.

"I don't figure we'll sort this out tonight. Or next week. Let's just take it a step at a time. See where it goes."

"Where can it go?" Kate asked, echoing her conversation with Cari. "Once Pegasus proves his stuff, we all head back to our separate units. Unfortunately, I've discovered I'm not real good at long-distance relationships."

"So you stumbled once. You didn't win. Does that mean you won't ever get back in the race again?"

He knew what buttons to push, she thought ruefully. She hadn't liked being called a coward. Nor was it in her to run away and hide from a challenge. Particularly when the stakes were as high as these.

Could she love this man? Did she want to?

The answer was staring her right in the face.

"Okay," she conceded with something less than graciousness. "Consider me back in the race."

"Good." With a satisfied smile, he slid a palm

around her nape. "Just to make it official, here's the starting gun."

"Hey!"

That one startled yelp was all she managed to get out before his mouth came down on hers. He kissed her hard and long, apparently determined to make up the ground he'd lost over the past few days.

His taste and his tongue sent little sparks of pleasure through Kate, heating her skin as they traveled her length. Dave added to the sensations by tunneling one hand into her upswept hair, wrapping the other around her waist and bringing her hard against him.

She curled her fingers into the soft, worn leather covering his shoulders. Her head went back, her chin tilted to find just the right angle. Within moments, she was breathless. Moments more, and she had to drag in big gulps of air when Dave broke off the kiss. She was still gulping when he reached down, hooked an elbow under her knees and deposited her on the tailgate with a small thump.

His skin was stretched tight across his cheeks, and his wicked grin signaled his intent even before he reached for the zipper tab at the neck of her flight suit.

"Dave!" She grabbed his hands, stilling them. "This is your idea of taking it slow?"

"I didn't say slow. I said one step at a time. And this, my very Kissable Kate, is the next step."

He tugged free of her hold, got the zipper halfway

down, and bent to nuzzle her breasts. The warm, damp wash of his breath came through her cotton T-shirt. Shivers rippled over every square centimeter of Kate's body. Sighing, she gave herself over to the pleasure.

Her sigh got stuck in her throat as he took little nips through the soft cotton. Pleasure gave way to hunger and Kate knew she was in trouble. But when he eased the fabric off one shoulder, common sense told her it was time to put the skids on. Unfortunately.

"Surely you're not thinking we'll get naked out here in the middle of nowhere, are you?"

"Oh, babe," he muttered against the curve of her shoulder, "I'm way past the point of being able to think."

"Dave! One of Jill's patrols could come cruising by at any moment."

"Nah." He nibbled his way back up to her throat. "I said a silent prayer to the mountain gods. Worked like a charm last time."

"Dave, we can't. It's too cold out here. And I want an official measurement. I'm not sure this truck bed is really over the perimeter line. We might have to—"

Suddenly, she went stiff. Her breath left on a gasp.

"Omigod! There it is!"

With his face buried in the silky skin of her neck and his senses already close to overload, it took Dave a second or two to realize she wasn't referring to a hidden sweet spot he'd triggered by accident.

"Look!" Kate exclaimed, thumping him on the back with a fist. "Over there! One o'clock high."

Swallowing a groan, Dave dragged his head up and threw a look over his shoulder at the faint green glow just visible between the peaks.

"Now it shows," he growled, not at all happy to have his reasons for driving Kate out into the desert vindicated. She, on the other hand, could hardly contain her excitement. Wiggling free of his hands, she yanked at her zipper.

"We've got to get back to the site. I need to access the solar observatory database, see if they're taking readings on this."

Regret knifed into Dave at the disappearance of her lush curves. Despite her desire to return to the base, though, she couldn't seem to tear herself away. She stood transfixed, her gaze locked on the distant haze. Dave guessed she was trying to calibrate the intensity of the light waves dancing in the atmosphere and causing those weird, moving shadows.

He had to admit they were pretty riveting. He'd pulled some temporary duty at Elmendorf AFB in Alaska, had been treated to the spectacle of the northern lights. These weren't anywhere near as intense, but they gave Dave some insight into why the rumor had persisted for so many years that aliens had landed near Roswell, New Mexico. Folks had probably spotted a green glow much like this one and let their fears prey on them. They wouldn't have had the benefit of scientific data regarding sunspots and magnetic energy and solar flares. Kate and Stu Petrie had treated Dave to an extended discourse on the phenomena, yet the dancing lights still sent prickles of unease down his spine.

"Do you think that eerie glow will impact tomorrow's flight?"

The casual question masked a dozen different concerns. That the team maintain the tight test schedule. That they wrap up the air portion and move on to the sea trials. That Pegasus get a chance to strut his stuff before being harnessed for plow duty in the trenches. If things turned sour down in Caribe, the Pentagon might have to move troops in and noncombatant civilians out pretty quick.

Kate gave the haze a final, frowning glance. "At this point, I can't say what the impact will be. All I can do is check the data and see if the observatory is projecting any significant activity in the earth's ionosphere. We don't want to take any chances with you or with Pegasus."

She started for the passenger door, stopped, and spun around. Grabbing his jacket collar, she yanked him down for a hard, fast kiss.

"Particularly with you, flyboy."

Ten

Kate didn't sleep at all that night.

She spent hours hunched over her computer collecting reports from every possible source. The solar observatory in Sunspot had recorded an increase in ionization in the earth's upper atmosphere, but no disruption of satellite or radio communications as yet.

By morning, she was hungry, hollow-eyed and more nervous than she'd ever been before jumping aboard one of NOAA's planes to fly into the eye of a howling storm. She knew every piece of equipment aboard the specially modified P–3, knew just how it would respond when buffeted by hurricane-force winds.

In contrast, Dave was going up in a new vehicle with only one operational test flight to its credit. The contractor representatives were confident they'd shaken the bugs out of Pegasus during the research and development phase—particularly after analyzing the data from the loss of the first two prototypes and incorporating design changes. But there was a good reason why the military didn't accept ships or aircraft or other highly sophisticated weapons systems without extensive field tests. Real-world conditions too often caused failure of systems that operated flawlessly in a controlled R and D environment. And high-energy solar explosions were about as real world as it gets.

As a result, Kate approached the 8:00 a.m. pretest meeting with considerably less confidence than she had previous such meetings. She was one of the first to arrive at the small conference room in the Test Operations building. Depositing her laptop and stack of briefing books on the table, she nodded to Russ McIver.

"'Morning, Mac.''

"Hi, Kate.''

"Are you going to load Pegasus with the equivalent weight of a full squad this morning?''

"That's the plan. Any reason to change it?''

Kate bit her lip. Pegasus was designed to carry a maximum of twenty fully-equipped troops or their equivalent weight in cargo. This would be the first test of how the vehicle performed fully loaded.

"No," she said slowly, thinking of all the weight and drag Dave would have to compensate for, "no reason to change it at this point."

The marine went back to flipping through the PowerPoint charts he'd prepared for the prebrief. Too restless to sit, Kate poured coffee into a mug emblazoned with the Pegasus test-cadre shield. Dave arrived a few minutes later and joined her at the pot.

"You look dead," he commented, eyeing her drawn face. "Gorgeous, but dead."

"Thanks."

By contrast, she thought wryly, he looked good enough to eat. His blond hair still gleamed from his morning shower, and his blue eyes showed none of the red tracks Kate's did.

"Did you get any sleep last night?" he asked her.

"Not much."

One corner of his mouth kicked up. "Me, neither. That bit of unfinished business we started out on the perimeter kept me tossing and turning all night. We *are* going to finish it, Hargrave."

Kate didn't argue. Sometime during the long hours of the night she'd accepted Dave's challenge. She was back in the race. Despite the tension that knotted the muscles at the base of her skull, she flashed him a ten-gigabyte smile.

"If you say so, Scott."

The rest of the cadre filed in, dumped their briefing books and hit the coffee. Everyone was in place when Captain Westfall arrived at precisely 0800. Chairs scraped back. Officers popped to attention. Even the civilians stood as a mark of respect for the naval officer whose drive and determination fed their own.

"Good morning, ladies and gentlemen. Take your seats, please."

After another shuffle, an expectant silence settled over the room. Westfall's glance moved around the U-shaped table and settled on Kate.

"Before we get into the actual mission prebrief, I've asked Commander Hargrave to give you an update on recent solar activity. We'll make the go/no-go decision for today's flight after we hear what she has to tell us. Commander."

Kate took the floor. The data she'd pored over last night was pretty well burned into her brain. She could talk her subject from memory, but had prepared a computerized slide presentation for the test team's benefit. Her palm slick from a combination of worry and nerves, she pressed the remote. The first slide cut right to the heart of the matter. It showed a soft X-ray image of the sun's "busy" side, with swirls of black clearly visible against the brilliant red corona.

"The National Solar Observatory at Sunspot, just a little over a hundred miles from here, has been monitoring a buildup of energy in the sun's magnetic fields. This increase in energy could lead to a solar flare, such as the one shown on this slide. This particular flare is in what we call the precursor stage, where the release of magnetic energy has been triggered.''

Kate hit the remote again and brought up another slide. In this one, the dark swirls all but obscured the red ball.

''In the second or impulsive stage, protons and electrons accelerate to high energy and are emitted as radio waves, hard X rays and gamma rays.''

The next slide depicted a glowing red ball with only a few black swirls.

''In the final stage, we can measure the gradual buildup and decay of soft X rays. Each of these stages can last as little as a few seconds or as long as an hour.''

She had their attention, Kate saw. Dave had received much of this information during their visit to the observatory. It was new stuff for the others.

''Solar flares are the most intense explosions in the solar system,'' she continued, bringing up the next slide. ''The energy released may reach as high as ten-to-the-thirty-second-power ergs. That's ten million times greater than the energy released in a volcano, and we all know the devastation that resulted when Mount St. Helens erupted.

''The problem is when the intense radiation from a solar flare enters the earth's atmosphere. It can disrupt satellite transmissions, increase the drag on an orbiting vehicle and generally wreak havoc with anything electronic.''

"Oh, great!"

The muttered exclamation came from Jill Bradshaw, but Kate saw the same concern reflected in every face at the table. A click of the remote brought up a bar graph charting the sun's magnetic-field activity for the past two decades.

"Solar flares generally occur in cycles," she informed her audience. "As you can see, 2000 and 2001 were peak years. This was predicted and planned for.''

"Planned for how?" Russ McIver wanted to know.

"A 1998 flare knocked out the Galaxy 4 satellite and disrupted some eighty percent of commercial cell phone and pager use in the United States. As a result, military and civilian communications agencies took a hard look at systems dependent on satellite signals and built in more redundancy. For example, radio, television, bank transactions, newspapers, credit card systems and the like are now spread across a wider spectrum of low- to mid-altitude satellites. Some might get knocked out, but the others would be at different points in their orbit and be protected from the solar blast by the curvature of the earth.''

Caroline Dunn sat forward in her chair. Her brown eyes grave, she studied the bar graph. "Looks like flare activity has been minimal since 2001. Are you saying there's a chance that could change in a hurry?''

"I'm saying there's a possibility," Kate replied carefully. She had to walk a fine line between predicting something that might not happen and minimizing the potential, only to have it blow up in her face. "Some of you may have noticed a green glow in the sky, similar to the northern lights only much less intense. It's caused by higher than normal ionization levels in the upper atmosphere."

"High enough to disrupt communications or interfere with the instrumentation on Pegasus?"

Kate answered Dave's question as truthfully as she could. "Not at present."

"But you're concerned another burst of ergs will come zinging my way?"

"Yes."

They were speaking one-to-one now. The others were still there, within their field of vision, but relegated to the background.

"Pegasus comes equipped with a lot of that redundancy you mentioned," Dave reminded her. "Backup communications, laser-guided navigational systems, fly-by-wire manual controls in the event of hydraulic failure."

"I know."

"There's also the fact I'm a test pilot. I've logged over a thousand hours in both fixed-wing and rotary-wing aircraft." His lips tipped into a grin. "I also survived almost every natural and unnatural disaster you threw at me during those hours in the simulator.''

''It's the 'almost' part that worries me.''

''That part worries us all,'' Captain Westfall interjected dryly. ''I need your best professional guesstimate, Commander Hargrave. On the basis of the data available to you at this point, do you recommend we press on with the mission or scrub it?''

Kate fingered the remote. She knew the situation in Caribe had added to pressure on the captain. On them all. She also knew how little room there was for a slip in the schedule even without the Pentagon's latest worries.

She had to accept the possibility that one of the swirling sunspots could generate enough energy to fry every circuit aboard Pegasus. There was also the chance Dave and his craft could wing across a clear blue sky.

She didn't look at Dave. This was her time in the box. Captain Westfall would ask for his input in a few minutes.

''Based on all data currently available, sir, I recommend we continue the mission. I'll monitor the situation continuously. If I receive any indication of increased solar activity, we can terminate immediately.''

The naval officer accepted her judgment with a nod and turned to Dave.

''Captain Scott, you're in command on this mission. You've heard the risk assessment. You're also fully aware that you're taking up a craft that's still in the test stage. The call is yours."

"I understand, sir. Taking educated, calculated risks is an inherent part of the test business. I agree with Commander Hargrave. As far as I'm concerned, the mission is a go."

A small silence gripped the room. Although Westfall had deferred to Dave, none of the officers present thought for a moment the captain couldn't—or wouldn't—pull rank and overrule the pilot if he so desired. Kate held her breath, half hoping he'd exercise that authority.

But when he stood and moved back to the podium, Westfall gave the green light. "Look sharp, people. We've got a mission to fly."

They finished the prebrief just before eleven. Pegasus was scheduled to fly at noon. Dave skipped lunch to conduct a final walk-around of his craft.

Kate found him in the hangar. He and the crew chief assigned to the craft were inspecting the tail section yet again. The engineers hadn't been able to determine the source of the vibration Dave had experienced on the first flight and Kate knew it worried him.

She stood beside a rack of equipment, waiting for them to finish. Her recommendation to proceed with the mission hung like a rock around her neck. It was the right recommendation given the available data, but if anything happened to Dave...

Her stomach lurched. A tight ball of fear lodged in the middle of her chest. The stark, unremitting fear forced her to admit what she'd tried so hard to deny these past weeks.

She'd fallen for the guy. Big-time. Despite her doubts. Despite Denise and Alma. Despite the need to focus strictly on the mission. Sometime between the moment she'd spotted the long rooster tail of dust churned up by his pickup the very first morning he arrived on-site and their soiree out under the stars last night, she'd tumbled smack into love.

And now Kate was about to send him up into a sky that could go supercharged with as little as eight minutes' warning.

Swallowing the acid taste of fear, Kate waited until he and the crew chief had finished with the tail section and had worked their way up to the nose. They had their heads buried in a tech manual when she stepped forward.

"Got a minute?"

His smile was quick and for her alone. "Sure."

She couldn't say what she wanted to in front of the mechanic or the rest of the hangar crew.

"I need to talk to you." Snagging the sleeve of his flight suit, she tugged him across the gleaming, white-painted floor. "In here."

"Here" was the men's room, the closest private

spot in the huge hangar. Lifting an eyebrow, Dave followed Kate inside. Luckily, no one was at the circular urinal.

The latrine was as spotless as the rest of the hangar, but if Kate had had time, she would have chosen a better spot than a rest room smelling strongly of Lysol to let him know how she felt. The fact that time was fast ticking away made the place and the scent irrelevant.

"What's up?" Dave asked.

The smile was still in his eyes, but Kate sensed the edge behind the question. No doubt he thought she'd come to tell him the sun was still acting up and the mission had been scrubbed.

If only!

"I've been thinking about last night," she said slowly.

"That's funny. So have I." Reaching out, he snagged her waist and pulled her closer. "Finishing what we started out there under the stars tops my to-do list for after this mission. Unless..."

He skimmed a glance over his shoulder.

"We're in luck," he said with a hopeful waggle of his eyebrows. "The door locks."

"Cool your jets, cowboy. I didn't drag you in here to make mad, passionate love to you."

"Well, damn! And here I thought I was going to lift off with a smile on my face. Okay, I'll bite. Why did you drag me in here?"

"I wanted to tell you... That is..."

Even now it was hard for her to say the words. She was still confused by the feelings this man generated in her, still unsure of where they'd go from here. But she couldn't let him take off without letting him know she'd had a change of heart. She wasn't just back in the race. She wanted very much to win this one.

"Come on, Kate," he prompted, as curious now as he was amused by her temporary loss for words. It didn't happen often. "Spit it out."

"All right, here goes. I think... No, I'm pretty sure I love you."

Surprise flickered in his blue eyes for a moment, followed in short order by laughter and delight.

"Well, well! That makes two of us who are pretty sure. What do you propose we do now?"

"This, for starters."

Wrapping her fists around the collar of his flight suit, she yanked him down for a kiss.

It took him all of a second to get into the act. Wrapping an arm around her waist, he dragged her up against him. They were hard at it, lost in each other's taste and touch, when Kate registered the thud of a palm hitting the rest-room door.

"Oh! 'Scuse me, folks."

"Use the latrine across the hangar," Dave growled without lifting his head. "This one's busy."

"Right."

There was a hurried retreat, the sound of the door swishing shut. Kate closed her mind to the small sounds, the astringent tang of Lysol, to everything but Dave.

Finally, she had to let him go. He still needed to run through his preflight checklists and she had to pull herself together enough to face the rest of the crew. She couldn't believe how difficult it was to ease out of his arms.

"I'd better get back to Test Operations. I want to have a front-row seat when you take off."

"Aren't you going up in the chase plane?"

"Not this time. I want to make sure I have a land link to the solar observatory."

In case the satellite links took a hit.

She didn't finish the thought. She didn't have to. With a crooked grin, he reached up and tucked a stray tendril behind her ear.

"Don't worry, Commander Hargrave. You'll be right there with me, in my head."

And in his heart, Dave thought with a funny little jolt.

So this is what it felt like. As if he'd stepped into a zero-gravity chamber a half second before the floor dropped out from under him. For the first time in his admittedly varied experience, he found himself floundering, not quite sure how to propel himself forward.

He'd figure that out after his flight, he decided. When he had Kate alone, in the dark, in some place that didn't stink of industrial-strength disinfectant.

Eleven

Kate left Dave at the hangar and returned to the dun-colored modular building housing Test Operations. Inside was the small room lined with digitized display boards that functioned as the site's command-and-control center during tests.

Using her laptop, Test Ops' high-speed computers and a battery of communications devices, she set up a series of redundant links to various weather sources. A voice link to Stu Petrie confirmed her real-time access to data being fed back through the solar observatory's array of equipment.

"We've reoriented the Dunn Telescope," the scientist informed her. "We're recording every burp and bubble of energy emitted by the magnetic fields. So far, the propulsive activity has remained relatively stable.''

So far.

The caveat didn't reassure Kate. As Stu himself had pointed out to Dave, intense bursts of energy from the sun didn't take long to reach the earth.

''I appreciate you allowing me to tap into your data system, Stu.''

''There wasn't much 'allowing' involved,'' the scientist responded with a chuckle. ''The order came straight down from the top.''

Kate could hear the curiosity behind the comment. The observatory had been read in on the need for real-time information, but not the reason behind it. Neither Dr. Petrie nor his boss had been briefed on the specifics of the Pegasus project.

''I want to keep that data line open for the next few hours,'' Kate told him. ''I've also got landlines and radio communications available as backup.''

''Don't worry. We'll get the data to you if I have to bicycle it down the mountain myself.''

Kate bit back the reply that bicycling would get the information here too late for it to do any good.

''Thanks, Stu. Let's hope it doesn't come to that.''

Her glance went to the digital time display on the wall of Test Operations. Eleven-twenty. Dave would be airborne in less than an hour and back on the ground by 4:00 p.m. if nothing went wrong.

Her mouth set, Kate grabbed her mug and filled it to the brim with black coffee. The coffee wouldn't help the acid already churning away inside her stomach, but she needed something to take her mind off the clock.

Cari joined her and grimaced at the residue left in the bottom of the carafe. "I'd better brew a fresh pot. This looks to be a long afternoon."

"No kidding."

"He knows what he's doing, Kate."

That was the best the brunette could offer. She didn't try to minimize the risks. She couldn't. If Pegasus proved his capabilities in the air, Cari would be the next one in the hot seat. Responsibility for the sea trials rested squarely on her slender shoulders.

With the brisk efficiency that characterized her, she filled the pot, poured the water into the well and added a prepack of coffee. When the water had started to gurgle, she turned to Kate.

"Remember what Dave said. He's a test pilot. He's been trained to think fast and respond instantly."

Kate nodded.

"We'll bring him home." Cari gave her arm a gentle squeeze. "We have to. I'll be darned if I'm going to miss my ride."

By three-fifteen Kate was almost beginning to believe they'd make it. Her eyes ached from staring at

the computer screens nonstop, her neck had a knot
in it that wouldn't go away, and her stomach was
pumping acid by the gallon. With one ear she listened
to every beep and blip of the computers. With another, she monitored Dave's voice as it came over
the loudspeakers.

"Chase One, this is Pegasus One."

"Go ahead, Pegasus."

"I'm climbing to thirty thousand feet."

"Roger, Pegasus. We're right with you."

Kate's glance flew to the computerized tracking
board. The last test objective yet to be met was to
ascertain the vehicle's performance with a full load
at, or close to, its maximum ceiling. To accomplish
that, Dave was now taking his craft in a wide, as-
cending circle high above the same resort the two of
them had golfed in.

And made love in.

They'd have to go back to the Inn of the Mountain
Gods, Kate thought, once this mission was over and
she could breathe again. Dragging her gaze from the
tracking board, she scanned the screen in front of her.

Suddenly, she froze. Her heart stopped dead,
kicked in again with a painful jolt. Her horrified gaze
ripped across the numbers painting across the screen
once, twice. Then she was shouting for Captain
Westfall.

"Sir! I'm declaring a weather emergency. We've
got to get those planes down!"

His steely-gray gaze shot toward her. She didn't have time to explain.

"Now, sir!"

He nodded once and keyed his mike. "Pegasus One, Chase One, this is Test Control. Terminate your mission and return to base immediately. Immediately. Do you copy?"

"This is Chase One. We copy."

Kate's pulse thundered in her ears until Dave responded.

"This is Pegasus One. I copy, too, Control. How long have we got?"

Westfall looked to her. Hitting the switch on her mike, Kate delivered the dire news.

"Seven to eight minutes. If you're lucky. Get that baby on the ground!"

"Roger that."

After an instant of frozen silence, the entire test cadre shifted instantly into emergency mode. The engineers sent their fingers flying over keyboards to back up every bit of flight data. Captain Westfall ordered the crash recovery team to stand by. Doc Richardson alerted his medical personnel. Jill Bradshaw instructed Rattlesnake Ops to yank every off-duty military cop from his or her bunk and prepare them to secure a possible crash site.

Kate heard their voices, felt their tension jump through the air like some evil demon, but she focused every atom of her being on the computer screen in front of her.

The numbers were off the charts now. The energy burst was coming and it was coming fast. All indications were it would hit right above them.

She forced herself to think, to clamp down on the terror icing her veins and *think!* The whole upper ionosphere was about to go supercharged. Dave couldn't get above it. He couldn't get around it. His one chance, his only chance, was to find a protective shield.

The mountains! He could use the mountains! If the burst occurred over the desert, as was now looking more and more certain, the mountains *might* act as a shield. The high peaks had certainly contained the green haze Kate and Dave had observed last night.

Every nerve center in her body screaming, Kate raced to Captain Westfall. Somehow she managed to spill out a succinct, coherent version of her theory. The captain took all of thirty seconds to weigh the pros and cons. His jaw tight, he keyed his mike.

"Pegasus One, Chase One, this is Test Control. You have two minutes to possible system shutdown. We recommend you change course and drop down behind the Sierra Blancas. Use the mountains as a shield."

"Test Control, this is Chase One. We copy and are banking hard left."

"Roger, Chase One."

One of the dots on the tracking screen turned sharply. The other remained on a straight course. Westfall keyed his mike again.

"Pegasus One, do you copy?"

"Roger, Test Control. I'm initiating…"

The transmission ended in a screech of static. Kate's heart jumped straight to her throat as the lights in the control center flickered. Computers beeped. Displays went fuzzy.

A second later, the entire facility went dark.

Twelve

Deep, impenetrable blackness surrounded Kate. There was no light, not so much as a glimmer of a shadow, to give depth or definition to the windowless operations center. She heard a thump. A curse. A terse order for everyone to remain still until the emergency generators powered up.

Her heart measured each second with hard, excruciating thumps. After what seemed like a lifetime, a muted hum signaled that the backup generators were kicking in. Seconds later the lights blinked on.

The scene inside Test Control could have been crafted for a wax museum. Lifelike figures were frozen in different poses, their faces registering shock, dismay, determination.

Kate wrenched her gaze to the computerized tracking board. It was blank. Completely blank. Both aircraft had disappeared from the screen.

"Oh, God!"

Her agonized whisper seemed to break the spell. Suddenly everyone moved at once. Captain Westfall's deep, gravelly command brought instant order to the chaos.

"All right, people, listen up! Control, get on the radio and see if you can raise Pegasus and/or Chase One. The rest of you check your data terminals. I want to know if any of the computers aboard either aircraft are still transmitting."

Officers and civilians scrambled to power up their computers. Kate had no sooner toggled the key on her laptop than the loudspeaker in the control center crackled. She spun around, her heart in her throat, as the loudspeakers emitted a loud burst of static. A few seconds later, a voice broke through the noise.

"...declaring an in-flight emergency. Do you copy, Test Control?"

Kate's nails gouged into her clenched fists. The voice wasn't Dave's. The transmission was coming from Chase One. Her momentary panic quickly gave way to a sharp, stabbing relief. If the C–130 was still in the air, there was a good chance Pegasus was, too.

The pilot's transmission was still echoing through the control center when Captain Westfall spun around and barked at the communications tech.

"Can you raise them?"

"No, sir. Not yet."

His jaw tight, Westfall could only listen with the others as the C–130 pilot tried to reach them again.

"Test Control, this is Chase One. We're transmitting on guard 121.5, using our backup battery."

Kate bit down hard on her lower lip. She'd spent enough time in the air to know 121.5 was a guarded frequency monitored around the clock by the FAA. It was always open, available for use by everyone from crop dusters to stealth aircraft in emergencies. The fact that the chase plane was transmitting via an open frequency told her instantly his secure communications had failed.

In the next moment, Kate and the rest of the team knew that the 130's comm wasn't all that had failed.

"Be advised we're declaring an in-flight emergency," Chase One repeated. "Our airspeed and altitude gauges are spinning like roulette wheels, the secure communications are fried, and we're flying by the seat of our pants. We're transmitting using our backup battery."

As Kate was all too aware, the backup battery contained only about thirty minutes of juice. The C–130 would have to go silent soon to conserve power for his landing.

"We had the target on our left wing…"

The transmission fuzzed, cut off for a moment, came back over the loudspeaker.

"...so we overshot the vehicle. Last reported sighting was at tango 6.2. I repeat, Control, tango 6.2."

Pegasus! He was referring to Pegasus. Kate's gaze whipped to the wall map that divided the vast site into specific patrol areas. Tango 6.2 was to the southeast, where the mountains trailed off into desert.

"This is Chase One, terminating transmission."

Kate chewed on her lip again until she tasted blood. A hundred unanswered questions thundered through her head. Had Dave made it to the mountains? Had the peaks shielded him, as they apparently had the C–130? Or had the chase aircraft overshot its target vehicle before Pegasus reached the granite peaks?

That question, at least, was answered a long, agonizing twenty minutes later.

The burst of solar energy fried communications towers and knocked out commercial radio, TV and cell phones in most of southern New Mexico. Buried cables were protected, although the switchers that routed calls took severe hits. Some calls went through. Others ended in static.

Hardened military communications fared considerably better. Jill used her radio to direct her people to activate the site's disaster-response plan. Within moments, each of the senior test-cadre members was supplied with a hand radio and could communicate with their counterparts in other agencies.

After several frustrating tries, Kate managed to get through to the National Solar Observatory. She was taking a fix on the exact area affected by the burst when Jill came rushing back into the control center. Her face set in tight lines, the military cop relayed the news they'd all been dreading.

"A local sheriff just notified the FAA of a possible downed aircraft. The air force picked up on the notification and relayed it to us. The craft was spotted going in just before the sky turned green."

Kate's chest squeezed. She couldn't move, couldn't breathe.

"The sheriff reports a column of black smoke rising from the approximate location," Jill continued grimly.

Captain Westfall clenched his fists. "Where?"

"Sector tango 6.2, sir."

Since the energy burst had fried the instruments in the chopper assigned to the Pegasus site, the initial disaster-response team was forced to employ land vehicles. Kate's duties didn't call for her to be part of the team, but no one, Captain Westfall included, challenged her determination to join the convoy. She raced out of Test Operations to retrieve her sidearm and survival gear.

Two paces outside, she skidded to a stunned halt. Jill was hard on her heels and almost ran over her.

"Some show, isn't it?"

Swallowing, Kate took in the green and yellow waves undulating across the sky. Normally the scientist in Kate would thrill at such a unique display. At the moment, she could only curse herself for underestimating their potential severity.

Sick over her miscall, she gathered her gear and ran to Rattlesnake Ops, where the convoy had already formed. Two Humvees, a wide-track fire-suppression unit, and specially modified all-terrain vehicles with machine guns mounted on the hood.

"I'll take the lead ATV," Jill informed the hastily-assembled response team. Her blond hair was swept up under a Kevlar helmet. She wore a bullet-proof vest under her battle-dress uniform. Her sidearm was holstered on her belt, and she'd slung an assault rifle over one shoulder.

"Our navigational and comm systems depend on satellite signals," she said tersely, "so we'll have to do this the old-fashioned way, using maps and compasses. Rattlesnake Four, you and your squad take the first Humvee. Doc, your medical response team have the second. Commander Hargrave, you're with the medical team. Mount up."

Jill had worked a deal with the military cops up at Kirtland Air Force Base in Albuquerque to modify the Hummers' engines. They'd required the increased speed to keep up with Pegasus during his land runs. Even with their modified engines, though, the vehicles couldn't chew up the desert fast enough for Kate.

It took the small convoy almost thirty minutes to reach the foothills of the Sierra Blancas, another twenty to hump through them to reach Tango Sector.

Less than two hours had passed since they'd lost contact with Pegasus. Every minute of those hours was etched into Kate's soul. She felt as though she'd aged a hundred years by the time the driver of her vehicle shouted to the passengers in the back.

"We're seeing a plume of black smoke dead ahead. It appears to be rising from a narrow gully."

Cody Richardson shouted back the question that burned in Kate's throat. "Any sign of the vehicle or the pilot?"

"Negative, sir. Major Bradshaw has just signaled to us to kick into overdrive. Hang on to the side straps, folks, it's going to get bumpy."

Ten bone-rattling moments later, the Humvee jolted to a halt. Kate was almost snarling with impatience as she waited for the rear tailgate to let down and the others to pile out. Disregarding the hand Cody held out for her, she jumped out and hit the ground with a jar.

Even before she raced around to the front of the Hummer she could smell the burning engine fuel. No one who'd ever survived a crash—or assisted at a crash site—could mistake that oily, searing stink. Her first glimpse of the dense black tower of smoke billowing into the sky sent her heart and her last faint hope plunging.

"Oh, God!"

The billowing cloud blurred. Hot tears burned Kate's eyes. A scream rose in her throat, aching to rip loose.

Shuddering, she fought it back. She had work to do. They all did. She swiped an arm across her eyes, swallowed the sobs that tore at her throat and reached a shaking hand into the pack containing a small, portable respirator and an oxygen pack. Anyone going within a hundred yards of that raging cloud of smoke would need both bottled air and protective clothing.

The crash-recovery team was already dragging on their shiny silver protective gear. Suddenly, one of them jerked an arm toward the fire.

"Isn't that Captain Scott?"

Kate spun around, terrified he was pointing to a charred, blackened body. She couldn't believe her eyes when she saw Dave scrambling down the side of the gully.

"'Bout time you folks got here!"

Keeping well clear of the smoke, he broke into a long-legged lope. Kate wasn't as restrained. She dropped her gear bag and charged toward the gully full speed.

The idiot was grinning!

Grinning!

That was the only thought she had time for before she plowed into him. He rocked back, steadied, and wrapped his arms around her.

The sobs Kate had forced down just moments ago ripped free. She couldn't hold them back, any more than she could keep from gripping his flight suit with both fists, as if to make sure he didn't disappear into that black cloud.

"I thought you were dead!" she wailed against his chest.

"It was touch-and-go there for a few minutes," he admitted, his voice a deep rumble in her ear. "But I'm okay, babe. I'm okay."

She didn't know whether it was his steady assurances, the knuckle that rubbed gentle circles on her spine or the abrupt arrival of the rest of the team that made her realize she had to get herself under control. Gulping, she pushed the sobs back down her raw throat and swiped her forearm across her eyes again. Dave kept one arm around her as the others peppered him with questions.

"How did you get down?"

"Did you have to bail?"

"Have you sustained any injuries?"

The last came from Cody Richardson, and Kate's euphoria took a swift nosedive. He'd insisted he was okay, but in tough, macho pilot lingo, that could mean anything from scratch-free to protruding bones. She pulled away to take a closer look while Dave parried their questions with one of his own.

"Did the C–130 crew land safely?"

"As far as we know," Jill informed him. "They

declared an in-flight emergency and were flying by wire, but we've received no reports of a downed aircraft other than yours.''

Dave let his breath whistle out. ''Good. They were a couple of hundred feet above me when the sky lit up. I was afraid the mountains didn't give them the same protection they did me.''

''Some protection,'' Jill murmured, her glance going to the burning funeral pyre.

''That was a hell of a call on Captain Westfall's part,'' Dave commented, ''sending us down behind the hills like that.''

''Captain Westfall didn't make that call,'' Jill informed him. ''Kate did.''

''No kidding.'' He squeezed her waist. ''Thanks for saving my butt, Hargrave.''

''To paraphrase a certain pilot I know, your butt is eminently savable, Scott. I'm just sorry I couldn't save Pegasus, too.''

''You did.''

''Huh?''

That less-than-intelligent response won her a quick grin.

''I lost some instrumentation, but I managed to bring him down. He's parked about a hundred yards down the gully.''

Kate's gaze whipped to the noxious black column. ''But the fire... The smoke.''

''My communications were fried. I didn't have any

way to signal my location, so I emptied some fuel from the vehicle, piled up brush and started my own personal bonfire. I figured someone would spot the smoke.''

Kate couldn't quite take it in. Dave had survived. So had Pegasus. They'd both come within a breath of having their wings permanently clipped, but both had survived.

''Now what do you say we put out the fire,'' he suggested briskly, ''throw a security cordon around the craft until we can get it back to base, and make tracks. I didn't have any lunch. I'm hungry.''

Still in a daze, Kate shook her head. ''He's hungry,'' she echoed to Jill. ''He wants food.''

''So feed him,'' the cop replied with a grin. ''Doc, one of my troops will drive you, Kate and Dave back to the site. I'll stay with the craft until it's secured.''

Dave released her long enough to retrieve the gear bag he'd stashed well away from the fire before rejoining her at the Hummer. Kate ducked her head and prepared to scramble inside. He helped her with a firm hand under her elbow and a whispered promise that raised instant goose bumps.

''Food isn't all I'm hungry for, my very, very Kissable Kate.''

Thirteen

It was long past midnight before full communications and power were restored at the base, Dave had finished debriefing his extraordinary flight, and Pegasus was once again bedded down in his gleaming white stall.

Two days, Captain Westfall announced to his weary staff, before the maintenance crew could replace every circuit that had blown in the test vehicle.

"That puts us behind the eight ball again on the sea trials. We'll have to cut the water-test phase to the bone," he instructed Cari. "I want you and Major McIver in my quarters at oh-seven-hundred with a restructured schedule."

Cari gulped. "Yes, sir."

"You can work here," Westfall said. "We'll clear the conference room and let you have it. The rest of you…" His glance roamed the circle of military and civilian personnel. "Get some rest. You'll need it, because once we leave for the coast and begin water trials, the pace is going to pick up considerably."

Kate couldn't imagine how! In the past two months, their tight-knit group had warded off an attack by a mysterious virus, lost one of their members to a heart attack and survived a megaburst of solar energy. Oh, yes, they'd also proved Pegasus could run like the wind and fly with eagles.

She muttered as much to Jill as the group dispersed. With a shake of her head, the site's chief of security agreed the pace was plenty fast enough for her.

"At least I'll get a break when we move down to Corpus Christi. We'll be operating out of a navy base, so they'll have overall responsibility for security. All I'll have to do is keep unauthorized visitors away from our little corner of the base."

"Wish I could look forward to a break. We'll be arriving at Corpus smack in the middle of hurricane season. Cari might just get stuck swimming Pegasus through gale-force seas."

"If anyone can do it," said a deep voice behind them, "Cari can."

Both women turned to find Doc Richardson waiting patiently for Jill to finish her conversation. Kate looked past him at the still-dispersing group.

"If you're looking for Dave," the doc commented, "he said to tell you he had something he wanted to take care of and he'll see you later."

"Later?"

It was close to 2:00 a.m. Kate hadn't slept more than an hour or two last night. Worry over that damned solar flare had kept her tossing and turning. That, and Dave's challenge that she get back in the race.

"Did he say how much later?"

"No." The doc's cheeks creased in a grin. "But he did ask me to keep Jill occupied for an hour or two."

"And your reply was?" Jill wanted to know.

"I told him I'm here to serve. Come with me, Major, and I'll let you look through my microscope."

"The last time I did that, I ended up flat on my back. With a virus," she tacked on dryly, but she didn't protest when Cody steered her toward the dispensary.

With a surge of excitement that chased away her weariness, Kate headed for her quarters. She had a good idea why Dave had asked Cody to keep Jill busy for an hour or so. If she moved fast, she could get in a quick shower and change out of the flight suit she'd been in for going on twenty hours now before the man arrived at her quarters.

She should have known she couldn't outrun a sky jock. Dave was already there. In her bed. Wearing nothing but a grin and his watch.

"What took you so long?" he complained.

Laughing, she leaned against the doorjamb. "How the dickens did you beat me here? Cody said you had some business to take care of."

"I did."

With a jerk of his chin, he indicated the box of condoms he'd invested in at the Inn of the Mountain Gods. They'd run through a respectable number of them, but there had to be at least five or six left.

"After our little adventure today, I just wanted to make sure we had plenty of backup and redundant systems."

Kate groaned. "That's the worst attempt to get a girl in the sack I've heard yet."

"I can do better," he assured her. "Come here, KK, and let me whisper in your ear."

"KK?" she asked, then remembered the nickname he'd bestowed on her. "Never mind, I got it. Move over, DD. Give me room to sit down and take off my boots."

He obliged, edging his hips to the far side of the twin bed. Kate sat on the edge, brought her foot up and let her glance sweep the length of his lean, muscled body. Her bootlace snapped in her fingers.

Dave didn't help matters by propping his head in

one hand and playing with her hair while she shucked her boots and socks.

"DD, huh? Let me guess. Darling Dave, right?"

"Wrong."

"Daredevil Dave?"

"Not even close."

"Gimme a hint."

"No hints. You have to figure it out for yourself."

Kate stood, unzipped her blue flight suit in one fluid move and stepped out of it. Her sports bra and panties followed her cotton T-shirt to the floor.

"In the meantime, cowboy, why don't we see just how redundant your systems are."

Very redundant, Kate decided some hours later.

She lay flopped across Dave's chest, boneless with pleasure and so sleepy she couldn't pry up even one eyelid. A dozen solar flares could have burst above her and blazed across the night sky and she wouldn't have seen them.

She did, however, hear Dave's soft whisper as he eased her off his chest and into the crook of his arm.

"This is one race we'll both win, Kate."

* * * * *

If you've enjoyed this novel then be sure to look for Merline Lovelace's next book,
The Right Stuff, *in Sensation next month.*

RULING PASSIONS
by
Laura Wright

LAURA WRIGHT

has spent most of her life immersed in the world of acting, singing and competitive ballroom dancing. But when she started writing romances, she knew she'd found the true desire of her heart! Although born and raised in Minneapolis, USA, Laura has also lived in New York City, Milwaukee and Columbus, Ohio. Currently, she is happy to have set down her bags and made Los Angeles her home. And a blissful home it is—one that she shares with her theatrical production manager husband, Daniel, and three spoiled dogs. During those few hours of free time from her beloved writing, Laura enjoys going to art galleries and films, cooking for her hubby, walking in the woods, lazing around lakes, puttering in the kitchen and frolicking with her animals.

Laura would love to hear from you. You can write to her at PO Box 5811, Sherman Oaks, CA 91413, USA or email her at laurawright@laurawright.com.

To my child, who grows inside of me
as I write this final Fiery Tale: Daddy and I love you.

Prologue

_____

Scotland
May

The sea took the shape of a woman's hip as it climbed into a wave: curved and pink in the setting sun. But Crown Prince Alexander William Charles Octavos Thorne had no use for women anymore, real or imagined.

Lungs filled with salty air, he sagged against a jagged rock and watched the surf crash against the beach and crawl toward him.

He didn't run from its progress, didn't move. Not even when icy water stung his foot.

He understood the sea's endless need to consume, to take, to hurt. For five long years he'd felt the like— too many times to count. Then there was today...

Three hours ago he'd received word that his wife had left town, left him for another man. Like the cold, pinkish waves before him, relief rippled through his blood. Relief and anger—for a woman who'd hated him the minute they'd married, a woman who'd acted like a bloody iceberg no matter how hard he'd try to care for her, a woman who'd wanted no children, no warmth, no friendship.

Alex tore off his shirt, let the cool air rush over his chest.

He'd been a man of his word, married a woman he'd hardly known, remained loyal and honorable to her, kept silent when she'd told his father and the court that they were trying to conceive a child—even kept up the charade that they'd been living together for the past two years.

But today, on the day she'd run off with another man, loyalty, honor and care went to Llandaron only. Alex had his country to think of now, damage control to see to. If the world found out the truth of his situation, the heart of the Llandaron people could be destroyed forever.

Pretense was his only saving grace.

He would move slowly, tread easily. He would use whatever money and means was required to settle this matter, while keeping the truth hidden for as long as possible. Next week he left for his summit in Japan with the emperor. He would make his wife's excuses, take care of business, and while he was there, call in a favor from an old school chum he trusted, who just happened to be a divorce barrister in London. Then at some point, he'd return home to Llandaron and tell his family—tell his father that he'd failed.

At that offensive realization, Alex's jaw tightened to the point of pain. If there was anything he despised more than failure it was admitting it.

Echoing his mood, twilight seeped in around him and the sea turned choppy, each boundless curl morphing from pale pink to violent purple.

From this day forward, he vowed silently, no woman would rule him.

And from this day forward, the prospect that he would rule dimmed.

The lifelong assumption that he would govern his country might now have to be put aside in favor of his brother, Maxim. For a queen and an heir were vital to the Kingdom of Llandaron. And Maxim had both.

Pain snapped at Alex's heart. He opened his mouth and released five years of unlivable ache. The gut-wrenching cries to the sea echoed, ricocheting back into his ears, making him start, stop.

Suddenly his eyes widened, focused. All thought drifted down, sank into the wet sand under his feet as out in the distance, a sailboat lurched across the coarse sea.

For one brief moment, before the boat disappeared behind the towering cove walls, he saw a woman, perched on the bow of the craft like one of the jewel-tailed mermaids from his childhood dreams, all mind-blowing curves and brazen, red hair.

She was facing him, her long hair thrashing about her neck and chest like silken whips. She seemed to stare straight at him—a bizarre sensation, as her eyes were impossible to make out. Unlike the delectable combination of senses emanating from her: air, water and fire.

From gut to groin Alex went hard.

A massive wave crashed just inches from him, spitting saltwater into his face, his mouth and eyes. He scrubbed a hand over his face to clear the mist, then quickly glanced up.

Both boat and mermaid were gone.

Awareness, raw and demanding battled in his blood, but he shoved the feeling away. He'd felt need before, perhaps not this strong, but he'd fight it just the same. No woman would rule him.

Jaw set, Alex stripped bare and dove into the frigid water, determined to remind the lower half of him—just as he had his mind—who was master.

One

Fog surrounded the sloop like a perilous curtain, while the influx of seawater slithered into the hull in a snake-like stream.

As she stuffed wet couch cushions into the cavity, Sophia Dunhill cursed herself for forgetting to plot her estimated position.

How could she have been so stupid? So scattered?

Maybe because with her grandfather's beautiful homeland in her sights, all thoughts of navigation had simply drifted from her mind.

She'd been sitting on the deck with the late-afternoon sun warming her shoulders, staring out at the small island nation just off the coast of Cornwall. She'd felt mesmerized by Llandaron. Her mountains and her beautiful landscape of trees, purple heather and rocks itching with beach grass.

The weather had been absolutely perfect. Blue sky, calm seas. Then everything had changed. Out of nowhere thick fog had rolled in like a milky carpet so fast she'd barely had time to think. And in seconds the *Daydream* had collided with the rocky coastline.

How was it possible? A sailor for a good ten years and she hadn't seen this one coming.

Panic surged in her blood as she bolted up the companionway steps to the deck and straight into the thick fog. She couldn't lose this vessel to her own stupidity and a pile of rock. It was all she had left of her grandfather. The beautiful sloop was his legacy, his dream—and the one thing that only they'd shared. It had to remain afloat. After all, she still had one leg of this voyage, her grandfather's voyage, to complete. She had to dock the *Daydream* in the small fishing village of Baratin where her grandfather was born before she could return home to San Diego, to her empty apartment and to the writer's block that had plagued her since his death.

Baratin wasn't far, just on the other side of Llandaron, and come hell or rough water she would make it.

With steady hands she hauled a spare sail across the deck and draped it over the gaping hole. But the water was too powerful. The padding wasn't going to hold for long. Especially bumping against the rocks the way they were.

A fleeting thought born out of panic, shot into her mind and she quickly shoved it away.

Abandon ship.

But to a sailor, abandoning ship was akin to abandoning a child. It wasn't done.

At that moment seawater burst through a deck plank like a geyser. The boat shifted, groaned in pain.

Abandoning her child.

Sophia's heart squeezed. She had no choice.

Grabbing the chart and ditch bag she'd packed, Sophia eased her way to the bow of the boat. Was she a coward to take the easy road? she couldn't help but wonder. For a moment she was reminded of her parents' funeral, of the decision she'd made that day to defy their will and go and live with her grandfather instead of her stern aunt Helen. After years of living with two domineering spirits, Sophia had felt desperate for freedom. She'd gone on instinct, and finding her grandfather had been one of the best decisions of her life.

Instinct was all she had to cling to now, and it was screaming at her to jump.

Sophia gave one last glance at the chart to make sure she knew which way to swim. Then, with her eyes closed, her breath a little too tight in her lungs, she listened for the sound of the waves just as her grandfather had taught her.

And after snugging up the straps on her life jacket, she slipped into the water.

He'd hoped to keep the world out.

At least for a while.

From the deck of his beach house, Alex Thorne leaned back in his chair, took a pull on his beer and reveled in the shroud of fog that enveloped him. Granted the mystical fog only lasted one hour in Llandaron. But it was an hour of no questions, no answers and it was pure ecstasy.

After returning home from London five days ago, there had been nothing but questions and the demand for answers. As always he'd dealt with each as succinctly and as nonemotionally as possible. His family didn't need details of his failed marriage, just the facts: he was divorced and back home to resume his duties, face his people.

Given his brusque nature, Alex had thought the news would flow easily from his lips. But it hadn't. Deep in his gut, shame had paved the road.

His brother, Maxim, and sister, Catherine, had offered their support and their love, while his father had listened with a tight expression, giving off only sighs and an occasional nod.

Alex didn't scorn the man's pragmatic reaction. In

fact, he understood it. He, too, was worried about Llandaron and how its citizens would take the news of his failure when it was soberly announced at the annual Llandaron Picnic on Saturday. He couldn't forget how year after year his people waited patiently for news of a child. News that would never come.

Could his people forgive him this, too? Or would they ask him to step down in favor of Maxim?

Alex took another pull on his beer and stared out into the fog-shrouded sea he bowed to whenever he needed some semblance of comfort. There was no getting past the fact that he loved his people more than his own life. And he was ready to do as they wished. Whatever they wished—

Suddenly, Alex stopped short, all thoughts spent, and leaped to his feet. Brow furrowed, he cocked his head to the side and listened.

A sound. A cry—coming from the water, faint, but desperate—echoed over the beach. A sound that made his blood run cold.

Gut in his throat, Alex bolted off the deck, dropped down onto the cool sand and raced to the water's edge. The fog was thick as butter, but the visual impasse didn't make him cautious. He could have run that stretch of beach blindfolded, he'd combed it so many times.

There it was again. A woman's cry. Louder now.

Without pausing to think, Alex thrashed into the

surf, then dove beneath the waves. He swam like a demon toward a cry muffled by the swirl of the sea.

When he surfaced, he fought for his bearings. He looked right then left, then behind himself as his legs worked like twin engines in the water.

It took all of five seconds for him to locate the source of that cry. Red hair, wide eyes, pale complexion. A woman thrashing about in the water, the strings of her life vest caught on rock.

Her shouts for help grew hoarse, weak. She was obviously tiring. The erratic tumble of Alex's heartbeat thumped in his ears as he swam like a sea snake straight for her. Once he reached her side, he wasted no time with words. He ripped the vest from the rock, then eased his arm around her waist and scooped her up.

But in his haste for shore, his leg caught, gripped by a colony of seaweed. The slimy mess wrapped his ankle like a hungry Octopus, dragging him down, dragging him under.

Cursing, he lost hold on the girl, for a moment lost his breath as he struggled under the whirling sea. Panic knocked him senseless as his pulse raced wildly in his chest. Floating below the surface of the green sea, he saw fleeting images of death, his death.

Then suddenly he felt a rush of water loop his legs, saw the red-haired woman down by his ankle, cutting him away from the slimy green god.

Up he sailed, practically flew to the surface of the

water like a helium balloon to the blue sky. Air smashed into his lungs. Coughing and sputtering, he fought to stay above the lurching sea.

Then, just when he thought fatigue might claim him, an arm eased across his chest, hooked him like a sad fish and he felt himself move.

The waves rose and fell around him like the footfall of a giant as they inched toward shore. The woman took her time, swimming slowly, taking the waves with gentle insistence, allowing them both a chance to get their bearings.

Though Alex's lungs ached, his breathing soon regulated and his pulse eased toward normal as he floated on the surface of the water.

By the time his feet hit wet sand, he could walk. But he didn't stay upright for long. When he felt the comfort of dry sand, he dropped down and stretched out. He heard the woman ease down beside him.

"You better be all right, Lancelot," she said breathlessly.

It took Alex a good thirty seconds to respond to the thoroughly American quip. "Lancelot?"

"The knight? The one who rushed in to save the damsel in distress?"

"Right," he mumbled, rubbing a hand over his wet face. "The one who rushed in to save the damsel in distress, then got his foot caught in the seaweed."

"Seaweed, stirrups…same difference." The woman put a hand on his shoulder. "You're okay, right?"

"I'll live." Alex forced his heavy eyelids open. "So, if I'm Lancelot that must make you…"

The words died on his lips. Framed in a halo of milky-white fog, just inches from his face, was a woman of such heavenly beauty he nearly thought he'd succumbed to the pull of the ocean depths. Eyes the color of the sea—pale green with tinges of blue—and miles of red hair, wet and in gentle waves.

His body tightened. It *was* her. He felt it in his bones—that same need, that same connection. How was this possible? The mermaid from four months ago, here. Washed up on his stretch of beach.

"I think that makes me an idiot," she said with dry humor. "Actually I'd say we're both idiots."

"How do you figure?"

"Me getting caught on that rock." She dragged her tongue across her lower lip thoughtfully. "You getting caught in the weeds."

If he snaked a hand around the back of her neck, pulled her down to him, would she part her lips for him, kiss him the same hungry way he wanted so desperately to kiss her? "That doesn't sound like idiotic behavior to me."

"No? What does it sound like, then?"

"Divine intervention. Perhaps we're both looking to get caught."

The fog seemed to suffuse Alex all at once. He had

no idea what had made him say such an insane thing, but it was too late to retract the statement.

The woman stared intently at him, as though she could see right through his skin. "I'm not looking to get caught, I'm looking to find freedom."

"God knows why, but right now they seem to be one and the same." He said the words as much to himself as to her.

Confusion swept her face. "Yes, they do. Why is that?"

She didn't give him a chance to answer, though he really had none to offer. This mood, this moment, was unreal, surreal. She lowered herself on top of him. Her arms snaked around his neck, her needful gaze melted into his own and she kissed his mouth. Just once, one soft, small touch.

Alex cursed the delicious weight of her, the fullness of her breasts pressing against his chest, the pouty lips just inches from his own.

With the fog as her refuge, she was doing something terrible and highly erotic to him, something he'd never felt before—or wanted to feel. Her eyes, the way she looked at him…she had him bound, deep in a trance—a mysterious, sensuous trance. And he needed to get lost there.

Mouth to mouth, body to body, fog blanketing them from the world. Pure paradise.

The freedom to be caught.

His pulse slammed her rhythm in his blood. This

had to be a dream. Or maybe it was a nightmare, he reasoned as pure heat came over him, dark and unstoppable. A nightmare where all the control he prided himself on was lost. Where his mind went, his reason, too.

Animal instinct took him. He shifted, had her on her back in seconds. He watched as she smiled tentatively, then lifted her chin, parted her lips. Was he insane? he wondered as her eyes drugged him, drew him in. Did he care?

The surge of need that rippled through him was completely foreign. Or maybe it had just been tucked away, waiting…

A deep, aching groan erupted from his throat as he lowered his head, brushed his lips over hers, just to test, to tease. And as he'd hoped, prayed, she met him.

Hot mouth, sweet tongue. Her fingers fisted in his hair, pulling him closer.

Alex couldn't think—didn't want to think. He whispered against her mouth, "What are we doing?"

With an erotic nibble on his lower lip, she uttered, "I have no idea. But it feels so good."

"Too good."

His mind went blank once again as she kissed him, deeply, urging him to follow, to play, to plunder. Total madness took him, and his kiss turned ravenous. She angled her head over and over, her hips pressing up, up against the steel in his jeans.

A need for control rapped at his mind. He pulled

away, just an inch, his eyes burrowing into hers. Sea-green hunger stared up at him, willed him to close his eyes and take—only take. And when a bleating cry of distress escaped her throat, he silenced her in the only way he knew how.

Around them, the ocean pounded the shore.

Around them, the fog swirled.

With a wildness he was just beginning to under-stand, she pulled at his T-shirt, fumbled with the but-ton on his jeans. Then before he could think, she rolled them both over until she was straddling his waist, fog lacing her face.

Pulse pounding, Alex eased down her bathing suit top, cupped her full breasts in his palms, rolled the swollen buds between his thumbs and forefingers. A hot gasp rushed out of her, and he felt her quiver over and over against his erection. He knew she was on the brink of release, totally free to take what she wanted.

He tugged at her nipples as she moved her hips against him in a rhythm as timeless as the ocean waves. Beneath them, sand flicked and flew. Alex moved with her, taking her to the edge as against his fingers, those rosy peaks turned crimson.

Suddenly she cried out, a deep aching sound from low in her throat.

Painfully hard, Alex rolled her on her back. He had her suit off, her thighs splayed before the next ocean wave crashed against the beach behind them. Breath heavy, eyes hungry, she wrapped her long, glorious legs around him, then slammed her hips upward.

Alex stared down at her. "Do you want this?"

"Yes," she whispered, panting.

Without another word, another thought, Alex rose up and plunged inside of her. He gasped as she stretched around him, wet and hot. "You feel like heaven."

A moan escaped and the words, "I'm no angel." She lifted and lowered her hips, moving him in and out of her body with wild, wicked strokes.

Complete madness took him. But he knew the madness couldn't last long, and that made him sick with anger. He wanted to be lost in this, in her, in this hallucination forever. But his body was weak from years of denial.

Sweat beaded on his brow as he drove into her, burrowing them both deeper into the sand.

She was so tight. So was he.

Her hands were everywhere at once; his back, his buttocks, gripping his shoulders. Until she stiffened, her legs releasing their hold on him and opening wide.

He could feel her climax coming, rumbling through her body like thunder, grasping him with her muscles. The feeling was so sweet he thought he'd lose his mind.

But instead he lost his control.

And as she convulsed around him, tightening, squeezing, Alex gave in, fell over the edge and exploded along with her.

As the heat of Sophia's body ebbed, so did the fog around them. For one full minute she silently prayed that it would take her with it, up into the sky where it was safe from reality and awkwardness. But as she'd learned early in life, the elements kept their own counsel.

The man beside her shifted, his hot skin grazing her own.

Unbidden, her body stirred in response. She stifled a groan. No, she was no angel. Burying her face in her lover's neck, she wondered how in the world had she allowed such a thing to happen. Granted, she wasn't someone who shied away from life—but making love to a total stranger was completely over the top.

And, yet, she wanted more.

More lying naked beside the most achingly handsome man she'd ever seen. More time where loneliness and uncertainty subsided and wonderfulness abounded.

More feeling like a woman, desired and consumed.

Reaching twenty-six years old with one pale love affair to her credit, she'd often fantasized about moments like this. She just never imagined one becoming reality. And now that it had, waking up wasn't as easy as opening her eyes to the morning sunshine and safety of her nautical bedroom back home in San Diego.

Sophia's thoughts faded as the man beside her disentangled himself from her grasp and sat up. His jaw was as tight as a lobster trap, his heather-colored eyes filled with dismay as he looked down at her. Her heart lurched and fell, and she felt very naked. Despite his gloriously handsome features, his expression was one of consternation.

But for his own actions or for hers, she wasn't sure.

With her cheeks turning pinker by the second, she snatched up her bathing suit and hurriedly slipped it on as she tried for a casual tone. "I suppose you won't believe me if I say that I've never done anything like this before?"

His eyes were blank now, no banter, no smile. "I must apologize."

His husky brogue washed over her, heating her skin once again under her wet suit. "There's no reason for an apol—"

"Of course there is." He cursed, drove a hand through his thick, black hair. "You were practically drowning out there—"

"So were you."

"—and I—"

"And we," she corrected.

He paused for a moment, his gaze moving over her. "Who are you?"

A fool? she felt an impulse to exclaim. A shameless

woman with absolutely no hindsight. A woman so desperate to live a little, she'd lost her mind...for a moment. "Maybe it's better that we don't know each other's names."

He released a haughty snort. "Impossible."

"Not really. Don't ask. Don't tell." *Just give me five minutes to disappear*, she thought dryly.

"I'm afraid that rule doesn't apply here."

"Why not?"

He stood up then, slipped on his jeans, all broad shoulders and lean muscle. Lord, the man could've been carved in bronze he was so well put together. Wavy black hair licked the back of his neck, razor-sharp features showed off his imperious nature to perfection, and then there were those amethyst eyes—needful, yet proud as a lion.

"Let's just say I'm old-fashioned," he said dryly.

"Well, I'm not," she countered. It was a lie, but emotional anxiety always brought out the worst in her. She wasn't about to spill her guts to this man. Not when he was making it crystal clear that their lovemaking was a huge mistake. She wasn't going to tell him her name, where she was from, that she was sailing the isles for her grandfather as she tried to come up with a decent idea for her next children's book.

No. She just wanted to run.

"I don't want to resort to commands," he began,

crossing his arms over his thickly muscled chest. "But I will."

Sophia's brows shot together; she wasn't sure she'd heard him correctly. "Excuse me?"

"I'm afraid I will have to command you to tell me who you are."

"Command me?"

"That's correct."

She grinned, let out a throaty laugh and shook her head, the tension inside her easing considerably. "That's very funny. You're funny. So that must make you what? The king of Llandaron or something?"

He shook his head brusquely. "Not yet."

Her stomach pinged with nerves, but she shoved the feeling away, forced out another easy laugh. "Well then, I suppose you can call me the queen of the sea."

"This isn't a time for humor, Miss..."

"I agree." She stood up, straightened her shoulders. This was getting ridiculous. They'd acted without thinking, made a horrible mistake. But it was over. She needed to get out of here. Now. Before this charade went any further. Before she made an even bigger fool out of herself. "Any more commands before I go find a boatworks, sire?"

His severe gaze fairly wilted her resolve. "Just one."

She swallowed, feeling the heat in her belly fire to

life—and hating herself for such a reaction. "Knock yourself out."

"I was careless. For that I apologize."

"Please, no more apolo—"

"You may be carrying my child, miss... The heir to the throne of Llandaron." He raised a fierce brow at her. "I'm afraid you'll have to remain with me, in my kingdom, until I know for certain."

Two

―――――

Alex watched the blood drain from the woman's beautiful face like wet paint from a canvas, and felt as though he wanted to ram his fist through a wall. He was the cause of the unease and shock she was feeling. He'd been too quick, too apathetic, in his quest to bring reality to the situation.

As though in the path of a rolling ball of fire, the woman leaped, glanced over her shoulder, then returned her stormy green gaze to him. "Listen, whoever you are. This, whatever it is, has gotten way out of hand."

Alex was calm as he replied, "You don't believe me?"

She sniffed, looked him up and down. "No, of course I don't."

"There are many ways to prove my identity."

"I'm sure there are," she said, her tone thick with agitated sarcasm. "But I'm not really up for more games today."

"Neither am I."

"Good." Her gaze filled with strength as her long, fiery hair swirled around them. "My boat hit a rock and is flailing around out there. I need to have it towed in before—"

"There's no need to worry about your boat. I will have it brought in for you."

"That's not necessary."

"I think under the circumstances—"

"Thank you, but I can handle it. Now if you'll excuse me." And with that she turned to leave.

But her hasty departure was something Alex couldn't allow. This was far from over, far from resolved. He grabbed her hand.

When she whirled back to face him, her expression screamed antagonism. "You've got some nerve, buddy."

A grin tugged at Alex's mouth. No one had ever spoken to him with such ferocity. Granted, she didn't believe he was the crown prince of the country, but still her pluck intrigued him.

"What do you plan to do while you wait for the repairs on your boat?" he asked.

She tugged her hand from his. "I haven't made any immediate plans yet."

Alex looked out toward the ocean, saw the boat thrashing around and made a quick assessment. "With damage like that, repairs will take a few weeks at the very least."

"We'll see. I'm pretty good with boats, so maybe I'll lend a hand."

"I don't think Mr. Verrick will allow such a thing, but of course, there is no harm in trying."

"Thanks for the advice. Can I go now?"

"Just one more thing. Where will you stay while your boat is healing?"

"I don't know," she said impatiently. "In town, I guess."

Alex shook his head, a vehemence he didn't know he possessed seeping into his blood. There was no way he was going to send this woman off to some hotel room. No matter how unwise, he wanted her close, where he could keep an eye on her, where he could protect her—where he could make certain she wouldn't leave Llandaron without his knowledge.

Not with the ominous possibility of his child growing inside her.

"You will stay here at my beach house."

Her brows shot together. "Just who do you think you are?"

"I told you who I am."

"Right. Future king. Right." She gestured around her. "I don't see any guards."

"I don't allow my guards in my private residence, nor are they allowed on the grounds."

"That's a little unsafe for the future king, isn't it?" she asked sarcastically.

"Perhaps. But after a lifetime of living 'beneath the shield of protection,' so to speak, it is what I have chosen."

She met his imperious gaze without flinching. "Look, buddy, what happened here was a mistake, okay? Can't we leave it at that? We weren't thinking. All that fog and having your life flash before your eyes can—"

"Can make one foolish?"

She pointed at him. "Exactly."

"Well, that doesn't stay the fact that you might be pregnant."

On a tiny gasp, her mouth dropped open and her gaze dropped to her belly. There was a long silence before her eyes finally met his once again. And when they did he saw pure unadulterated shock. Then, like a shifting breeze, anxiety and wonder filled those sea-green depths.

She said quietly, almost to herself, "Did you ever think that maybe I'm on the pill?"

"I don't think so."

"And why would you think that?" She lifted her

impish chin. "Am I so undesirable that I wouldn't have a steady boyfriend?"

Undesirable? Alex fairly chuckled at the thought. The word sounded like insanity coming from that full, sweet mouth he wanted to taste again. Just as the word *boyfriend* rang like an irritating bell in his brain.

His jaw tightened. He didn't want to think of her with another man, he didn't want to think of her taking birth control for an active love life. Both thoughts made his gut twist. But such feelings were dangerous.

"I wasn't meaning to insult you," he said tightly. "I just assumed... Well, you've been out to sea for at least four months. Alone. The need for companionship—"

She cut him off, her tone shaky, "How in the world could you know that I've been at sea for four months?"

"I saw you." The image of her standing on that boat, hair wild, all mind-numbing curves, slammed into his mind—along with the white-hot need that accompanied it.

"When?" she demanded. "When did you see me?"

"In Scotland. Back in May. I was on the beach. You were standing on the bow of your boat."

As the salty wind whipped around them, her eyes darkened to a rich green, pink stained her cheeks. "That was you?"

Alex nodded, his pulse jumping to life in his blood.

So she'd seen him, too.

Sophia knew her face was turning bright red in front of this man, and she hated herself for it. She wasn't one for embarrassment or awkward situations. In fact, she pretty much ran headfirst into conflicts so they could be resolved and done with. But around this gorgeous creature she wasn't herself. And the fact that she'd had dreams, even fantasies about seeing him, bare-chested and formidable, etched into Scotland's rocky coastline for a full month afterward, made her even more disheartened.

"Who are you? Really?" she asked him, tucking a strand of hair behind her ear.

"Crown Prince Alexander William Charles Octavos Thorne." The grin he gave her made her knees soft as cream. "Really."

"You're lying."

He shook his head. "I don't lie."

Breath held, she studied him in the light of the fading sun. Her grandfather had always said she was a great judge of character. But this man was harder to read than most. He seemed to have iron bars shooting up around him.

But even so, in those heather-colored eyes, in that solemn set of his jaw she saw honor—she saw truth.

She turned away, back toward the sea, with a groan. This was impossible. Impossible. Such things didn't happen in real life. A prince, for heaven's sake.

Had she really gone and done something so outrageous as to make love to a prince?

Her hand went to her stomach.

A child... An oh-so-familiar ache surged into her throat. She'd been an only child, treated as an adult with all the responsibilities that came with it since the age of five. Ever since, she'd dreamed about having a family, a brood of kids. Teaching them to read, to sail, to swim and, most important, to be silly and carefree—to be a kid.

But having a child this way...

And with royalty...

For a moment Sophia thought that maybe she'd fallen asleep on the deck of the sloop that afternoon. Under the hot sun. Maybe her mind had played tricks and this was all just one crazy dream. The crash, the fog, the man...

With a dash of hope in her heart, she reached over and pinched her arm. A sudden sting told her that she was very much awake.

"And your name?" he asked.

Sophia glanced up at him and muttered a bleak, "Sophia Dunhill from San Diego, California."

With a grim smile the prince took her hand. "Come back to my house, Sophia, dry off, then we'll have your boat rescued."

"Good God. Not another American," the king exclaimed.

Leaning back against the palace library's black-walnut mantel, Alex crossed his arms over his chest and watched his brother, Maxim, and his newly-pregnant sister, Cathy, turn to their American spouses and break out into laugher.

Ten minutes ago Alex had left his spunky little mermaid to her bathing. She'd sworn up and down that she would stay put "at least for tonight," she'd said. He didn't know whether to believe her or not, but what he did know was that if he hadn't taken a break from her presence, he would have pulled her into his arms and made love to her again.

Now, just the thought of her nude, in his bath, up to her neck in vanilla-scented suds...

His hands balled into fists under his crossed arms. Control had to return, must return.

"Unlike my brother and sister," Alex began with a frown. "There is no...romance here, father."

The king gave his regal wolfhound, Glinda, a pat on the head, then leaned back in his favorite armchair and took a swallow of brandy. "I should hope not. This would be a very unwise time to go running around with—"

"Some American, Your Highness?" Maxim's wife, Fran, said on a chuckle.

Alex watched as the king tried to jolt his pregnant and very American daughter-in-law with a withering look, but it came out as a lopsided grin instead. And when the pretty veterinarian returned the smile and patted him on the knee, the old man actually blushed.

The sight of his father turning from staunch dictator to blushing teddy bear stunned Alex. He'd never seen that side of his father. Not since he'd returned home, at any rate. It didn't take a masters in psychology to deduce that this "American" had done the softening up.

Maxim turned to Alex, grinned. "So, she turned up on the beach, did she?"

Alex nodded succinctly. He wasn't elaborating. The particulars of his encounter with Sophia on the beach didn't need to be shared. As it was, the truth wouldn't stop playing over and over in his mind; visions were more than enough. "Her boat needs extensive repairs."

"And you volunteered to put her up until it's fixed?" Cathy's husband, Dan, asked with a grin to match Maxim's. The new head of palace security was not only a former U.S. Marshal, but far too inquisitive for his own good.

Alex muttered tightly, "That's right. It was my stretch of beach she washed up on. I would say that holds me responsible."

Dan and Maxim exchanged wry glances.

"Didn't you used to dream about mermaids when you were little?" Cathy asked, taking a sip of her cranberry juice.

"He certainly did," Maxim said.

Fran smiled broadly and snuggled closer to her husband who had her very sleepy wolfhound pup, Lucky, on his lap. "How very romantic."

Dan turned to his wife. "So what were these dreams about, Angel?"

Alex sighed heavily. "When did these family dinners start?"

They all ignored him as Cathy explained, "Alex was always a stoic child. He rarely told us anything...private. But when he started having these dreams, the same one, every night for a full year, he couldn't keep it to himself. I was rather young, but I still remember how my big brother, my very stoic, grumbling brother, looked when he'd tell us about this dream."

"All right, that's enough," Alex said, his voice laced with warning.

Maxim chuckled. "Not nearly."

Cathy smiled and continued, "He would sit on the roof of the stables and look out at the ocean and tell us all about her. Long red hair, green eyes, pale skin stepping out of the sea with her arms outstretched."

"Don't forget about her magical powers," Maxim prompted.

Quite caught up in the whole mess, the king inquired, "What's this about magic?"

Dan and Fran nodded quickly, both inquiring, "What about her magical powers?"

Alex groaned, stalked over to the bar and filled a

glass with whiskey. How could such a stupid, adolescent dream come back to haunt him this way? And where were the silent and very sedate family dinners he'd always enjoyed—and had counted on tonight?

Cathy's words came out like a sigh. "He said that when she looked at him he felt as though he could fly, as though he was free, as though he could do and be anything."

Alex cursed, his knuckles white as he gripped the glass of whiskey.

Dan snorted. "What do you make of that, Max? Poetry or something?"

Maxim shrugged. "I'm not certain. But it sounds as though he was in love with her."

Alex glared at his brother and sister. "You know, there are plenty of humiliating stories I can share with your spouses."

Fran grinned widely, her eyes lighting up. "Oooo. Like what?"

Maxim gave his wife a kiss on the cheek. "He's bluffing, sweetheart."

"You want to try me, little brother?" Alex countered.

"How about after dinner," Fran suggested on a chuckle. "When we're all full and not as prickly." She turned to Alex. "So, what does this Sophia look like?"

Alex shook his head at his new sister-in-law. She was quick, very quick. Turning the conversation back to him and this mystery they all seemed to want to solve. He should be steaming mad. But no man could be angry with this woman for long—that was clear. Smart, beautiful and glowing with pregnancy.

He stilled, his mind returning to a beach house not far away. Would Sophia glow from carrying his child?

"Red hair by any chance?" Fran asked softly.

With a wave of the hand, Alex tossed out without thinking, "Red hair, green eyes and pale skin. Don't know about the magical powers."

Everyone fell silent, only the crackling of the fire and the subtle tinkling of ice cubes in glasses could be heard. Alex could fairly feel them gaping at each other over what he'd just said.

"Why would she not come to dinner tonight?" the king asked at last.

"She wanted some time to herself," Alex said tightly. "And after...the stress of losing her boat today, I thought it best not to overwhelm her." He didn't add *in her condition*—or potential condition.

The king drained his glass, then announced, "I would like to meet this young woman."

Cathy nodded. "I think we all would."

"How about a picnic lunch on the hill tomorrow?" Fran suggested. "With Aunt Fara and Ranen, and Glinda and the pups, too."

Chest tight, Alex stared at his family as they planned and plotted a way to meet his new houseguest. Everything was being taken out of his hands today. What happened at the beach with Sophia; his strange need for her. And now the insistence of his family. He felt as though he was just an onlooker, a bystander, in his own life. As though some force of nature had taken over.

But before Alex could even attempt to snatch back any semblance of control, his father stood up and barked his command. "Very good. A picnic on the hill. That's settled, then. Let's go in to dinner now."

Sophia stepped out of the bath feeling only mildly relaxed. Here she was, in the crown prince of Llandaron's opulent bathroom of pristine white and rugged navy, attempting to soak off the day's craziness.

But how could she soak away unease and hope, not to mention a need unlike any she'd ever felt before?

Her shrink back in San Diego would have a field day with her behavior today. Normally their sessions were comprised of past regrets and pains: her lonely childhood, her parents' death, her devotion to her beloved grandfather, her wariness to get involved with, then subsequently lose someone she loved.

But this...

This situation that she'd found herself in was beyond all analysis.

Sophia stepped over to the gold-encrusted mirror above the sink, dropped her towel and stared at her reflection. Bright eyes, pink lips, flushed cheeks. She had the look of a woman who'd experienced lust and excitement and satisfaction. The look of a woman who'd just had life breathed into her.

The double meaning in those words had Sophia touching her belly.

A soft smile moved through her. She and Alex had made love at a very risky time. But was such a miracle even possible? Could a life be growing inside her from a moment in time that was as wonderful as it was insane? And if so, what in the world was she going to do about it?

She lifted her chin, her gaze again to the mirror. She would do as she'd always done—face life head-on, face her fears and live each moment with no regrets.

No regrets.

"Sophia?"

Sophia gasped at the masculine call, reached down and snatched up her towel. Alex was back from dinner. Way too early. No doubt to check on her, make sure she hadn't run away.

With a quick shiver, Sophia glanced over her shoulder at the bathroom door. She swallowed hard. It stood open a good foot. He was right outside, and his close proximity made her feel as though she couldn't move, as though her feet were stuck to the bathroom tiles. "I didn't expect you back so soon. Could you close the door, please? I'll be out in a minute."

She heard him snort. "Don't tell me you've become shy all of a sudden."

"Not all of a sudden," she mumbled.

"Is that right? And today—"

"Today I was temporarily blinded by—"

"Lust?" he offered.

"More like a near-death experience. Now, are you going to close the door or what?"

"Not just yet. I'm rather intrigued by the 'or what.'"

On a frustrated sigh, and without thinking, she stalked to the doorway and faced him. "You are impossible!"

"And you are…"

"I'm impossible, too. Now, what can I do for you?"

His fierce gaze raked boldly over her. "You shouldn't ask a man such a question wearing only that scrap of cotton."

Sophia pulled her towel closer. "Are you telling me that I can't trust you to be a gentleman?"

"That's exactly what I'm telling you."

Heat moved through her, but she kept her tone cool. "Let's get one thing straight, sire. Today was a lapse in judgment. It's not going to happen again."

He nodded succinctly. "Fine."

"Fine?"

"I don't supplicate, Sophia."

"Good. And I don't kowtow to royalty."

His mouth twitched with amusement. "Just so we

understand each other...." He gestured behind him. "Now get dressed and come out. I brought you dinner."

She glanced past him, saw several steaming, silver chafing dishes on the glass dining table. "I appreciate the thought, Alex, but I'm not very hungry."

"You will eat, Sophia," he insisted with a vague hint of disapproval.

"Maybe you didn't hear me a moment ago, but I won't be commanded to do—"

"This isn't about you." A muscle twitched in his jaw, his eyes growing dark as eggplant. "You will not starve my child."

Sophia's body stiffened with shock, her mind reeling. Alex's words, his command, cut her deep, deeper than she could have imagined. Just the thought of harming a child, her child, a child that might be growing inside of her at this very moment, brought tears to her eyes.

She blinked them back and took a calming breath. "I'll be out in a minute."

He nodded, a hint of warmth passing over his dark and very dangerous gaze. But it was gone quickly. And after a moment he took a step back and closed the bathroom door.

Three

Holding two mugs of coffee, one black as mud, the other creamy and decaffeinated, Alex followed Sophia out onto the beach house's sprawling deck. "What are you thinking so seriously about tonight?"

"My future."

"And what do you see?"

She shrugged. "It's very uncertain, isn't it?"

"I suppose it is," he said, sliding the mugs of steaming liquid onto the teak sombrero table.

All around them, the night sky gleamed clear, but for the brilliant clusters of stars winking down at them. A cool sea breeze blew across the beach, shifting specks of sand here and there.

Alex motioned for Sophia to take a seat at one of the rustic dining chairs, but she shook her head, then headed down the stairs. When she reached the bottom, she gave a weighty sigh and sat down on the last step, dug her toes in the sand.

"I'm not used to being on this side of the sand," she said. "But it's very beautiful."

Alex watched her stare out at the ocean as it crashed against the shore in cloudy tufts, biting his tongue from telling her just what *he* found beautiful on this side of the sand.

Instead he followed her down the stairs. "Why have you been sailing the isles for four months, Sophia?"

"I don't know if you'd understand the reason."

"Why?"

She glanced over her shoulder, gave him a half-smile. "You seem too, well...practical."

"You have the wrong perception of me," he said, dropping down beside her on the step.

"Wacky, wild and crazy, are you, your highness?"

"I can be." He glanced out toward the sand, the place where they'd made love not long ago. "Tell me about your journey," he said, trying to shove away the surge of desire that was running through him at a hectic pace.

Her voice softened. "Well my parents died when I was young, and I didn't think I had any family besides my horribly overbearing aunt. I was so afraid of her. She was so much like my parents. Too protective, too concerned, yet totally invulnerable." She released a sigh. "But then I found out that I had a grandfather."

She pulled her knees into her chest, smiled. "He came and got me. He took me in, raised me on his houseboat, taught me to embrace challenges instead of being afraid of them. We spent nearly every day on the water. The man was beyond wonderful. He treated me like I was special and loved. He made me smile every day that he was alive."

Alex had never heard someone speak in such a way. Open and honest with absolutely no pretense. He wasn't sure what to make of it. "When did your grandfather pass away?"

"Last year."

"I'm sorry, Sophia."

"Me, too. We were almost finished with the *Daydream*. His one wish in life was to sail the Isles."

Alex smiled with understanding. "You are doing this for him?"

"Yes," she said softly. "Llandaron is the last leg on my tour. But…"

"You didn't get all the way around her?"

She nodded.

He was schooled in the ways of diplomacy and tact, but comfort didn't come easy to him. He eased a wayward strand of red hair off her cheek and said, "You will."

Sophia turned to look at him. "I have to, Alex. Llandaron was very important to my grandfather. Especially Baratin. He was born there, lived there until he was thirteen."

Alex paused, shot her a glance of utter disbelief. "You have family here?"

She shook her head. "I don't think so. Not anymore, anyway. Gramps never spoke of family."

"Dunhill. That doesn't sound familiar to me."

"No it wouldn't. That was my father's name. My grandfather was my mother's father. He was taken away from Llandaron by his aunt when his mother died."

"What was your grandfather's name?"

"Turk. Robert Turk."

Shock slammed through Alex, rendering him temporarily speechless. Robbie Turk. He hadn't heard that name in years; to one of his clansmen it was the closest thing to blasphemy. But there was nothing for it now. The man's granddaughter had come home, and the man's family had a right to know.

With a thread of protective instinct fueling his blood, Alex snaked an arm around Sophia's waist. "Come back upstairs now and have your coffee. It's getting late."

Sophia stared wide-eyed at the scene before her. In America a picnic typically consisted of something like fried chicken, potato salad, strawberries, Jell-O mold and all the ants you could handle from within a five-block radius.

What was unfolding on the oh-so-picturesque bluff above Llandaron was no picnic. It was a fantasy, a royal affair, a scene from some Merchant Ivory film. Not that the members of the royal family were wearing white lace and carrying parasols. Actually, they were casually dressed. Khaki and blue, a little lavender to match the heather growing wild around them. No, what made the picture so superb, what made a girl catch her breath, was the beautiful table setup, the elegant wait staff and the killer scenery.

Like a sentinel, the bluff sat quietly overlooking miles of ocean, only showing off its grassy cap to those who had the good fortune to climb it. Thickly rooted trees gave plenty of shade to the family and to the long teak table spread with fruit and meats, oysters and wine, cheeses and fresh bread.

"Don't worry." Alex took her hand and squeezed it. "They don't bite."

"I'm fine, Alex," she said with a confidence she really didn't feel.

"Nothing makes you tremble, right?"

"That's right."

To be honest, she really wanted to impress these people. Which was totally unlike her. Normally she couldn't give a whit what others thought of her—a trait passed down by her grandfather—royal or not. But the people that Alex was guiding her toward were his family, and she wanted them to like her. If she really was carrying his child, this group would be its family. And there was nothing she wanted more for her child than a loving family.

Alex led her into the center of the gathering. "I want to introduce you to my father first."

"The king?" she whispered.

"Yes." He raised an amused brow at her. "I thought you weren't afraid—"

"I'm not afraid. I just thought that maybe we'd start out with someone easier. Like a duke or a countess or something."

He chuckled, squeezed her hand again. "Come on."

The king of Llandaron sat on a large white armchair, legs apart, his countenance fierce and formidable. He was broad-shouldered and battle-scared. But the deep lines etched into his face were not from combat; more likely from years of negotiations and treaties. Whatever the reason for his powerful presence, when self-proclaimed brave soul Sophia stepped into his gaze, she actually felt her knees buckle a little.

"Your Majesty," Alex began. "This is Sophia Dunhill, Sophia, my father, King Oliver Thorne."

Sophia inclined her head as she'd seen many do in the movies and hoped it was appropriate here. "It's nice to meet you, Your Majesty."

The king looked her over. From the tips of the

brand-new sneakers she'd bought that morning to the new jeans and white peasant blouse that had accompanied them and up to her makeup free face and loose hair.

"Odds fish, Alexander," the man exclaimed. "She really does have the look of your mermaid about her, doesn't she?"

Caught completely off guard, Sophia fairly choked as she whirled to face her escort. "Your what?"

The king's hearty chuckle filled the air.

Alex's lips thinned. "It's nothing," he muttered, taking her hand again. "Thank you for that, Father."

"You are most welcome, my son."

"Let's find some shade, shall we?" Alex said dryly, leading her away.

Sophia managed another tilt of the head and a quick, "It was good to meet you, Your Majesty."

The king called merrily after them, "And you, my dear."

"Are you going to explain yourself, sire?" Sophia asked Alex as he led her toward the buffet table.

"After lunch."

"Fine. But I'll hold you to that."

"I'm sure you will.

Sophia grinned. "Listen, before we eat, I'd like to meet the rest of your family."

He sniffed proudly. "And after that bit of lunacy with my father there's nothing I'd like less."

But he led her over to a group of jovial men and

women, anyway, introduced her to each, then gave every last one of them the evil eye and stern instructions to keep all discussions of mermaids and past childhood apparitions out of the conversation.

As the group gave a not-so-convincing, yet collective, nod, Sophia made a mental note to ask Alex about the second part of his warning as well as the first.

But the inquisition would have to wait until after lunch she quickly realized as Alex, his handsome brother, Maxim, and rugged brother-in-law, Dan, were locked into a debate over football and the lack of quality players on this year's teams. This left Alex's violet-eyed sister, Cathy, and beautifully pregnant sister-in-law, Fran, with Sophia.

It was odd, but Sophia felt an immediate kinship with the two women. Fran was also from California, down-to-earth and welcoming. Cathy was nothing like the stuck-up princess Sophia had expected. She was incredibly kind and warm and strong willed. They were the girlfriends that she'd never had and always wished for, and the urge to spill her guts about what had happened between Alex and her was strong.

But she was a wary creature by nature and kept what had happened yesterday where it belonged: in the fog.

"So, you came here to care for the king's wolf-hound?" Sophia asked Fran.

The pretty blonde pointed to the sleeping dog behind the king's chair. "Glinda had a brood of beautiful pups." She stroked the head of the large puppy at her feet. "If you can believe it, Lucky here was the runt."

"You got to keep one of her pups? How wonderful."

Fran smiled broadly. "Got a pup, a prince and a baby out of the deal."

Cathy laughed. "Plus a sister and a pain-in-the-neck brother-in-law."

"Don't say that," Fran warned in good humor, touching her burgeoning belly. "His child can hear you."

"Oh, Lord, and so can mine."

The women laughed and rubbed their stomachs. For some stupid reason, so did Sophia.

Fran saw her and frowned. "Are you okay?"

Blushing, Sophia quickly dropped her hand from her flat belly and smiled. "Fine. Just...hungry." She stood up. "Can I get either of you something?"

"Maybe just some biscuits and cheese," Fran said, and Cathy nodded.

Sophia headed for the buffet, calling herself all kinds of idiot. She didn't need to get attached here— to the people, to the land, to Alex and even to a child she wasn't sure she was carrying.

Maybe after lunch she'd head over to the boat works, see how the *Daydream* was faring and get her mind on the realties of her life.

"Sophia," she heard Alex call from behind her.

When Sophia turned, Alex, an older couple and another wolfhound pup were all walking toward her. A strange palpitation started in her blood, fast and uneasy as she stared at the wrinkled old man beside Alex. His eyes—strangely memorable eyes—fairly bored a hole in her heart as around them the sea released a salty breath.

"There are two people I haven't introduced you to, Sophia." Alex grinned. "They have just now arrived. I think you'll find this introduction fascinating."

The thin, exquisitely beautiful older woman took Sophia's hand, her violet eyes warm and inviting. "My name is Fara."

"My aunt," Alex supplied.

Sophia smiled, feeling incredibly tentative and not knowing the reason for it. "How nice to meet you, Your Highness."

"And you, Sophia."

Alex's aunt was terribly sweet and welcoming, but Sophia's focus was all for the frowning man, weathered and worn, at the woman's side.

If this had been a dream, Sophia would have reached out for him for he looked so familiar. Or maybe he felt familiar...she wasn't sure.

"And who might you be, lass?" the man uttered, his voice gravel-like and thick with that husky Llandaron burr.

"My name is Sophia Dunhill." She couldn't stop herself from asking, "Who are you, sir?"

He stuck out his gnarled hand. "The name's Ranen. Ranen Turk."

Sophia mouth dropped. So did her heart. She stood there, blank, amazed, shaken. "What did you say?"

"Just my name, lass."

"Turk?"

"Aye."

"Sophia?" Alex said, clearly concerned.

Fara put a hand on her shoulder. "Are you all right, my dear?"

But Sophia barely heard either one of them. Waves of utter disbelief were threatening to capsize her mind. "Did you know a Robert Turk from Baratin?"

The man's face turned instantly sour as he ground out, "Don't speak that name to me, lass."

"Did you know him?"

Ranen scowled, his nostrils flaring. "My younger brother, he is. Deserted his family. A bloody bastard, he is."

"Ranen, please," Alex said sharply as his arm eased around Sophia's waist.

She leaned into his hold. "I don't understand."

"How do you know Robert?" Fara asked, caught somewhere between her concern for Ranen and her interest in Sophia.

Sophia couldn't take her eyes off Ranen. "He's...he's my grandfather."

Ranen's eyes widened to saucers, but he said nothing. For a good thirty seconds, the only sounds that could be heard were the rush of ocean to shore and the distant chatter of the picnickers.

Sophia fought for the right thing to say, the right questions to ask.

But she ran out of time. For after a moment Ranen turned on his heel and walked away.

The fax in front of him blurred.

Alex tossed the offending paper onto his cluttered desk, slung his head back and sighed. He had no mind for work right now. Four hours ago, he and Sophia had returned home from the picnic. Conversation had been tight and sparse. She'd looked pale and confused and had gone to her room almost immediately upon entering the house.

He'd wanted to comfort her, wanted to explain why he'd chosen to surprise her with Ranen's existence today, but he was inexperienced with apologies. Especially ones regarding a personal mistake.

Yet he couldn't just sit here and do nothing.

Dismissing the work on his desk, Alex left his office and went downstairs. The house was quiet, save for the muffled sound of the ocean. About thirty minutes ago, Sophia had emerged from her bedroom, towel in hand. She was going for a swim, she'd informed him soberly. The fog had receded, and she would stay close to shore.

That promise had done little to appease him, but he knew she needed the exercise. He knew she needed the comfort of the sea. He'd felt such a need many times himself.

Alex breathed in the salty air the moment he stepped outside his front door and onto the deck. Twilight had painted the canvas of sky a magnificent violet. But he didn't give the scenery more than a glance. He wanted to find her, had to find her.

As promised, she was swimming close to shore, taking the easy waves with natural grace. Alex watched as she dove under the water, then emerged, her hair slicked back, profile stunning, shoulders soft and wet. She made one drop-dead silhouette, and he couldn't stop himself from recognizing that it was the perfect recreation of his childhood dream.

Nor could he stop himself from going to her. Under the Van Gogh sky, he jogged toward the water's edge, stripped off his shirt and shorts. He tried to tell himself that a quick dip would bring back his sanity. When he dove beneath the waves, he told himself that the cool water would heal him.

But when he found himself face-to-face with her, standing inches away in belly-deep water, he had to admit that he was a fraud.

The truth was, he wanted to be near her. Just like the ginger-haired mermaid in his dream, when he was around Sophia he felt alive and free.

"Pretty brave of you, Highness," she said, wiping away the droplets of water streaming down her face.

"Why is that?"

"Returning to the scene of the crime—aka, the near-death experience."

"Well, you saved me once. I expect you'd do it again if the need arises."

"I don't know. Look what kind of trouble that brought last time."

A wave pelted them both, sending them sideways a foot. "You'd let me drown just to protect yourself against—"

"Pain?" she offered, smiling.

"I was thinking pleasure."

She shook her head. "We're not going there again, Alex."

If only that were true, Alex mused. If only they possessed that level of control. He was willing to bet his life that neither one of them did. But he offered her a flippant "Anything you say, Sophia," anyway.

She wasn't buying. "You say that as if you fully expect me to cave."

"Cave?"

"Like you expect me—at some point, when I can't stand it anymore—to reach out, grab you and haul you against me."

His chest tightened, as did the rest of him. "Perhaps there's no expectation. Perhaps there's only curiosity and...hope."

He saw her lips part, saw her tongue dart out and swipe her bottom lip. Then felt his own reaction, deep in his groin.

"I'm curious," he continued, his pulse jolting in his blood. "What would happen after you hauled me against you?"

"I don't know," she murmured silkily. "I'd kiss you, I suppose."

"Hard or soft?"

Her eyes darkened to a deep green. "Maybe both."

"What then?"

"I don't know."

"Yes you do." He moved closer but didn't touch her. "Would you wrap your legs around my waist?"

"Probably."

Alex could hardly contain himself. He was ready to pounce. His hands were balled into fists under the water, his groin painfully tight. But he fought for control. This had to come from her.

"Sounds nice, Sophia, but—"

"But?" she uttered incredulously. "But what?"

"It's a pretty bold move."

"And you don't think I'm bold?"

He grinned, moved closer, within inches. "No."

Her brows snapped together as the wind whipped her wet hair about her body. "Excuse me?"

"I'm just saying that taking what you want without the protection of the fog and with no excuses is—"

"You don't think I'm up to it?"

Alex didn't have a chance to answer. He was being thrust forward, long, toned legs wrapping his waist, beautiful, moist mouth closing in on his.

And he took, wanting all she could give.

His hands raked up her thighs until he found her sweet backside. He gripped her tightly, squeezing, feeling her curves as around them night fell and ocean quaked. She made a soft whimpering sound, and Alex took her tongue into his mouth, holding his ground, digging his feet into the sand to keep them upright.

She tasted of saltwater and heaven, pure perfection. He held her tighter, possessively. She was his. Right now at any rate, right now, she belonged to him.

They twisted and struggled as they kissed like long-lost lovers eager to learn each other's taste and scent once again. Until Sophia broke the spell, broke the kiss and raised her head.

"Have I proved myself, Your Highness?"

Jaw as tight as the rest of him, Alex released her. "You are very bold, Sophia."

She nodded, her breathing still labored. "I'm going in now. You coming?"

"In a minute."

She turned away, waded into shore, then stopped and turned back. "You'll be all right out here by yourself?"

"I always have. I always will."

He saw her flinch slightly before saying, "Good night, then."

Alex watched her go, all the way up the sandy beach and into the house. When she was safely inside, he turned and dove into a wave. His mind was blistered from their silly game, and his groin screamed with pain.

But it wasn't merely madness and unrequited pleasure that plagued him. Those two shackles he could deal with, had for his entire marriage—as he was no rogue, no cheating husband.

No, it was something far more dangerous.

For the first time in six years, he felt connected with life—open to lust, to need, to pain and to want.

And Sophia Dunhill was his keeper of the keys....

Four

Sara Squirrel hugged the acorn close to her chest and smiled....

Her back to a small beach rock, Sophia sighed into the ocean breeze, scribbled over the rotten sentence and started again.

When Sara Squirrel woke up that morning she just knew that today was the day she was going to find her family....

A moderately satisfied smile curved Sophia's mouth. Better. Not great. But better than the last attempt.

Was it possible? she wondered, fiddling with her finely sharpened pencil. Could the wild lushness of

Llandaron be causing the dense walls of her brain to come tumbling down? Or was it the allure, the kisses of a tall, dark and very handsome prince?

The blush of a silly teenager with a crush on her heart crept into Sophia's cheeks. With a snort, she shut her notebook and dropped back against the stone. It had been one week since she'd jumped ship and come to shore. One week since she'd made love to Alex. And in that week, she'd rarely thought of anything but him—those probing eyes, those crushing lips on hers and, of course, the amazing possibility that they'd made a child together.

Life would've been much easier if the pull she felt for him was nothing more than physical. But it wasn't. The way he challenged her, made her think and wonder about things she'd never contemplated before—they all conspired against her, making her desire for him as a partner, as well as a lover, intense and undeniable.

And she, who only wanted freedom. She who never needed anyone.

Or thought she didn't.

Sophia stared out at the sea, watched the heavy waves curl into a peak and crash to shore. She shivered with the weight of their descent.

"Been avoiding us, have you? Or is it just me?"

Sophia whirled around, startled. Standing above her on the rock was Ranen. At his feet, sat the panting wolfhound pup with wide, sweet brown eyes she'd seen with him at the picnic.

"Jeez," she said with a breathless laugh. "You scared the life out of me."

"Sorry about that." With the agility of a man half his age, Ranen jumped down from the rock. The pup followed suit. "In fact, I'm right sorry about a couple things. But you won't make me name them all, will you, lass?"

Her heart warmed at his words, vague though they were. "Of course not." She understood his pride as she'd understood her grandfather's.

"So, have you seen anything besides His Highness's beach house in the last week?" he asked quickly.

"I went down to the boat works this morning, as a matter of fact."

"How long before your rig is back afloat?"

"Two weeks."

He nodded, quick and tight—and familiar. He was so much like her grandfather it almost ached to look at him. Yet it was strangely comforting, too. This man who was all the family she had left and was too angry, too stubborn to recognize it.

As though offering her comfort, the brown-eyed wolfhound pup sidled up to her and lay down. Warmth spread from the pup's body to Sophia in seconds, soothing her senses, calming her heart.

"Her name is Aggie," Ranen said, leaning against the rock.

"She's lovely."

"Follows me everywhere, she does. A regular pain in the arse."

Sophia chuckled as she stroked the pup's wiry fur and said without thinking, "My grandfather used to say the same thing about our cat, Smoke. But if that cat wasn't on his lap purring at least three hours a night, Gramps was totally out of sorts."

It was little surprise that Ranen chose not to respond. Instead he pointed to her notebook. "What are you working on there?"

"A new story. Hopefully." She shrugged, explained, "I'm a writer. Children's books. And I'm desperately trying to stomp out some writer's block."

"Sounds pretty serious."

"It can be if it goes on long enough. And I've had the problem ever since..."

She paused, sat uneasily in the sand.

"Since when?" Ranen probed.

"Since my grandfather died."

Sudden anger lit the old man's eyes. He cleared his throat. "So the old bugger passed on, did he?"

Sophia nodded, her throat tight with feeling. "Last year."

With a tight jaw, Ranen dropped down beside her on the sand. He was silent as he stared toward the ocean. Sophia so desperately wanted to ask him about her grandfather's life in Baratin and why there was a rift between them, why they'd never spoken in all those many years.

But she didn't get the chance when Ranen offered, "My grandmother was a writer."

"Really?" Her voice rose in surprise.

"Poetry."

"I'd love to read some."

He shrugged. "Perhaps I'll give you a few to look over. If I can find 'em, you understand."

"Oh, that would be wonderful, Ranen."

"Tosh," he grumbled. "Perhaps I could take you by the house today. But first, Aggie and I are going to the Llandaron Picnic. It's a yearly gathering. Whole town'll be there. And since you're here in town, you must come along with us."

Just the thought of going to a town function made her feel weary and unsure of herself. She didn't know her place here—if she had a place here. And she sure wasn't prepared to answer questions about Alex and her if they arose. "I'd like to, Ranen. Really I would. But I have so much work—"

"This isn't an invitation, lass. But orders from the king." He stood, brushed the sand from his already dusty pants. "Crown Prince Alexander is speaking, and he's going to be needing all of our support."

"Support? For what?"

Two bristly brows shot together. "He hasn't told you?"

Sophia shook her head.

"Four months ago, the prince and his wife divorced. Now he must explain the situation to his people and hope that they accept him without a princess, without an heir."

A bundle of nerves rustled in Sophia's belly—exactly where a child might be, an heir might be. "Why wouldn't they accept him?"

"'Tis the way things have been for ages, lass. No man has become king without a wife. No man has remained king without an heir."

Nerves turned into strong stabs of fear. No wonder Alex had reacted so strongly, so intensely to the possibility of her being pregnant. "And Alex wants to be king."

A look of unwavering seriousness suffused his features. "More than anything."

And if she was carrying his child...

Sophia closed her eyes for a moment and tried to slow her racing pulse. But it was no use. If she were pregnant, her child would belong to Llandaron.

And therefore so would she.

Apprehension has no place here.

Alex drummed the words into his mind. And he knew that, if need be, he would repeat them until they became reality.

In all his thirty-five years, he'd never been fearful of standing up in front of his people. But today so much was at stake. His future, the one he'd grown up to expect, could be coming to an end. This is, if his people rejected him in favor of his brother. And in all honesty, they wouldn't be wrong in doing so. Every king to sit on the throne of Llandaron had preached the same edict: country, order and peace were secured by tradition and law.

And for Alexander Thorne, he would respect that directive and abide by the wishes of his people.

The stone steps leading up to the podium were long and heavy, but he managed them. And under a cloudless blue sky, he turned to face his people. Rows upon rows of interested faces staring up at him, waiting. No doubt they expected a greeting, a royal order to enjoy the picnic and the day, not an update of his marital status.

For a split second Alex thought his voice had gone, his will, too. But when he noticed a cloud of red hair and an infectious smile gazing up at him from the crowd, the tension inside him eased.

A reaction he never would have expected.

He'd made specific instructions that she shouldn't be told about the event. He didn't want her to hear about his failure. He didn't want her to see his people reject him.

With her, he felt a supreme amount of pride. Whether it was wise or not, her opinion mattered to him.

But there was nothing for it now.

With a nod to his people, he began....

Sophia eased back against the cool leather seats of the limousine. She'd never ridden in such luxury, and she rather liked it. Outside the tinted windows, the quaint town shuffled by at a leisurely pace as the driver made his way toward the beach.

Beside her, Crown Prince Alex sat in regal silence. No doubt reviewing his performance this afternoon.

"I have always been ready to give my life for my country," he'd said. "Today, I give my heart, my soul and my future."

A slow shiver inched its way up Sophia's spine. A man with impassioned words and an unselfish nature made a woman's—well, made this woman's—knees weak.

Sophia ventured a glance in his direction. Stubborn jaw, aquiline nose, fiery violet eyes beneath thick black brows. Yes, he was something to behold, both in looks and in character.

She let her breath ease out of her lungs as she tried to calm her racing pulse. Never in her life had she wanted to jump into a man's lap, kiss him senseless, feel that rush of heat in her belly as he returned her ardor, his fingers threading in her hair.

There was no doubt about it. She was in trouble. For not only had Alex Thorne won over his country's heart today, he'd taken Sophia's right along with it. A heart she'd always thought an impassive muscle when it came to romance. A take-it-or-leave-it sort of thing.

But with Alex, she wanted to take.

"Are you all right?"

Sophia turned at Alex's query, nodded. "Fine. How about you? After a day like that I'm betting you're pretty keyed up."

He grinned in his way; that confident quirk of the mouth. "It went well."

"I would say so."

"I'm glad you came, Sophia."

"So am I. You were really wonderful."

He snorted, shifted back against the seat. "I was laid bare."

"Well, no man ever looked so good naked."

She sucked in a breath, her words echoing in her ears. For someone who was trying to play it cool, she was failing miserably.

Further proof positive was Alex's killer grin and husky, "Thank you, Sophia."

"Don't get cocky, your highness," she said with mock reproach. "You know what I mean."

He sighed heavily. "Yes, but I wish I didn't."

She couldn't help but laugh. "We get in trouble together, did you ever notice that? Verbally and otherwise?"

"Otherwise," he lamented. "Ah, yes, I miss otherwise."

Chuckling, she gave him a playful swat on the arm.

"You know, Highness, since you've been laid bare today—as you put it—maybe you can come completely clean."

"What do you have in mind?"

"Maybe now you can finally tell me about this mermaid business your father mentioned."

His smile faded. "I'd rather not."

"You did promise."

"Yes, I did." He waved an impatient hand. "All right, here it is then. When I was a boy I had a dream...several dreams, in fact...about the ocean and a certain..."

"A certain what?" she pressed eagerly.

"Mermaid coming out of the water," he ground out.

A slow smile eased its way to Sophia's lips. "The king said that I look like this mermaid?"

Through gritted teeth, he muttered, "Yes."

"Is it my hair?"

"Among other things."

"Like what?" she asked, batting her eyelashes.

He chuckled halfheartedly. "You're a tease."

"And you're much too far away."

His left eyebrow rose a fraction. "Excuse me?"

Groaning, she said, "I told you we get into trouble verbally and—"

She never got to finish that sentence as Alex reached out and dragged her to him. For just a quick second, as she stared up into violet desire, Sophia thought about doing what she'd only fantasized about doing: hurling herself into Alex's lap, wrapping her arms around his neck and kissing him senseless. But if she started this again, where would it end? What if she weren't pregnant and had to leave? And what if she was and this was only a physical connection. After all, he'd just gotten out of a relationship and it was perfectly clear he wasn't interested in another. Was she willing to risk her heart on an affair?

Alex brushed his thumb over her bottom lip. "If you want to kiss me, Sophia, all you have to do is tip that chin up and close your eyes and I'd be happy to oblige."

"You are way too full of yourself, you know that?"

Alex lowered his head, kissed her softly on the lips. When he pulled back it was only an inch. "I'd like to be full of you."

His kiss sent swirling currents of heat into her belly. He was so persuasive with just a look, a glance, a touch. She knew she was staring longingly at him, willing him to just take her without discussion so she didn't have to think or give in.

"Alex—"

"Yes, lass?"

Sophia melted at the husky, lusty burr, glanced toward the partition where the driver was in full view. "Are we close to home?"

"Ten minutes or so."

"Ten whole minutes?"

He chuckled softly, then reached over the side panel and grabbed an iced bowl of fruit. "Here, let's both have a strawberry. Keep our mouths occupied."

As he held one to her mouth, heat shimmied down her belly, pooling low. She didn't want berries, dammit! Couldn't he see that she wanted kisses, only his kisses?

Why wasn't she acting the way she had that first day on the beach? Taking what she wanted with no fear?

No answers came as Alex rubbed the berry between her lips with gentle insistence. She could feel his eyes on her as she opened her mouth, let him slip the fruit between her teeth.

When she bit down juice splattered all over her chin.

She grinned. "You planned that."

"Do you think I'm that powerful, Sophia?" he asked, gaze sliding downward. "That I can command a strawberry to burst? For sweet, pink juice to dribble down your chin and onto your blouse?"

"Yes." She looked down at the droplets of juice winding a path down, down, toward the valley between her breasts. "My blouse…"

"Let me get that."

"Do you have a towel or napkin or something?"

"No, I don't think so." Alex reached up, depressed

a button on the ceiling. Up went the privacy window. "But I have an idea."

Sophia held her breath as his fingers brushed the top of her shirt. But before he unfastened a button, he glanced up. "Do you mind?"

Refusing to think, rationalize or wonder, she shook her head. Alex grinned and moved in, had three buttons unhooked in a breath. Sophia's heart jolted as little by little cool air met her heated skin.

"Sophia…" Alex lowered his head and brushed a kiss over the inner curve of her left breast. "You taste so sweet, Sophia."

"It's the strawberry juice," she said breathlessly.

"No, it's you."

With skillful fingers, he eased aside the lace cup of her bra, then nuzzled his way to her nipple, hard and aching. Sophia arched her back, silently begging him to taste, to tease. And he did. He took, just as she had been so unable to do a moment before. He took for both of them, and she was thankful.

A fire roared to life within her, like a wild creature set to run from its trap. And if it lost a limb, lost its heart, so be it.

Or lost its mind, she mused as Alex cupped her breast in his palm and took her swollen nipple into his mouth.

Sophia couldn't control the moan of pleasure that ripped from her throat. She didn't even try. And the unfettered sound spurred Alex on. His suckling became intense, almost rough as his free hand dropped to her belly, inched lower to the apex of her thighs. Sophia bucked against his palm. Alex pressed harder.

Then a dose of reality slashed into their little dream world as the limousine came to a halt.

"We've stopped," Sophia whispered, her breathing ragged.

"Aye." The word came out as a growl.

"I suppose this means we should, too."

On a curse, Alex lifted his head, then his gaze. "I want to know you inside and out, Sophia."

"We already know each other that way—"

"No." He cupped her face gently. "Not as I imagine. Not fast and furious. I want to take you slow and sweaty and—"

She shook her head. "Don't say any more." Slow meant thinking. Slow meant wondering about the future, hoping for more than she had a right to. *That* she didn't want.

Alex sat up, fell back against the seat. "All right. I won't say any more. For now. For today. For tonight."

To his right, the limousine door opened. But before he got out, he shot her a wickedly serious stare. "But I can't control this…whatever is happening here…for much longer."

On legs filled with water, Sophia followed him out of the car and into the house. She could still feel his kisses on her tight, aching skin, hear his soft burr echoing in her ears.

I can't control this for much longer.

Neither could she. Lord, neither could she.

Five

"This is a right of passage," Fran announced as she and Cathy escorted Sophia through the green doors of Gershins Taffy Shop with such reverence one would think they were entering a great cathedral instead of...

"A candy shop?" Sophia said, glancing around at all the brightly packaged offerings.

"It's not just candy," Fran counseled sagely. "It's more like a little piece of heaven."

"Mana from heaven?" Sophia teased with a hint of a smile.

Cathy tossed Fran a pitying look. "She's been so deprived."

Fran nodded her agreement. "She just hasn't tasted it yet. Once she does, she'll understand."

Following her new friends down a thin aisle lined with barrels of sweet-smelling confection, Sophia couldn't help but laugh. "Are you guys trying to tell me that this is some kind of magical taffy?"

Cathy snorted, snatched up a piece of rich caramel-colored taffy from a nearby barrel and thrust it to her. "Just remember, skeptics rarely get seconds."

Sophia laughed again as she took the candy and unwrapped it. She was having way too much fun with these women. A relatively new experience for her.

As a writer, she worked at home and had little social life, so friends were few and far between. Even as a child, she'd led a pretty isolated life on her grandfather's houseboat. An existence that had actually suited her well. For she felt welcomed and cared for there as she hadn't anywhere else. And that was proved when she started going to school. During the day, she would do her work, eat her lunch with a few of the quiet girls, but when that bell rang at the end of the day, she was out of there—back to the place she finally felt was home.

She honestly never thought she'd feel welcomed and cared about again. But around Fran and Cathy she did. So when they'd come by the beach house an hour ago and asked her to join them in town, she'd jumped at the chance.

Sophia paused, her mind quickly turning to mush

as she bit into that piece of chocolate taffy insanity that Cathy had given her. The muffled word, "Ohmigod!" slipped from her sugar-sweetened lips, followed by, "This is…"

"I know!" Cathy exclaimed with a huge grin, unwrapping a smallish tube of green-apple taffy.

"It's…it's like…" Sophia stumbled with her words, with an accurate description for the cream and chocolate and salty sweetness exploding in her mouth.

Fran put a hand on her shoulder. "We did warn you."

Sophia shook her head. "Seriously, I've never tasted anything like this. It must be the saltwater around here or—"

"Don't try and figure it out," Fran advised.

Cathy nodded. "No, don't. It's just like a man."

Fran's gentle laughter rippled through the air. "I can't wait to hear this."

"Don't try and figure a man out," Cathy said, unwrapping her second piece of apple taffy. "Just sit back and enjoy the moment."

"Oh, that's good." Fran popped the piece of root beer taffy she was holding into her mouth. "That's very good."

But Sophia was having a little trouble with the analogy. Images of Alex and her flickered like firelight against the back of her mind. Kisses and sweet caresses. Amethyst eyes probing her very soul. Words of desire and true fulfillment whispered in her ear.

How could she just enjoy the moment? Alex was like the taffy that sat temptingly all about her. She would always want more. She could so easily become addicted.

Fran nudged Cathy with her elbow. "I think we might've said the wrong thing."

"Or the right thing," Cathy said. "Let's see—men, taffy, enjoying the moment, a dreamy-eyed, pink-cheeked girl."

Fran grinned. "I see where you're going with this."

Coming out of her haze, Sophia looked from one smiling woman to the other. "I sure don't."

"Are you falling for my brother?" Cathy asked plainly.

Sophia fairly choked, but she managed to utter the word, "What?"

"I know he's a handful—"

"That's just what Max says, too," Fran tossed in.

Cathy continued, "But he is also brilliant, generous, kind—"

"You guys—"

"Funny, protective and—"

"Incredibly sexy?" Sophia said wryly.

Fran and Cathy paused, stared at Sophia. Then two matching grins turned to bubbling laughter. Hands on hips, Sophia tried to look staid, but it didn't take. After a moment she was laughing right along with them.

Cathy looped an arm through Sophia's, grabbed a sack of assorted taffy and started for the cash register. "She's one of us, that's for sure."

Sophia pointed to the bulging candy bag. "You are going to be sharing that, right?"

"Yep. Definitely one of us," Fran said, snatching up a handful of chocolate fudge taffy and following them.

The headline of the London newspaper stared back at Alex with raw, black eyes.

Former Wife of the Crown Prince of Llandaron Marries President of Garrison Bank. Couple Expecting First Child in May of Next Year.

The words seeped into Alex's blood, making his pulse pound a hostile rhythm. Why was he so angry over a story about a woman he never loved, having a child he was never meant to have?

No doubt, because the waves of failure had ebbed for a little while and now they were back full force.

No, it wasn't his ex-wife or her child that made him see red—it was himself, his own inadequacies and the questions that would never retreat: was he capable of making a woman happy? And if so, did he even want to attempt such a feat?

His mermaid drifted through his mind.

Yes, with her he wanted to. But was it because she might be carrying his child? Or was it more?

Did he want an heir so desperately he was willing to risk his soul again?

Alex leaned back in his chair, the answer to his silent query coming fast, almost viciously.

Never.

It was 6:00 a.m. on the following Saturday morning when Sophia knew that her life had changed forever.

One hour ago she'd woken up with a strange pang of nausea. Groggy, she'd slipped out of her bed and into the bathroom where she'd immediately thrown up.

At first, lying against the cool tiles, she'd wondered what she'd eaten the night before to warrant such a reaction. After all, she'd always had what her grandfather referred to as a cast-iron stomach. Steak, mashed potatoes and a pot of hot chocolate…nothing too dangerous.

Then, like a wrecking ball to a sturdy building, a thought had slammed into her foggy brain. A strangely soothing thought.

Lord, she mused now as she leaned back against the tub, could she really be—

"Sophia?" The call startled her, made her breath catch, and was followed by a knock at the door. "Are you all right?"

"Yes, fine," she answered quickly.

No doubt too quickly, for Alex sounded a tad uneasy when he asked, "Can I come in?"

Her pulse jumping to life in her blood, Sophia actually shook her head at the closed door. She wasn't ready for this, for him. Not yet. Not until she knew for certain.

"I'm okay, Alex," she said firmly. "Really. Go back to bed."

He chose not to hear her. The door squeaked open a crack and he peeked in, his eyes filled with concern. "What's wrong?"

Coming to her feet, Sophia said, "Nothing," then turned the faucet to cold and grabbed for her toothbrush.

Seeing him, his face, made everything seem different. As insane as it might be, she wanted to tell him that she might very well be carrying his child. She wanted him to wrap his arms around her and kiss her, joy illuminating his handsome face.

But what if there was only an expression of moderate pleasure and he never moved from his spot by the door—no hugs, no touching.

He would love the child, but never the child's mother.

"You look as pale as a sheet," Alex said, moving closer to her.

"I'm okay. I'm feeling much better now."

Again, he paid her assurances of "fineness" absolutely no attention. Instead, he snatched a washcloth off the towel rack and held it under the running water.

"What are you doing?" Sophia asked.

"Just stop talking and sit down."

"Alex, this really isn't necessary—"

"Why don't you let me decide that. Trust me, all right?"

That soft grin he tossed her way disarmed her, made her cast off any feelings of apprehension about the word *trust,* the two of them and their future.

She returned his smile. "Okay, Alex."

He took the toothbrush from her hand with gentle insistence and deposited it on the counter. Then with true tenderness, he eased her down on the lid of the toilet and began to wipe her face.

The cool cloth felt delicious against Sophia's heated skin, and she let her eyes drift closed. "That feels nice."

"What did I tell you? I bring no pain, only pleasure."

"Promise?"

Sophia felt the washcloth move over her mouth, then heard Alex say, "I will do my very best, lass."

"I know you will."

Silence took the room as Alex continued his ministrations. Fresh, cool water on her forehead, cheeks and neck. Sophia was almost asleep with he asked, "Did you have pizza again with Fran and Cathy last night?"

"Nope. Steak and potatoes."

"Perhaps there was a spice in the potatoes that didn't agree with you."

"Possibly."

"Or perhaps you're getting sick."

"Sick?" she mumbled.

"The flu."

"I don't think so, Highness."

There was a slow silence, then, "Sophia?"

"Hmmmm?"

"Open your eyes."

In her dreamy state, she did as he commanded. But once she saw him, saw the look in his eyes, she wished she hadn't.

Eyes a vivid violet, lips thinned, jaw tight as a trap, his words came out as a growl. "All I ask is that you tell me the truth."

Her stomach clenched tight. "I don't understand what you mean."

"Yes, I think you do." He stood up, dropped the cloth in the sink.

"Alex—"

"Just the truth, Sophia." Something fragile, almost desperate flickered in his eyes. "Please."

"I don't know the truth."

"What does that mean?"

This was going too fast. She wasn't prepared to say anything now. Foolish what-ifs sliced through her brain at a mile a minute. Why couldn't he have just stayed in bed? Why couldn't she have gotten sick after he'd left?

"Sophia?"

"This could be the spices in the potatoes, this could be stress, this could be the flu."

"Dammit, Sophia, talk to me."

Her heart was thumping so madly she was sure he could hear it. "And this could be a child."

"Dear God."

"I'm late. Two days."

Six
———

Later that day, Alex stood outside the bathroom door, fighting the urge to pace. He had always prided himself on being a cool, calm and exceedingly rational person. But right now, he was so far removed from any of those three traits he barely recognized himself. For behind the bathroom door, his future was being decided.

Or perhaps it had been decided the moment he'd seen Sophia standing atop the deck of her grandfather's sloop four months ago.

Alex plowed a hand through his hair. He'd wanted a child for so many years, the actual possibility of such a dream seeing the light of day filled him with a desperation he hadn't known he possessed.

Yet, if Sophia was carrying his child, what did that mean? What was their future? No matter what the situation or how needful he felt for the woman, he had no intention of giving himself to anyone ever again. That much of his future was already decided.

He turned to the door once again, raised his fist to knock, then dropped it.

Bloody torture.

Was it too early for a drink? He glanced at his watch. Eleven o'clock in the morning.

Quite probably.

"Alex?"

Alex's head came up with a snap just as the door opened. Sophia emerged from the bathroom, face pale, lips thin. He searched her eyes for some sign, an answer. But he couldn't read her.

She managed a tremulous smile and a noncommittal "Hi."

Here they stood in the brightly lit hallway of his beach house, neither of them comfortable, neither prepared for what was about to be discussed. And all that Alex was capable of was a nod.

She took a deep breath. "I took the test."

"Sophia, you're killing me here," Alex practically growled, his chest tight, tense.

"You don't have to worry."

"What the hell does that mean?"

"Just that you have no extra burdens."

"Burdens?" he exclaimed, leaning back and giving

an impatient sigh. "I never said that having a child would be a—"

Nervously Sophia ran a hand through her hair. "You didn't have to, Alex. I know what you've been through with your ex-wife."

"What does that have to do with anything?"

"Just that your marriage was a difficult one. Five years is a long time to..." She touched his arm. "You've made it perfectly clear how much you're enjoying your freedom."

"This isn't about freedom from a child, Sophia."

She let her hand drop to her side, her tone running cool. "It's about freedom from women."

Alex didn't agree or disagree. He wasn't interested in a therapy session or rehashing a past that was past. He only wanted answers. And he usually got what he wanted.

"The test was negative?" he said, jaw tightening as his past rose up to clip him on the cheek. "Is that what you're saying?"

For a moment she only stared at him, her eyes guarded. Then she said softly, "Yes."

Alex had expected to feel at least a grain of relief at such news. After all, he and Sophia were lovers, not parents. But in his heart there was only deep regret and profound disappointment.

"So, I'll be leaving, then," Sophia said, her chin lifted. "As soon as the boat is finished, I'm heading to Baratin, then home."

Another shot of regret poked and prodded his heart at her statement, but with this, with her, he wouldn't acknowledge the feeling. It was best for her and for him that she go, follow the course she'd set for herself.

No matter how crazy it might make him.

He nodded in her direction, then turned to leave. "I must return to my offices now."

Under a gorgeous midafternoon sky, camped out on the grand lawns of the palace, under a shady cherry tree, Sophia took the white stick with its two blue lines out of her purse and stared down at it with a mixture of terror and wonderment.

She'd lied.

A child—Alex's child—was growing inside her, and she'd told him that her pregnancy test was negative.

Shame worked through her at a heady pace. She'd never done anything so horrid, so cruel, so selfish in her entire life. All in the name of fear.

After she'd heard him speak at the picnic last Saturday, heard the story of his unhappy past with a woman who had cared so little and taken so much, Sophia didn't want to add to his burden, give him something that he didn't want.

But all that had changed this morning when he'd told her that he wanted a child, just not the mother. Fear unlike anything she'd ever known had enveloped

her. Alexander Thorne was a prince and a very powerful man. If he wanted to, he could take her child
from her. All in the name of Llandaron.

This was so unlike her, she mused. She didn't run
from problems.

Sophia plucked at the grass. Was she doing the
right thing? For her child?

From behind her, something leaped at her shoulders. When she glanced back, a pink tongue darted
out, lapped at her face.

The tension in her broke and she laughed out loud.
"Well, how did you get here, little girl?"

The beautiful wolfhound pup cocked its head to the
side and barked.

"Ahhh. Ran away, did you, Aggie?"

The answer came in the form of another lick to
Sophia's face.

Smiling, Sophia stroked the pup's head. "Well,
you're always welcome here."

On what could only be described as a contented
sigh, Aggie did a double turn, then lay down, curled
up at Sophia's side.

"Looks like she's got a crush on you, lass."

Sophia grinned. She knew that voice. Coming toward her on the lawn was Ranen and Alex's stunning
aunt Fara. The older woman looked as if she just
stepped off the pages of *Harper's Bazaar* with her
chic short haircut and perfectly pressed white
pantsuit.

"Ranen has been trying to get that pup to lie down all day," Fara informed her, a glowing smile about her lips.

Sophia threw up her hands. "I used no bargaining chip, I assure you. No bacon in these pockets."

Ranen snorted. "Likely story."

Fara pointed to the blanket spread out over the thick grass. "May we sit with you? This tree offers a lovely shade."

"Of course."

The twosome sat side by side, backs to the tree trunk, hands close but not touching.

Fara sighed as she looked about her. "You know, when Alex was a young boy, he would climb the cherry tree outside his window and sit up there for hours."

"You're kidding?"

"No. He was something of a dreamer."

"I can't imagine that."

Fara smiled and inclined her head. "Of course, he acted the somber child when we were near. His title and station demanded that it be so. But when he was alone, he could relax somewhat."

Ranen nodded his agreement with a taut jerk of the head. "He had his dreams, that one. He wanted a wife he could love, a brood of wee ones he could teach to explore and read and love the ocean as much as he does." The old man gave Sophia a look of cheerless understanding. "But he knew what was right—what had to be done."

"Which was marry a woman he didn't know?" Sophia asked, her voice sounding tired even to her own ears. "Have an heir? Rule his country?"

Ranen nodded. "Takes a disciplined mind."

"So all those dreams had to die?"

"Perhaps they didn't die." Fara smiled a little sadly. "Perhaps they were put aside. Until…"

"Until?" Sophia asked.

"Something or…someone came along to help him see those dreams once again."

A blush surged into Sophia's cheeks, and she looked down at the blanket, at the pup, anywhere but in the woman's eyes. She saw too much. What if she looked further and saw what was in Sophia's heart, all that she had done—and had not done?

Until someone came along to help him see those dreams once again….

Yes, she wanted Alex to find that part of himself again. That amazing, carefree part she'd so rarely seen. But was that her destiny? Was that *her* child's destiny?

To help a man who didn't want help?

Reaching out, Fara touched Sophia's hand. "You know, chances are best taken, my dear."

"I know," Sophia acquiesced. "It's just that—"

"You'd be wise to follow your own advice, Highness," Ranen interrupted.

The older woman looked over at him, startled, confused. "What in the world does that mean?"

Ranen suddenly jerked to his feet. "You know exactly what."

"I do not."

With a pained frown, the man turned and walked away, grumbling something Sophia couldn't make out.

"I'm sorry about that, my dear," Fara said, her voice weak.

Sophia felt the woman's hand tremble over her own. "Are you all right, Your Highness?"

"He is…he wants me to…" She shook her head. "I told you that chances were for taking. But I'm not altogether sure about second chances."

Fara said no more, and Sophia didn't push her. The two of them had heavy hearts and what were obviously difficult decisions to make. So as the sun began to vanish from the sky, casting the palatial grounds in shades of terra-cotta and gold, Sophia grasped Princess Fara's hand, hoping not only to give but to receive just a little bit of comfort.

It was half past eight that night when Alex walked through the door of the beach house. He felt weary and frustrated. His workday had been a slow, arduous one where all thoughts had raced to one subject and one subject only. Sophia. Like it or not, he couldn't get used to the idea of her leaving, and it made him insane that she had this power over him. This insatiable need he had to see her, hear her, touch her would not die no matter how hard he tried to—

"Hi, there. You hungry?"

The eagerness in her voice, the sweet welcome, made his chest constrict. "You must be a mind reader."

Her mouth curved into a smile. "That'll teach you to be careful of all those...thoughts you carry around with you."

"Are you picking up anything else?"

"Hmm." She cocked her head and glanced up at the ceiling as though trying to concentrate on his thoughts. It was all a coy little joke, but it sure gave Alex a moment to take her in.

Dressed in a navy-blue knit dress, feet bare, her hair pulled back in a loose ponytail and soft makeup on her flawless face, she looked incredibly beautiful—elegant yet casual—every round curve she possessed shown off to perfection.

"Oh, my," she exclaimed suddenly. "I've just picked up on something."

"Wild thoughts?"

"And wicked."

"Well, that's the trouble with being around you."

She looked puzzled.

A chuckle escaped Alex's throat. "Wild and wicked thoughts are a guaranteed occurrence."

"Oh." Stains of pink appeared on her cheeks. "Well, thank you, I think."

"Make no mistake, Sophia," he said, walking toward her until he was just a foot away. "That was a compliment."

"And I'm betting that you say stuff like that to all the girls." She grinned, shrugged. "Or princesses or countesses or whatever you date."

"I don't date. And no, I rarely tell a woman my thoughts—sexual or otherwise."

She appeared shocked by his bold honesty, as he was himself. He didn't tell a woman his thoughts. So why had he told this woman? She was no princess, no countess, just a green-eyed, red-haired commoner from San Diego, California who had stolen his control the moment he'd laid eyes on her.

"Why don't we sit?" Sophia suggested, taking a step back, showing him the dining table fully dressed up with plates and wineglasses and a pot with steam wafting out. "The stew's getting cold."

"Stew. Good God, I haven't had stew in thirty years."

"You don't like it?" she asked, melancholy lacing her tone.

"No. Love it." He took off his jacket and sat down at the table. "I just haven't had the pleasure of late. Hearty, earthy dishes are rarely served at social functions or at the pretentious restaurants I'm forced to frequent."

"Of course."

"A grave error, I've always thought."

She gave him a soft, appreciative smile, then sat down beside him, not across from him as he would've expected, but beside him. And the gesture pleased him immensely.

"I know good politics when I hear it," she teased, ladling him out a healthy helping of stew. "You're a wonderful diplomat, Alex, and you're just trying to make me feel good about serving peasant food to a prince."

Alex couldn't help himself. He eased a finger under her chin and lifted her gaze to his. "If I was trying to make you feel good—" he leaned in, kissed her softly on the lips "—there are so many better ways."

"Are there?" she asked breathlessly, her gaze shifting to his mouth. "Like what, for instance?"

He grinned and leaned toward her. But this time instead of kissing her he took her lower lip between his teeth and gently tugged. A soft moan escaped her throat, and her eyes remained closed.

The ache inside him raged like an animal. He wanted more, and clearly so did she, but he wasn't about to ravage her at the dinner table—not when she'd gone to all the trouble of making him dinner.

No, he would wait until later.

"You taste like heaven, Sophia," he said, sitting back. He snatched up his spoon and dug into the stew. "And this is heavenly," he murmured again before slipping a spoonful of stew into his mouth. "Thank you."

Sophia watched him eat, her own appetite defunct. But from the kiss or the lie she'd told that morning, she wasn't sure. What she did know for certain was that it was time to stop running.

Today, sitting beside Fara, she'd really thought about what she'd done and said—and had not said—to Alex. She'd realized that her reasons for deceiving him, no matter how just they'd felt at the time, were cowardly. And she was no coward. Her child deserved a family. And Alex deserved the chance to be a father.

He didn't love her, she knew, but surely he wouldn't keep her from their child. At least, she prayed he wouldn't.

Sophia waited until Alex was finished with his meal, with his wine, then took a breath and jumped. "I have something I have to tell you, Alex."

He drained his wine glass. "This sounds serious."

"It is."

"Your boat is going to take another month for repairs?"

She was set to flinch, ready to reply with something quick and cool, thinking his words were meant unkindly. But when her eyes met his, so hot, needful, soulful, she realized he hadn't meant his query as a concern. In fact, the expression on his face was one of hope. He wanted her just as she wanted him. Neither one of them was ready for this...this whatever-it-was between them to come to an end.

There was nothing she wanted to do more than take his hand and lead him into her bedroom, beg him to make love to her all night. Her body craved him, and she was through denying it. But before she could be intimate with him again, she had to tell him the truth.

"What is it, Sophia? What's wrong?"

Shame filled her soul, but there was nothing for it. "This morning when I told you the pregnancy test was negative..."

As her voice faded, so did the heat from Alex's eyes. Apprehension took up quick residence.

"Continue," he said, his tone now commanding, all arrogance, as though he were speaking to a servant who was about to make a confession.

With every ounce of strength she had in her, she forced out the words. "I lied to you."

"What?" he fairly hissed.

"It wasn't true...what I said. It—"

"You...you are..."

"Yes. I'm pregnant, Alex."

He pushed away from the table with such force, his water glass capsized and dropped to the floor with a crash. Sophia stared at the broken glass, at the water as it seeped into all the cracks and crevices of the floor. She felt as though she'd just broken something in Alex, and in them, with her admission.

"How could you do this?" he demanded, glaring at her burning, reproachful eyes.

She felt as if her breath was cut off, but she stumbled on. "My only excuse—if that even matters now—is that I was scared."

"Of what?"

"The future. My future, the child's future."

"Your future?"

"Yes. I want to be with my child—"

His eyes narrowed dangerously. "If there really is a child. You've lied to me once, Sophia, how do I know you're telling me the truth now?"

Silently Sophia reached into her purse, took out the test and boldly held it out to him.

He snatched it up on a growl, then scanned the white stick with its two blue lines as though looking for the fine print. When he saw what he needed to see, he released a weighty breath. "This changes everything, you have to know that."

"I know that this child is your child. And I understand what that means."

Concern had surpassed the anger in his gaze. "Do you, Sophia?"

"Maybe not to the full extent. But I realize that we'll have to live here in Llandaron—"

"Not just in Llandaron."

"What do you mean?"

"The child must live with me."

"Alex, let's not get ahead of—"

"As will you."

"Alex—"

"Sophia," he said, every angle and line and plane of his body proclaiming his demand, "you must marry me."

Seven

The mattress felt like bricks tonight, unyielding and unforgiving.

Sophia threw back the covers, allowed the cool night air rushing through her windows to brush over her skin. Normally, the sound and smell and caress of the ocean breeze did wonders for her bruised psyche.

But not tonight.

She glanced at her bedside clock. Midnight.

Just four hours ago she'd confessed her secret to Alex. And after the initial anger and shock had worn down, she'd listened as he'd told her that they were to be married.

Heck, with that kind of shock, of course the breeze wasn't doing much but keeping her cool.

So used to having his commands met, Alex hadn't even given the idea over to discussion or refusal. He'd simply walked out the front door, headed down to the beach and stayed there for hours. Sophia had heard him come in after she was in bed.

Married to the crown prince of Llandaron, she mused. Married to Alex. An uneasy smile graced her lips. Yes, she wanted this man. Yes, she wanted to raise her child with its father. But the uncertain future ahead filled her with fear. As did the uncertain feelings of a certain prince. What did he want? What did he really want?

Clearly, he was acting on instinct and protocol. Maybe marrying the mother of the heir to the throne of Llandaron was a law or something. Who knew. But Sophia didn't come from that kind of world; arranged marriages to royals, men and ladies of the court you'd spoken to once or twice, stuff like that. In her world you married the person you were in love with or not at all.

Sitting up, Sophia swung her legs over the side of the bed. Maybe Alex wasn't willing to talk to her about this future he'd already dictated, but she sure as hell couldn't allow the sun to come up on another day without some kind of understanding.

Clad in a thin white tank and blue pajama bottoms,

she made her way down the hall to his room. But once outside the door, she paused for a moment.

If she wasn't sleeping, odds were he wasn't, either, right?

She knocked softly on his door.

She heard him sigh, then utter a husky, "This isn't a wise idea, Sophia."

"We need to talk, Alex."

"Go back to sleep."

"I'm not sleeping. I can't sleep. Obviously you can't, either." And with that, she opened the door and walked inside, no permission, no thought.

A grave mistake.

A fire blazed in the black marble hearth beside the mahogany four-poster, illuminating the man in the bed to knee-buckling perfection.

Chest ripped with sinewy muscle, arms powerful and lightly tanned, Alex lay there, his back to the ornately carved headboard, watching her, totally nude, save for a navy-blue silk sheet lightly draped over his hips. His black hair was mussed, his jaw darkened with stubble, and his eyes shone like two brilliant and very sensual amethysts.

Without reserve, Sophia stared longingly at him, wishing she could join him, wanting him to open his arms and command her to bed.

"I told you this was unwise," Alex said, his lips twisted into a cynical smile.

"Why? Because you're in bed with no clothes on?"

"Something like that, yes."

"I'm not embarrassed, Alex." Desperately turned on, she thought inanely, but not embarrassed.

"Good to know."

"After all, we've seen…each other…"

He snorted, laced his hands behind his head. "Following that line of logic, I think it's only fair that you remove your clothes, as well."

"Excuse me?" she fairly choked.

"It's only fair, don't you think?"

"Aren't you too angry with me to want me?"

His gaze raked boldly over her. "I don't think that's possible. I don't think I could ever be that angry."

Sophia's heart jolted—or maybe the sensation came from someplace below her abdomen, deep within her core.

This setting, fire and ocean waves, broad shoulders and eyes that tugged at her clothes as much as they tugged at her heart…it was so disturbing. If it was possible, her skin actually ached for him, ached for his touch. Every inch of her calling out to every inch of him. When? Now? *Yes…*

But she couldn't take even if he was willing to give. Not yet. Not until they worked out this crazy marriage command he'd tossed her way.

"Alex we need to talk."

He gestured to the edge of the bed. "Have a seat."

"I'm fine standing."

"Don't be ridiculous. You look chilled. The fire is warmer over here."

Warm? Right, she mused. Try blazing, scorching, inferno. Try...

Irresistible.

But like a kid to candy, she went, walked over to the side of his mahogany "throne," sat down on blue silk and tried not to breathe differently.

"Now," Alex began, still sprawled back against the headboard, hands behind his head, chest wide and splendid, attitude commanding. "What has you coming to my room at midnight?"

"This subject of marriage."

"What about it?"

"Let's get serious."

"I assure you, Sophia, I was nothing if not serious."

She asked the silly question she'd posed in her mind earlier. "Is there some kind of law stating that you have to marry your child's mother?"

"There is no law."

"Then we don't have to be married to share a child, do we?"

"Granted, there is no legal basis for my decision, but we *are* talking about the monarchy here. There are unspoken rules we live with, and we must abide by them." He released his hands from behind his head and crossed his arms over his chest. "This is not a contemporary situation, Sophia. My child will be heir to the throne. He or she must be brought into a union, not a single-parent home."

"You are really ready to go through with this again? Marry a woman you don't love for your country?" She waited with bated breath for his answer. And it came quick, and painful.

"Not for my country, for my child," he corrected, pride in his tone.

"A worthy sacrifice for your child. Marrying its mother." She hated the bitter tone in her voice, hated it and was embarrassed by it. But, Lord, she understood this man's reasoning, too. She would give up anything for her sweet baby as well.

"Sophia?"

"Yes?"

"Don't make the mistake of thinking that I have no feeling for you."

She put a hand up in protest. "Alex, you don't need to—"

"It is true that I cannot love you," he interrupted. "I don't have that capability, that gift. 'Tis a lost gene." He shrugged. "But there is something between us. Call it what you will—heat, need, desire—"

"All physical."

He shook his head. "Not necessarily. Need and desire can reach far past the physical."

So, he cared about her, liked her, needed her in some cosmic way. But the truth remained that he wouldn't be offering her marriage if she wasn't pregnant.

Her mind showcased a telling slide show, with pictures from the afternoon the *Daydream* hit a rock all the way up to now, sitting on Alex's bed.

She put her head in her hands and sighed. "I can't believe I've allowed all this to happen."

"That may be the case, Sophia, but it is happening. And we must do what's best for the child now, yes?"

"Of course. Yes. I just—"

"Good. Then it's settled. Our child will come into a family."

Sophia glanced up, into the fire, her heart squeezing painfully. A family. For almost a year she'd been without the only family she'd ever really loved. She was lonely. And God help her she wanted the whole Thorne Clan. But what was more important, her baby deserved them.

"Sophia, what are you thinking?"

She turned to look at him, all handsome and royal and...unattainable. "That I would sacrifice anything for my child. Even my own..."

"What? Happiness? Desires?"

"Yes."

"I can satisfy one right now if you'll allow me."

Her heart skipped, literally, skipped a beat. This man's appeal was devastating, and to fall into his arms sounded like pure heaven right now. But was it enough? Would she regret it later when she was lying beside him thinking about what he could never give her?

But the answer didn't surface within her, and she felt too tired to search for it.

She stood up. "I think we're done here."

He bowed his head. "Waiting until the wedding night. Yes, much better."

"Good-night, Alex," she said firmly.

He grinned. "Pleasant dreams, Sophia."

And as her pulse skittered in her heated blood, Sophia walked away from her future husband, out of his bedroom, making sure to close the door securely behind her.

"I like the cream chiffon."

"The pale-green silk is so beautiful on her," Cathy said, holding up the dress in question.

Fran gaped at her. "Green silk? She can't wear green on her wedding day."

"Why not?"

"Ladies," Sophia said from her perch at the edge of Cathy's hand-carved sleigh bed. "Let's try and remember that this whole thing is a charade not a romantic moment in time."

Both women stopped what they were doing, turned away from the full-length mirror and promptly gave Sophia two very child-like frowns.

Sophia couldn't help but laugh, though the sound was anything but gay. "I'm just saying, let's be realistic here."

"I'm being realistic." Fran cocked an eyebrow. "You *are* falling for him, Sophia, and to me that's pretty darn romantic."

Cathy nodded, hugging the green silk dress closer to her chest. "And he's definitely falling in love with—"

"Don't say it," Sophia interrupted dauntingly. "Don't even think it. He's marrying me for our child."

It had been Sophia's intention to keep her pregnancy a secret, at least for a while, at least until Alex could tell his father. But around Fran and Cathy, she felt as though secrets were an impossibility. The terrific twosome brought out a bonding, sisterly impulse in her. And wrong or right, she'd just wanted to tell them that she was one of them now. So, when they'd picked her up to go shopping that morning, she'd spilled the entire thing.

All about the baby and the marriage.

Cathy and Fran couldn't have been more delighted or more supportive. Just as they were being now, Sophia thought with a melancholy smile.

Fran pitched the cream chiffon over a chair and came to sit beside Sophia on the bed. "Perhaps the baby is the impetus for the marriage, but—"

Sophia shook her head. "He told me quite clearly that he's incapable of love."

"That's just fear talking," Cathy assured her, placing the green dress over the cream and joining them on the edge of her bed. "You must understand this, if Alex lets his guard down, if he acknowledges his true feelings for you, he could be hurt again."

"What do you mean?" Sophia asked.

Cathy touched her shoulder. "He didn't love his ex-wife, but he certainly cared for her and tried to make the relationship work."

"And look what happened," Fran finished. "She walked out on him, humiliated him, made him feel as though he'd lost control and couldn't trust himself or anyone else again. Wouldn't you be scared to listen to your heart, put yourself on the line again, too?"

"Of course, but—"

"Give him a chance," Cathy urged, coming to her feet. "Give this marriage a chance. It could be the best decision of your life."

A wave of hope washed over Sophia as she listened to Cathy and Fran. Alex *had* been through hell, and he was gun-shy now. That was understandable. But the question still remained; past or future, could he ever relinquish that control that bound him and fall in love with her?

No one was capable of answering that question today. Right now, she just needed to focus on the present. On creating the best family she could. And if she was lucky enough to find, to have, what Cathy and Fran had, she would be forever thankful.

With a flash of smile at her new sisters—her new family—Sophia said merrily, "I think we should go with the green silk."

Here he was. Once again. Dressed in princely robes and stern expression, standing in front of the same priest who had performed his marriage rites the last time—that fateful time.

Alex inhaled deeply, calling for calm.

This time was different though. He had to admit it. Instead of the one thousand friends and relatives that had been in attendance five years ago, today there were only a mere 150 gathered in the ancient palace church.

Aside from the drop in number of invited guests, this time Alex had no misconceptions about his marriage, no hopes for an impossible future and a beautiful child already on the way.

He also had her.

The vision that stood before him.

As the priest continued with his wedding sermon, Alex took in the view. Beneath a veil of pale-green tulle and crystals, Sophia smiled tentatively up at him.

Never in his life had he seen a woman so lovely. She wore a floor-length dress of pale-green silk that clung to every curve she possessed, yet upheld the modesty the day dictated. Her long red hair hung loose about her shoulders in soft curls, and her skin glowed with health and the beginning of pregnancy. But what really made his body ache for her, were her lips, full and rosy and just a little bit moist.

A bitter chuckle rose in his throat. He'd wanted to feel absolutely nothing today. But that idea had been thoroughly crushed when he'd seen his bride walking down the aisle toward him. Like the fool that he was, he'd felt too much. He'd felt attracted, mindful and incredibly protective of her.

"Do you take this woman…" The priest interrupted Alex's thoughts as his crackly query boomed through the hushed church.

Did he take this woman?

Had the man of God heard him, seen the pictures in his mind, Alex wondered inanely? Yes, he wanted to take this woman. Bloody hell, he wanted—

The priest inclined his head, whispered, "Your Highness?"

Alex brushed aside all thought for a moment and answered the old man. "Yes, I do."

"And Sophia Rebecca Dunhill," the priest continued. "Do you take this man as your husband? To love him, honor him and obey him…"

Sophia arched a brow at him when the priest said, "obey him."

Alex grinned at her, couldn't help himself. He wondered if she would say yes to everything but the promise to obey. She was so spirited, so passionate, and she would give him trouble always. But damn if he didn't like that about her.

Sophia was looking straight at him, her eyes clearly saying she didn't plan to obey anyone at anytime, but her smile was warm. "Yes. I do."

"Then by the power vested in me by God, I pronounce you husband and wife. You may kiss your bride, Your Highness."

Alex's chest felt as if it would burst. His bride, his wife. A shadow rushed through him, sallow and anxious. But he fought it. He fought it because a welcome pleasure was now upon him.

Reverently Alex lifted his bride's veil. "Your Highness," he whispered before lowering his head and covering her mouth, giving her a tender kiss.

She tasted like sweet mint, and he wanted so much more. But he only took a moment, as they were in church with the eyes of all his acquaintances and relatives upon them. Then he grasped her hand in his and guided her down the aisle and out into the vast courtyard where the afternoon reception was to take place.

White roses and purple heather sprung up everywhere. In vases on the tables, in oak barrels bordering the antediluvian courtyard. Servants wandered in and out serving champagne and caviar on toast. Guests milled about drinking and eating and, Alex mused, no doubt comparing this wedding to the last.

When the king, dressed in all his impressive royal

plumage, made his entrance, the assembly bowed low. He hastily waved them back to their celebration and headed across the courtyard. His eyes bright, he made his way over to Alex and his bride.

Alex shook his head in bewilderment at the beaming smile of his father's face. Oddly enough, the man hadn't reacted at all foully to the news of his marriage or the child he'd conceived with Sophia. In fact, he'd actually asked if he could have his staff take care of all the wedding details.

"Sophia," the king fairly gushed, taking both her hands in his. "You are one of my daughters now. I hope this pleases you as much as it pleases me."

"It does, Your Majesty," Sophia returned earnestly. Smiling a little sadly, she added, "I lost my own father when I was a child, then last year…"

"Ah, yes, Ranen's brother."

She nodded.

"Not to worry, my dear. Now you have us both. Two old grumps looking out for your welfare."

"Thank you. I'm truly honored, sire."

"Well, if that's the case, we must have a dance." The king looked at Alex. "If your husband has no objection."

The word gripped Alex's heart like a vise. "No objection at all."

Alex watched as his father took Sophia out to the floor for a slow waltz, watched as Ranen guided Fara

to the floor to join them, watched as the guests followed suit. Soon, everyone was dancing.

Almost everyone, at any rate.

"Congratulations, brother." Maxim came up to
stand beside him, beer in hand. "But shouldn't that
be you out there dancing?"

"I'm no dancer, as you know."

"True enough." Maxim sighed as he stared at the
dance floor. "Sophia's quite a beauty."

Alex nodded. "She is that."

Sidling up to Alex on the opposite side, Dan cuffed
his brother-in-law on the shoulder. "Wife and child.
You're really one of us now."

"It would seem so."

"Ah, the joys of pregnancy," Maxim regaled.
"Morning sickness—"

"Mood swings," Dan offered on a chuckle.

"Late-night fudge cravings."

Dan shook his head. "We haven't had those. It's
been fried chicken for Cathy."

"Sounds rather taxing," Alex said, his voice calm,
his gaze steady as he watched a Spanish duke ask
Sophia to dance.

Dan snorted. "Don't let our typical male com-
plaints deceive you, buddy. We love every minute of
it, don't we, Max?"

"It's true. Nothing's better than having the woman
you love carrying your child."

His brother's words stung, straight to his very soul. "Yes…" Alex uttered coolly.

"What's with the long face, Alex?" Dan chided good-naturedly. "You hit the jackpot today."

If that Spanish bastard held Sophia any closer, Alex thought darkly, he would rather enjoy breaking both the man's legs. True, he'd never taken to dancing. So what. That Spaniard had no right to take such liberties with his wife. Maybe Prince Alexander Thorne wasn't capable of love, but he sure as hell was capable of jealousy.

Sophia was his now, for better, for worse, forever.

But when she glanced over at Alex, her eyes imploring him to come to her, dance with her himself, he turned away. Jealousy was a weakness he couldn't afford. Not now, not ever, if he was going to stay sane and strong in this marriage. He couldn't afford to have her see such an emotion as jealousy in him. He'd already given up too much control and was already too bloody involved with her as it was.

Alex turned to his brother, did something that he would never have dreamed of doing. "I need some air."

"What?" Maxim exclaimed.

"I'm going back to the beach house."

"Alex what the hell? You can't just leave your bride here by her—"

Alex's lip curled. "Please don't tell me what I can and cannot do, little brother."

True, leaving this reception was uncalled for and completely devoid of his customary sense of duty. But he didn't care. The first marriage and the second were fusing in his mind, making him mad. He needed to detach himself.

"Alex," Dan began, his voice smooth and relaxed as though he were trying to pass those traits off onto a foolish groom. "Why don't we all have a drink and relax."

"Thanks, but I'll be drinking alone tonight."

He turned to leave, but Maxim grabbed his arm. "You don't care how this will look?"

"I will tell the king that urgent business has called me away."

"But what should we tell Sophia?"

Alex shrugged him off and muttered a terse, "Anything you want," before walking away.

Eight

A brilliant sphere of moon lit the beach with a ghostly glow. Though she felt almost desperate to get to him, Sophia took patient steps toward the living statue that faced the tortured ocean waves.

Arms crossed over his chest, legs splayed, jaw tight, Alex didn't even glance at her when she came to stand beside him.

"I thought I'd find you here," Sophia said casually.

"Why did you come looking?"

She didn't flinch at his curt reply. After all, it wasn't in her nature to cower when others got angry or impassioned. Besides, this man was her husband now, with all his flaws and all his fears.

"Alex, you know why I'm here." Her mind whirred with reasons, with truths. She wanted to tell him that she cared about him and knew that he was uneasy over the leap they'd just taken. But she could tell he wasn't ready to hear that.

So she grinned and said, "I needed to get out of there. Your father can throw one crazy party. The band actually refused to play any more waltzes until the bandleader performed a rap song."

"Is that so?" he said dryly.

"No." She rolled her eyes, sighed. Obviously, humor wasn't going to work, either. "That's not so. The truth is, I was ticked off that you left me back there with your entire family and a hundred of your closest friends, and I wanted to give you a good dressing down."

After a moment he turned to look at her, his eyes a strange mixture of frustration and heat. "You want to give me a dressing down, huh?"

A delightful shiver of sensuality moved through her. "Something like that."

"Well, perhaps we should go inside then."

She shook her head, though her feminine instinct hovered briefly over his suggestion. "No, not yet. We need to settle this. I want to know why you walked out on our reception."

"I had something I needed to take care of."

"Right, you had a business emergency." She snorted. "Oh, please."

Alex's eyebrows shot up in surprise. "Is that what Maxim told you?"

"He could barely look me in the eye when he said it."

"Hmm. Perhaps I shouldn't have put such a burden on him."

"Perhaps not." She cracked a smile, wanting to be irritated with him but finding it impossible. "You know, you're entirely too cocky, Your Highness."

Something close to a grin tugged at his mouth. "Yes, I know."

As the waves hit the shore, Sophia sighed. She wasn't sure which direction to take here, how best to get through to him. But she had to try something. "Alex, if this is going to work, don't you think we should at least try and be friends?"

"I don't want you as a friend."

"You're not being reasonab—"

"I said I don't want you as a friend."

"How do you want me, then?" she exclaimed, gathering frustration now.

"Dammit, Sophia!"

"What?"

He groaned, his eyes flashing in a familiar display of impatience. "This line of conversation is making me insane. Why are you here? What is it that you want from me?"

"I just want you to talk to me."

"About what?"

With a quick shrug, she said, "I'm a good listener, and maybe talking about your past, about your feelings, could really help."

Through gritted teeth, he uttered, "I'm not looking to be saved from the past."

"What, then? Are you looking to hold on to all that stuff with your ex-wife as protection or something?"

His laugh was forced, bleak. "I thought you were a writer not a psychiatrist."

Never in her life had Sophia been in such a battle of wills with such a formidable partner. Her grandfather was a stubborn man, but not like this. Not completely closed off to feeling and pain and history.

Obviously, Crown Prince Alexander wasn't used to giving in to anyone. But she was growing tired of fighting him.

"All right, Alex," she said, turning away, ready to head back up to the house. "You win. I won't beg."

But she didn't get very far. Alex's hand darted out and caught her wrist, turned her to face him. "Bloody hell, Sophia. Don't you understand? I'm the one who wants to beg here."

"You?"

"You sound shocked."

"I am. I can't imagine you ever resorting to something so—"

"So what?" He suddenly pulled her close to him, body to body, as the ocean breeze swirled the skirt of her wedding dress around them. "So base? Desperate? Humble?"

"No. So honest."

He stiffened as though she'd struck him. Cursed as if he'd been wounded. Then after a moment, he lowered his head, pausing just centimeters before taking her mouth. "I am being honest. I've never denied wanting you. Not to you or to myself."

Sophia could hardly get her breath. Her entire body was reacting to the closeness of him, his clean, spicy masculine scent, his heart-wrenching frustration. "This has escalated past the physical, don't you agree?"

A thin, tight muscle pulsated under the skin below his jaw as he whispered huskily, "It cannot."

"Do you think this is easy for me, either, Alex?"

He didn't answer, merely nuzzled her lips with his own, causing her lips to part and a rush of wet heat to pool low at her core.

She struggled to speak, tasting him as she went, feeling as though her mind had fled time and reason and was now drifting with the waves behind them. "I've lost everyone I've ever loved in my life. Do you think I want to become attached to someone? Trust someone? Open myself up to getting hurt again?"

"I would never hurt—"

"Don't make that promise."

His hands raked up her back and into her hair. "Sophia, you lost your family through natural causes, not because they didn't want to stay—"

"But my pride is still at stake," she said roughly. "This marriage is terrifying and risky for both of us. But we've done it, Alex. I've spoken my vows, and I know this—I won't run from you...ever."

His hands fisted in her hair. "And you don't make that promise."

"I can," she insisted, pressing her hips against him, feeling the rock-hard evidence of his need. "I can because I want you that much."

"Sophia..."

"At least I have the guts to go after what I want."

"Damn you!"

He said no more, just scooped her up in his arms as though she weighed little more than a grain of sand and stalked back to the beach house.

The last time they'd been together, their lovemaking had been quick, wild, even a little dangerous.

But this time, Sophia promised herself, as Alex carried her into the bedroom, this time they would go slow. Enjoying each other without reproach or thought or worry because they both desperately needed this reconnection.

The distance to the bed was little, but Alex didn't ease her down on the mattress as she expected. No, he was a man of surprises and sensation, and when he let her down, it was to stand in front of him. It was to look at her, take her in, drink her in with those woman-killer eyes of his.

"You looked so beautiful today," he said, his tone rough and ragged. "When you came down that aisle, I nearly lost my mind."

She offered him a coy smile. "I'm sorry for that."

"No, you're not." The full moon outside the bay window gave off their only light, but it was enough to see Alex's wicked grin.

Sophia shook her head. "No, you're right, I'm not sorry."

In one stride, he moved to stand behind her. Missing him, his warmth, she started to turn toward him, but he stopped her with one word.

"Please."

Such a statement coming from that mouth made her freeze, made the excitement in her build all the more. What was next? What was he going to do next?

"This is our wedding night, Sophia," he whispered close to her ear as he started unbuttoning her dress, his fingers cool against each inch of skin he exposed. "This is our wedding night and I have no gift."

"You don't need to give me anything," she assured him, her breathing heavy with longing.

"Yes, I do. You deserve all for marrying a man like me."

Sophia's heart ached for his pain and torment, just as her skin ached for his touch. He had everything a man could ask for: riches, power, the adoration of thousands. But his sense of worth and his pride had been twisted by a horrible marriage.

He wanted more from this marriage, more from Sophia than he would ever admit—she knew that as well as she knew her own name. But she also knew she would have to be patient, loving, tender and open to get him to see the truth. Maybe then he would take what she was so willing to give.

At that thought, her silk dress fell into a sea-green pool on the floor. Cool air rushed her skin and she pressed her back against his chest, looking for his arms to fold around her. But Alex wasn't finished removing her clothing. With deft fingers, he flicked the clasp of her bra, lifted the lacy straps from her shoulders and let that, too, drop to the hardwood floor.

Sophia sucked in a breath as she felt his hands move lower, his fingers finding the edge of the white lacy thong Fran had insisted she wear. With a gentle tug, he eased her panties down, over her hips, down her thighs and ankles until she was totally naked before him.

"No gift," he uttered again as he reached around her waist, palming her abdomen.

Sophia placed her hand over his, at the place where his child grew inside her. "This is the best gift you could ever give me."

"Sophia, lass," he uttered hoarsely, his kisses searing her neck and shoulders while he moved his hand lower, then lower still.

A moan, guttural and fierce ripped from Sophia's throat as Alex's fingers slipped between the silken curls at the junction of her thighs.

"Open your legs for me," he whispered in her ear.

He needed the control like he needed to breathe.

And she gave it to him.

She pressed herself back into him again, this time feeling his erection, hard and pulsating against the top of her buttocks. On a purely feminine growl of satisfaction, she did as he commanded, stepping out, parting her legs for him.

A trembling sensation came over her as he reached around, cupped her breast, kneading the plump flesh, while his other hand palmed her, then penetrated her, slipping first one finger, then a second inside her. Liquid honey met him, and she heard his sharp intake of breath next to her ear.

"Hold yourself open for me, Sophia," he commanded.

A soft whisper of embarrassment gripped her heart. She'd never been touched this way, never been so exposed. But she was falling head over heels in love with this man. He was her husband, her lover, and if she ever wanted him to be free with her, she would have to set the tone, here and now.

Her breath shallow, she eased her hands down her stomach, way down to the center of her body and did as he asked, parting her slick, pink folds for him.

"So hard," he whispered in her ear as he rolled

one aching nipple between his fingers. "So wet," he said as he used his thumb to stroke the very core of her.

Sophia was starting to feel as though she couldn't stand on her own anymore, couldn't give to anyone but herself anymore. Electricity and heat surged through her abdomen, the pulsating sensation almost painful.

But she took the wondrous pain, bucking against his fingers, moaning into the sea air rushing through the window, knowing that she couldn't hold on, hold back much longer. She could only surrender to him as she was surrendering to her love for him.

Suddenly, shudders of pleasure hit her full on, sending a wave of heat screaming through her body.

Her breathing became ragged as she took it all, reveled in it all. And when the convulsions eased, she felt depleted—yet wanted more.

She wanted Alex.

Whirling on him, she gripped the back of his neck and pulled his mouth down to hers. Her kiss was hungry and demanding as her fingers inched up, threading into his hair. She felt his erection straining against his pants, pressing into her belly. There was something so erotic about being naked when he was fully dressed, but the need to feel him, all of him was too strong to deny.

She fumbled with his jacket, the buttons on his

pants, but she was too slow, too awkward. And she wanted his mouth again.

Alex must've heard her silent plea, because he gathered her in his arms, slanting his mouth over hers, taking her tongue into his mouth, playing and giving and tormenting as he moved them onto the bed.

Her back licking the cool silk sheets, she watched as he ripped off his jacket, watched as his eyes turned a smoky shade of wine, smiled as he gazed down at her hungrily.

Slowly he eased over her, gave her a slow, drugging kiss on the mouth before dipping his head to her breasts.

How could he be this loving with her, she wondered, this open about his wants and needs, yet keep his heart so closed?

The query left as quickly as it came, for Alex was drawing slow, lazy circles around her breast with his tongue. Sophia let her head fall back, her eyes close as he made his way slowly, so slowly, to the hardened peak. And when he did, when he laved her nipple, then suckled it deep into his mouth, she cried out.

Perfect torture.

She arched her back, her hips, anything to tell him that she wanted him closer, inside her body where he'd be warm and safe.

He glanced up then, as if he'd heard her thoughts, his gaze fierce. "Tell me you want me, Sophia."

"So much, Alex," she said, her tone impassioned.

''Tell me this is okay for our child. We aren't hurting—''

''No, it's perfectly fine.''

He stood then, stripped himself of pants and boxers, then eased her legs apart. As he moved over her, his hands slowly raked up her inner thighs, massaging as he went. Sophia hummed with need, anticipation, her memory roaring back to the first time he'd been inside her. The heat, the sensation, the—

Alex entered her with one silky stroke, filling her with thick, hard steel and a tenderness he would never admit to. But she could feel him, his desire and his heart beating inside her.

She wrapped her legs around his waist, moving with him as he started off with slow, heady strokes that soon graduated to raw, ravenous thrusts.

The core of her, that small bundle of nerves Alex had taken to heaven earlier was shimmering with heat once again. Her nails digging into his back, she slammed her hips upward over and over, reveling in the sound of their bodies slapping with slick play.

A guttural sound escaped Alex's throat and he covered her mouth with his as he went deep, surged deep, then shattered with the intensity of his climax.

A second later Sophia followed him.

Sunlight lumbered through the window, bathing the room in lazy beams of white. Tagging along, came a soft ocean breeze, urging the navy curtains bracketing the window into a graceful dance.

Eyes still closed, Alex reached up and stretched. He hadn't felt this good, this relaxed in a long time. If ever. Last night Sophia had been wild and wanting and completely giving of herself without embarrassment or shame. Highly addictive.

His bride, his wife.

Alex waited for the unease of her new title to wash over him. But it didn't. Instead, it settled deep in his bones, seemingly content with just being fact. Strange. And a little bit disconcerting.

Surely one night of glorious lovemaking hadn't turned his mind from his vow. No, he still coveted control. He could have both, he quickly assured himself. The warmth of his wife without the push for self-discovery, forgiveness and promises.

Just the very thought of warmth and his wife had Alex's blood pumping hard. He knew he had given her a new experience last night, and he wanted to give her more, anything she desired. Anytime she desired it.

But when he opened his eyes, reached for her to give her that pleasure, he found only sheets and the space beside him empty as a tomb.

A straining sense of doom clawed at his gut. One he couldn't shake off even as he jolted out bed and headed for the living room.

Once there, doom turned to agitation. She was nowhere in sight. Nor was she in the bathroom, kitchen or out on the beach.

The clock above the stove struck eight. Where had she gone so early on a Saturday? On the morning of their first day as husband and wife.

Answers came, ones he didn't want, ones that were so embedded in his mind now, that they couldn't be shut off. Had she lied last night about staying with him? he wondered, anger and misery saturating his senses. Had she had second thoughts about their marriage, about raising their child amongst royalty—with him?

His lips thinned dangerously. Had she walked out just as—

"Morning, Highness."

Alex turned sharply at the singsong call, caught his smiling and incredibly beautiful wife in the doorway.

"Where have you been?" he asked, his tone excessively harsh even to his own ears.

"Someone woke up on the wrong side of the royal bed this morning." From behind her back, she pulled out a basket. "I was just out hunting for some breakfast. We have nothing in the fridge."

He heard her words, but they did little to appease him. He started to pace. "You shouldn't go out alone. You're the crown princess of Llandaron now."

"Relax. I went into town, grabbed a few things and headed back. No harm done."

"No harm done?" he said through gritted teeth.

"You could've been kidnapped or worse. You must understand your—"

"My what? My place?"

"Yes!"

"Alex, I'm going to pretend I didn't hear you say that." She walked over to the counter, set the basket down and started unpacking. "I'm guessing this isn't really about me being kidnapped. But I suppose you aren't going to tell me what it *is* about, right?"

She was too bloody patient, too grounded, and she saw far too much. He continued to pace, barking, "There is nothing more to tell."

"Right. Okay. Let me just say then that this princess thing is new and unfamiliar territory, and from now on I'll have a palace guard with me if I go into town alone." She glanced over her shoulder at him. "All right?"

He mumbled a terse "Fine" her way, then asked briskly, "So, what did you trek into town for?"

She rolled her eyes and smiled. "Blueberry biscuits and honey butter."

Alex stopped dead in his tracks, his heart twisting inside his chest. "How in the world could you..."

"Your favorite breakfast, right?"

She'd done it. That one, very sweet, very intimate act she'd just performed was the stopper in his bottle of restraint, the bottle he'd reluctantly left open to breathe the moment he'd met her.

Finding out about his favorite breakfast, that was something a wife did for her...husband.

But they were husband and wife, he quickly reminded himself.

It was just that, such a gesture—it was what a *loving* wife did for her husband.

Alex stalked over to her, looked into her eyes. Did she love him? He knew she cared for him, was attracted to him, but love...

"Why would you do this?" he asked, searching her gaze.

She frowned. "What do you mean 'why'? Because I thought you'd enjoy it."

He couldn't allow her to love him.

"I appreciate the gesture, Sophia." His tone was tight and forced. "But you—"

She dropped onto one of the bar stools with a huff, her patience obviously draining. "But I crossed the invisible and ever-changing line you've drawn between yourself and the rest of the world, is that it?"

"I just don't want there to be any confusion."

"Confusion over what?"

"No matter what we do in there," he said, pointing toward the bedroom. "You must never forget who I am."

"Crown Prince Alexander?" she asked tightly.

"A man who will never love you, Sophia."

Nine

"**A**ren't you supposed to be on your honeymoon, lass?"

"One would think," Sophia replied, stretching out in one of Ranen's bedraggled armchairs with Aggie, the large wolfhound pup, curled up on her lap. "I didn't know where else to go."

Ranen reached over to touch her hand, then quickly retreated. "You are always welcome here, lass, you know that."

She didn't, but was so thankful to hear it. For better or worse or somewhere in between, Ranen was family and the closest thing she had to her grandfather. She needed the strength of him and the consolation of his small, comfortably worn house right now.

"Would you like to tell me what happened?" he asked, filling a pipe with fragrant tobacco and setting it to light.

She shrugged to hide her discontent, but ended up spilling it, anyway. "It's Alex."

"Go on with yourself, lass."

"You know, I take this marriage very seriously."

"And you think the prince does not?"

"I think he takes the *union* seriously, but the marriage..." She sighed heavily. "I've fallen in love, Ranen."

"I know."

"But he won't allow himself to fall in love with me."

"Tosh. You're wrong about that, lass."

Hopes and wishes surged through her at his words, but she shook her head. "I don't think so. He's made it pretty plain."

At that, Aggie yawned, stretched, her front paw lifting into the air and dropping down directly on top of Sophia's hand. Sophia couldn't help but smile at the sweet, almost sympathetic gesture.

"He's fighting you because he's falling in love with you," Ranen said, pointing his pipe at her for emphasis.

Her heart, her senses, darted back to the glory of last night. Alex had been so giving, so wonderful. The way he'd touched her with such veneration, looked at her with such care. In those wondrous hours, he'd felt every inch her husband.

And though the ceremony and reception had been less than ideal, he had truly given her the perfect wedding night.

Perfect wedding night, she thought sadly, for one very imperfect couple.

"If that's true," she said softly. "If he's really fighting me because he's falling in love with me, who do you think will win in the end? The very controlled prince of Llandaron or his feelings of love?"

The question seemed to startle Ranen, and he leaned back against the unlit fireplace and harrumphed loudly. "Can't say. Can't rightly say. Both are worthy opponents."

Didn't she know it? Alex and his mind set were at odds almost daily. Sometimes she feared they would destroy each other, leaving no victors, no spoils.

The situation reminded her of those trials and tribulations of her mom and dad. Constantly at odds, no one winning, everyone losing.

"What is it, lass? You look a mite disconcerted."

Sophia spoke with quiet but desperate firmness. "I just want my child to come into a loving family, not like—"

"Yours?"

She nodded. "My parents hardly spoke to each other. They weren't even friends, Ranen."

"Don't fret anymore on it today, lass. Llandaron is a special place. Magic lurks here."

"I could use a little magic."

He raised a bushy eyebrow. "Well, it grabs hold of you when you need it most."

"Then why hasn't it found you?" The query came out in a rush, unprepared but honest.

A query that took Ranen completely unaware. "Me?"

Sophia saw the twinge of aloofness brush over Ranen's eyes, but she pushed on. He was her family; she cared for him deeply and she wanted him to be happy. "Looks to me like that Llandaron magic you're talking about has been trying to grab on to you for quite some time, but you keep running."

He simply glared at her, frowning.

"I'm not afraid of that look, Ranen. Your brother had a mighty fierce one of his own. And whenever I did something wrong, he gave it to me good. So, try something else."

"I think you've been eating too much of that taffy Fran and Catherine are so bloody keen on," he growled with frustration. "Clogged your brain, it has."

"This has nothing whatever to do with taffy, old man. It has to do with love."

"Love?"

"You love Fara."

Ranen's mouth fell open, and his pipe dropped to the floor.

"And Fara loves you."

"This is foolish talk—"

"I know she does."

"Tosh," he said impatiently.

She leaned forward. "You need to do something about it before it's too late."

"I know what I need and what I don't. And I don't need you coming here, telling me—"

The look of defiance Sophia shot his way made him stop where he was and listen to what she had to say. "Regret is an unhappy state of affairs, Ranen."

He shook his head. "The niece giving the great-uncle unsolicited counsel. It's...it's..."

"It's family, Ranen. And family is a blessing."

For a moment the old man only stared at her, and she wondered if he was going to order her out of his house. But then an amazing thing happened. Maybe it was a little of that Llandaron magic kicking in, who knew, but Ranen's face split, actually split into a wide, toothy grin, and he said, "You're a right winning lass, you are, Sophia."

The compliment touched her deeply, in that place left vacant by family long gone. And it fueled her, as well. To stick things out and make things right, make things better, best, with the man she loved.

All for the child she loved....

* * *

He'd found her.

Finally.

He'd been to the beach house, the boat works, then to Ranen's place looking for her with absolutely no luck. Then, he'd come to town for a pint at the pub, and there she was. Out on the cobblestone sidewalk beside Gershins Taffy. One of the older palace guards was sitting beside her, and fifty or so town's children surrounded them.

At first Alex had wanted to go to her, but as he'd gotten closer to the crowd, he'd thought better of it. She was talking and laughing with the boys and girls, asking all about their favorite animals and what they'd like to see that animal do. Fly? Dance? Belch...? When she'd said that Alex had laughed so hard he'd nearly caught the attention of the group, so he'd backed up to a safe distance.

One thing was certain. The children adored her, wanted to be near her. She had a special rapport with them. He'd never seen anyone so willing to play without reserve or embarrassment before. Not even when he was a child himself.

She would be a wonderful mother to their child.

Alex felt his gut tighten. In seeing Sophia that way, he couldn't help but wonder what kind of father he would be when the time came.

It was at that moment that Sophia caught his eye. Alex flinched at the unease he saw in her gaze. She was probably wondering why he was there, whether for good or bad. But his presence obviously made her nervous and, he noticed with deep regret, made all of that brilliant childlike pleasure drain from her spirit.

He didn't blame her for reacting to him in such a way. After the magic of last night, then the boorish attitude he'd offered her this morning, he wouldn't blame her if she chose not to speak to him. But Sophia wasn't that sort. She was a brave, bold, gutsy creature. She would not ignore him or shame him by cutting him in front of his people.

After thanking the children and giving them all a winning smile, she disentangled herself from the group and walked over to him. Her guard followed but kept a respectful distance.

"Good afternoon, Your Highness."

He reached out, took her hand and kissed it. "And to you, Your Highness."

Her gaze tripped a little, and she eased her hand from his grasp.

"You looked like you were having fun," he said, trying to find an easy subject.

"The children are very sweet and very patient. They were helping me with my writing."

"Having some trouble focusing?"

"Yep."

Alex glanced around casually, just to see who observed them, then said in a low voice, "As am I, Sophia."

At his telling admission, she looked up at him with understanding, steady eyes. "What do you suggest we do about it? Stay away from each other?"

He could feel her anger, her frustration and felt ashamed for having been the cause. "That's not very practical, is it?"

"Not really."

Around them the people of Llandaron were beginning to stop and stare. Under normal circumstances, like a drink or meal or shopping trip into town, his people gave the royal family a wide berth. But as this royal had just married their new princess the day before, they weren't being as generous.

Alex offered her his hand. "Shall we walk?"

After seeing the growing flock, she nodded. "All right."

With the palace guard trailing behind them, Alex led her down several streets until they arrived at Short Street, a charming, little way, quite private. He stopped and gestured to a white bench, whereupon Sophia sat and he followed suit.

"How about if we try not to think," Alex began, "or to reason anymore?"

When she turned to face him, surprise registered on her face. "Really?"

"Yes."

"What about false judgments, Alex?"

He stiffened at her frankness, but as it was deserved

he acquiesced. "I will abstain from all judgments, m'lady."

"For how long?"

He grinned. "As long as we can."

She smiled tentatively. "So, we don't think or reason, we just…"

"Experience."

"And enjoy."

"Yes."

"All right."

He took her hand again, smiled when she didn't pull away and said, "Will you come somewhere with me?"

"Where?"

"It's a surprise."

Sophia could hardly believe her eyes.

Before her on the computer screen was a tiny peanut-shaped object inside a wedge of blackness. At first she'd hardly seen it. But then, slowly, as the doctor moved the probe around her abdomen, the object had seemed to grow darker or lighter, somehow catching her eye, drawing her to it.

Sophia felt a lump in her throat, but she managed to say, "That's my child?"

Sitting beside the ultrasound monitor, the royal doctor nodded his head. "It's a bit early, but yes. This is your child, Your Highness."

Tears welled up in Sophia's eyes. She was no wilting flower, granted, but a life was growing inside her. One she and Alex had created together. And that statement was almost overwhelming because she loved him so much.

"And the heir to the throne of Llandaron," the doctor finished reverently.

She gave the doctor a nervous smile. Yes, her child would be heir. He or she would be a prince or princess of Llandaron.

How life had changed in a matter of mere weeks, she mused as Alex inched closer to her, his gaze fixated on the screen, his hand wrapping around hers. Five months ago she was alone, no family, few friends, no stories to tell. And now she had a husband, a family, an uncle, a country, a direction, a heart full of stories and, most important, a child.

Brow furrowed, Alex pointed to the screen. "What is that, Dr. Tandow?"

"The baby's heart, Your Highness."

Alex squeezed her hand, no doubt unaware that he was doing so. "It's beating rather fast. Is that—"

"It's perfectly normal, Your Highness," the doctor assured him.

"Beautiful," Sophia cooed.

"Yes, Your Highness."

Your Highness. Lord, would she ever get used to such a title? For it didn't suit her at all. A strange name for little, scrappy Sophia Dunhill from San Diego, who used to sit out on her grandfather's boat and drip Popsicle juice all over herself.

"I think I'll leave you both alone now." The doctor stood then, inclined his head. "Your Highnesses."

When the man had left the room and closed the door, Sophia turned and looked up at her prince. He looked so devilishly handsome in his black dress shirt and pants. His dark hair a bit mussed, his jaw slightly dusted with stubble, and that tan skin against those sexy amethyst eyes.

And he belonged to her.

He brushed a thumb over her cheek. "Good surprise?"

"The best. Thank you."

"Consider it an apology."

"For what?" She knew what he was apologizing for, but she wanted to hear him say it, needed to, deserved to. If they were ever going to get anywhere with this "no judgment, no thinking" plan of his, they needed to start with a clean slate.

He grinned. "My asinine behavior this morning."

She found it impossible not to return his alluring smile. "Ah, yes, that."

"Do you accept my apology?"

"Hmm," she began, feeling a rush of wickedness invade her blood. "I feel there should be some kind of punishment involved, don't you?"

He leaned down, gave her a soft, drugging, nipping

kiss that left her mouth and the lower half of her burning with fire.

"Was that the kind of punishment you meant, m'lady?" he asked huskily against her lips.

"You're certainly on the right track," Sophia uttered through a breathy chuckle.

"You require more?"

"Definitely."

"Kisses or...?" His hand moved under her blouse, up, up until his fingers brushed her lace-covered breast. "Caresses?"

She swallowed hard. "Caresses are good."

It was the most erotically romantic moment of her life. Crazy as it was. Never in a million years would she have thought that lying on a metal table, fully clothed, kissing her husband while the doctor waited outside and could walk in on them at any moment, was romantic.

But it was.

Wild and wickedly romantic.

After stealing a quick kiss, she whispered, "Maybe Dr. Tandow would let us borrow this room for say...an hour."

Alex smiled, his thumb sweeping lightly over her hardened nipple. "Although, the thought of staying like this, holding you, making love to your mouth for a good long time in this very public place sounds intriguing, I have plans for us."

"Plans? Wasn't this—"

"This was merely…an appetizer, Sophia."

"You mean an appe*teaser.*"

A wide grin overtook his features before he broke into a full-on chuckle. "Why don't we go now?"

He helped her sit up. "Let's go back to the beach house and change into evening clothes. I'm taking you to dinner and a movie tonight."

"A date?"

"Indeed."

"Dinner, movie…then what?"

He leaned close, whispered in her ear, "More making up."

She shivered. "Making up or making out?"

He chuckled, the sound deep and rich. "You make me…"

"What?" she demanded, standing up before him. "Crazy?"

"No. Happy."

The word had come out fast, in a rush, unexpected and powerful. Alex looked appalled at what he'd allowed himself to say. But the word had been music to Sophia's ears, and she wasn't about to let him recant. So, before he could even open his mouth to speak, she grabbed his hand and pulled.

"Come on, Highness, let's get you home."

Ten

Beside the rousing fire, tangled in silk sheets and each other, Alex pulled Sophia closer, reveling in the feel of her skin against his own. It was truly amazing how her curves and valleys fit him to perfection.

Satiated by their fierce lovemaking, yet growing needful once again, Alex gave her a soft kiss on the mouth and whispered, "Tell me."

She dragged her smooth thigh across his groin. "You'll laugh."

As her minor shift of position charmed the lower half of him into rock-hard erection, he uttered hoarsely, "Do I strike you as the kind of man who is moved easily to laughter?"

"Good point."

With a slash of smile, he again pulled her to him in a heady show of possessiveness that had him questioning his rapidly deteriorating self-control. Why couldn't he pull her close enough? he wondered. Like inside him, where his heart pounded and his blood pulsed only her rhythm? And why couldn't he get enough of her? It was maddening. He was Alexander Thorne, the man who would have control at all costs. And here he was relinquishing that power willingly.

But then, he'd promised not to think.

"Whatever it is, Sophia," he said, brushing his lips across her forehead. "I'll take care of it."

"All right." She sighed. "It's bread pudding with cream."

"Hmm." He glanced out the window at the predawn sky. "I might have to take care of that craving tomorrow."

"There's no pubs open after 3:00 a.m. in the village?"

"I'm afraid not. I could wake the palace, however."

"No, I wouldn't dream of doing something like that." She lifted her head to the top of his shoulder and nuzzled his neck. "It can wait until tomorrow."

Her touch, the genuine way she moved, made him weak. A man who knew few weaknesses was humbled by this amazingly beautiful redhead with her quick wit, sharp mind and loving tongue.

"Is there anything else you crave?" he asked.

At that, she eased up on her elbow, palm to chin, and gazed down at him. "What are you offering?"

Alex skimmed his thumb over her pouty lower lip and arrested the urge to taste her. At least for the moment...while she gazed at him in that way.

Bloody hell, did she have to look at him with such openness? As though she wanted to read the words on his soul? Why couldn't this romance have just remained easy and untroubled and fulfilling the way he'd suggested earlier in the day?

Because Sophia wasn't a woman to be content with "easy."

And he wasn't a man who had ever been fulfilled—not until she'd come along at any rate.

"Such suspense, Your Highness," she said softly, interrupting his thoughts, hauling him back to the present, back to her and the feel and smell and look of her.

His control fell, utterly lost now.

With one quick movement, he had her on top of him, sitting on top of him, her long, muscular legs straddling his waist. "I offer myself," he said, feeling her warmth, her silky wetness pressing against the head of his hard shaft. "But I expect my own craving to be satisfied, as well."

"Of course."

"And I crave something sweet."

Her smile was brazen. "What do you have in mind?"

A growl escaped his lungs as he gripped her hips and hauled her toward him, her buttocks raking over his chest, then collarbone until she was close, so close to his waiting mouth.

Sophia felt helpless yet powerful at the same time. Tonight had been a groundbreaking experience. The way Alex had touched her, talked to her, made love to her—his soul had come along for the ride...whether he'd wanted it to or not.

She was no fool, however. She hadn't said a word about her observations. And she wouldn't. She would only relax and enjoy.

But right now, as Alex found her, opened the hot, aching center of her, relaxation was an impossible ambition.

Sophia sighed, deep in her throat, anticipation washing through her. What would he feel like? she wondered madly. What would it feel like when his mouth, his tongue touched her? No man had ever been this close. No man had ever taken her to such an intimate place.

Love intermingled with desire as she reveled in the fact that her husband, the man she loved, was the first.

Then her mind went blank as Alex gave her one hot, raking stroke with his tongue. Shivers of painful delight racked her senses. Heat, electric and throbbing, pulsated in her blood as she waited for more, more...

Then it came. Light, quick strokes, back and forth over the hardened peak nestled in her core.

"Alex..." she whispered breathlessly, wanting him to understand that she was all his, that he made her feel and cherish and crave like she never thought she could.

"I know, sweetheart. I know."

His hot breath against the wet, throbbing bundle of nerves he was so intimately ministering to had Sophia calling out. Alex gripped her buttocks tightly, but lightened his caress as wicked and wonderful shock-waves rippled through her. Coursed through her at a heady pace.

But she didn't wait for the delicious feeling to sub-side. Instead, Sophia pushed away from his grasp, lifted her hips and lowered onto him.

"Sophia..." he uttered, his voice turning ragged.

She sucked in a breath, feeling the steely heat of his erection inside of her. It was like going home every time. And she knew so assuredly with each touch that she'd found the mate to her heart.

If only Alex would realize it, too.

Her thoughts and the blues they brought with them were taken as Alex gripped her hips and shifted her forward, deepening his penetration.

Dawn broke before them on their sandy spot, the sun rising out of the ocean like a giant peach. Sophia snuggled closer to Alex under the blanket, letting the gentle morning breeze send her hair fluttering about them both.

Was it actually possible that life was coming together? she wondered, staring out at the calm sea with its docile waves.

There was no denying that she'd fallen for this whole fairy-tale land just as she had fallen for its first family. She was so thankful for the time and the care of her new sisters, for the welcome of her father-in-law and for the second chance she had to get to know her uncle.

But most of all she was thankful for the chance to be part of a family, part of Alex's family.

"What were you like as a child, Sophia?"

The question, and the timing of it, startled her. Not simply because she'd had thoughts of family before he'd asked it, but because she and Alex had remained silent for quite a long time.

It had been a half hour ago when Alex had suggested they go down to the beach. After making love a third time, they'd both been satiated, yet neither one of them had wished to sleep.

Perhaps they'd desired each other's company in another way, she'd thought.

So, naked and warm, and wrapped in an enormous blanket, they'd come to the water's edge. And here they sat together on the sand, just being close without words. That was, until now....

"As a child," she mused aloud. "I would say I was curious, and I always tried to follow through on what I started or what I made a commitment to. And I tried to be creative, as well."

"That sounds like you. But—"

"But?"

"I think you might be missing something."

She turned, quirked her brow questioningly. "Oh, really?"

He nodded, grinned, then spoke in a thick brogue, "Me thinks you were also a stubborn little lass."

"And what make you *thinks* so?"

He chuckled, low and deep. "Are you seriously asking me for examples, Sophia?"

"All right, all right," she confessed crossly. "I might've been a tad stubborn—"

"A tad?"

"Fine. I was stubborn. Stubborn as they come. Mule-like in my stubbornness. Happy?"

His mouth twitched with amusement. "Ecstatic."

Sophia laughed, shook her head. She loved talking to him this way, irreverently and relaxed. Like this, they were friends as well as lovers.

"You know what, though?" she said, snuggling closer to him inside the blanket. "Despite the afore-mentioned stubbornness, I always took time, whether it was the appropriate time or not, to dream."

With true gentleness, Alex eased them both back on the sand and gathered her in his arms, the blanket cushioning them from the elements. "And what did you dream about, Sophia?"

"The future." Of finding someone I could really love, someone like you, she wanted to say.

"And what did you see in your future?"

"Well, when I was five, I dreamed that I'd grow up to be the world's biggest Barbie collector." She laughed softly. "Then later, I thought about becoming a doctor or a therapist. But when I started writing stories, I knew that was it for me."

Alex was quiet for a moment, then he said, "You were fortunate to have lived your dream."

Tender ground, she knew, and she wasn't about to tread boorishly. "What were you like as a child, as if I even need to ask?"

"Don't be so smug. It could surprise you."

She snorted. "Try me."

"I was clever."

"Of course."

"Handsome."

"Naturally."

"And probably too bloody serious for my own good."

Sophia gave a mock gasp. "No!"

With a husky grumble, Alex was over her in seconds, his black hair mussed and gleaming in the morning light, his beautiful mouth firm and sensual. "Mocking the crown prince of Llandaron…"

Lifting her hips, pressing against his arousal, she whispered, "What'll that get me? Ten years in the stockade?"

"I think you need twenty to straighten you out," he growled with mock severity. "But I'll rethink the stockade."

"You have something else in mind?"

"Torture. Highly sensual, guaranteed to make you misbehave again…and again."

This game had her tied up in knots, every inch of her skin on fire, while the lower half of her pulsed with need. She had barely enough breath to utter, "I can live with that."

But Alex didn't shoot back another sexy quip. Nor did he slip inside her as she'd expected, hoped, wanted. Instead he grew solemn, thoughtful.

"Sophia?"

"Yes?"

"I want our child to dream."

The fraught statement nearly undid her, as did the earnest tone in her husband's voice. Tears formed behind her eyes, hot and emotional. But she pushed them back. Tears were not what Alex needed right now.

"He," she smiled, "or she *will* dream."

"We will make sure of it."

"Yes."

Alex lowered his head, gave her a slow, drowsy kiss. "Yes."

Wrapping her arms around his neck, Sophia tipped her chin up and just gazed into his eyes. She saw so much when he allowed her to; his heart, his pain, *his* dreams...

Then suddenly, from out of nowhere, she gasped. "I have the perfect idea for a story."

"What?"

"For my new story. I've been struggling, not sure if I'm writing the right story. But now I know. I know what the right story is, Alex."

He kissed her lips again, then her cheek, whispering in her ear, "I love to see you happy like this."

And I love you, she thought, closing her eyes, feeling his mouth rake over her skin as his hands explored the curve of her back and buttocks.

"You were the impetus to the idea, Your Highness," she whispered breathlessly.

His lips brushed the pulse points on her neck, then trailed downward over her collarbone to her breast. "I inspired you?"

"More than you'll ever know," she uttered hoarsely as her husband sacrificed their blanket, their refuge, to the wind and took her swollen nipple into his mouth.

"I'm proud of you, big brother."

"For seeking your advice on the best in nursery

finery?'' Alex asked Cathy as they entered Belles and Beaux, Llandaron's most exclusive shop for babies.

Of course, it was tradition for the heir to the throne of Llandaron to sleep in the royal bassinet, the linens made especially for the little prince or princess by the nuns of St. Augustine, who lived just an hour away on the eastern coast. And Alex would accept this gift with thanks. But he was determined to purchase a few things for his child on his own. A crib, blankets, a few toys. Maybe some books, as well. He wanted to read to his child. He'd been told that babies were capable of hearing outside the womb at five months, and he wanted to make sure that his child got to know his father's voice as soon as possible.

''I'm proud of you for taking such an interest in your child,'' Cathy said, tugging him from his thoughts, looping her arm through his and steering him around the shop. ''I never thought I'd see the day when you stepped foot in a baby store.''

''It's nothing to get roused about, Catherine,'' he said with a trace of irritation. ''Sophia's busy writing. I thought I'd help out, surprise her with a few things, that's all.''

''Tosh, as Ranen would say.'' Cathy laughed richly as she led him over to a display of handmade cribs. ''You want to please her, make her happy.''

''Catherine…'' he began, his tone laced with warning.

''Why be ashamed of it?''

"I'm not ashamed—"

"Good to hear it. Because, big brother, you're turning into a wonderful husband whether you want to or not."

The sweet scent of designer baby powder in the air seemed to intensify all at once, swirling around Alex. No doubt the sensation had been brought on by the word *husband.* In the past the word had made his heart harden in anger and bitterness. In the past he had given the word little credence as it had always represented another's control. But lately, around a certain redhead, the word had only puzzled him, made him question, made him wonder.

He turned to Cathy who was watching him intently and asked, "Do you think Sophia would prefer the white or this pale green?"

"What do *you* think she'd like?"

"Stop playing games, Catherine. I don't have infinite amounts of time to spend here."

"That's right," she said, fingering a very sweet pale-pink baby blanket. "Shouldn't you be working right now? I've never heard of you taking time off during a workday."

He tossed her a black glare. "You're really making me regret inviting you along."

She touched his shoulder, smiling gently. "I'm sorry. I don't mean to tease. It's just that..."

"What?"

"Have you realized yet that your dream has come true, Alex?"

"I don't know what you mean."

"About how that beautiful mermaid rose up out of the water, red hair shining, green eyes blazing, and with one look made you feel like a different person, like you could fly."

As a salesman walked discreetly past them, Alex lowered his voice to a harsh whisper. "I'm only going to say this one more time, it's not like that between Sophia and me."

"No?"

"No."

"What's it like, then?"

"We are married and we have a child coming."

"As simple as that?"

At this point Alex was fairly ready to put his fist through the blue-and-pink-checked wall. It wasn't that he hadn't observed all the similarities between his childish dreams and today's realties. God help him, he had. Only too often. But what did it all matter? So, he had found and married the woman of his dreams...

Alex came to a screeching halt in his mind. Where had that come from? How had he allowed such a thought to register? *Woman of his dreams...* Men like him didn't entertain such foolishness.

"What do you think of this bookcase?" he quickly

asked, hoping Catherine would let the previous subject lie. "Shall I order the complete set?"

But she wouldn't let the subject lie. She took a step closer, her gaze riveted on him, her voice a whisper. "She's not Patrice."

"What?"

"She's not Patrice. And you're not the man who was unhappily married for five years anymore."

He glared at her, frowning. "I know this, Catherine."

"I don't think you do, Alex. I think you carry the weight of that relationship around with you day and night. I think that you're afraid if you give yourself, all of yourself, to Sophia, and things go wrong, you won't be able to hold your head up this time."

Frustration suddenly matured to scalding fury. Through clenched teeth, he replied sharply, "I won't discuss this subject further."

Catherine refused to back down. "You haven't discussed it at all."

"I don't know if I like this new, modern, speak-her-mind Catherine."

"Well, get used to it, buddy." A glint of amusement tugged at her mouth as she tried to pull him out of his bad humor. "Because you not only described me, but your sister-in-law *and* the most outspoken of them all—your wife."

Again, Alex was stopped in his tracks. This time by a vision of Sophia. Gloriously naked beside him, wrapped in a blanket, her hair down and wild, her eyes bright with exasperation as he jested with her about her stubborn nature.

Just the thought made his bones ache for her.

"She is a stubborn lass, isn't she?" he muttered to himself.

But Catherine heard him and chuckled. "My poor Alex. You've really gone and lost your heart."

Grimacing, he returned to the gentle sparring they enjoyed so much. "What I've lost is my head when I called and asked you along today. Now, are you going to help with this or not?"

"Sophia would love the pale green." She leaned up and gave him a peck on the cheek. "But something tells me you already knew that."

Alex gave her a mock snarl, then turned to call over the salesman.

Eleven

The cup of tea to Sophia's left was untouched and growing colder by the second. But it was a welcome sight. It was the first time since her grandfather's death that tea or a muffin or whatever she happened to have sitting beside her writing pad wasn't thoroughly consumed before she'd written her first sentence.

But not today. In fact, not any day this week.

…Della Denkins passed out just three dreams that night. But every child she blessed woke up full of hope, full of happiness and full of heart.

Sophia glanced up from the kitchen table and her last ten pages of story with the oh-so-prized "The

End'' affixed to the bottom and smiled broadly. She'd done it. Almost a year of writer's block and she'd finished this story in just under a week.

A story she was so proud of. A story she would dedicate to her husband and to her child. For it was not a story about a talking animal this time or a lost boy looking for a new friend.

It was a story about dreams.

A sudden pang of hunger rose up to claim her, taking her mind off dreams for a moment in favor of reality. This intense empty-stomach feeling was something that was happening pretty often as of late. First the slight nausea, then a ravenous appetite. Both of which could never be ignored.

Oh, the joys of pregnancy, she mused with a smile as she stood up and went to the fridge. Two extra large sandwiches coming up. Alex did love peanut butter...

That morning he'd mentioned that he might be coming home for lunch if he finished up with the chancellor on time.

Sophia grabbed the jelly and peanut butter, then scooped up the bread from the counter. He'd be here. Just as he had every day this week. And just as they had every day this week, they'd share a sandwich and a story about what each of them had done that morning.

Time was being so kind to them. Wooing them along in a romantic haze. Every day they'd talk and laugh and share about what they wanted for their child. Every night they'd make love in Alex's bed, then afterward he'd pull her close and they'd fall right to sleep.

They were having a marriage. An honest-to-goodness marriage. And while Sophia was giving Alex time to feel and understand himself, he was giving her, and them, a chance.

Her heart full, Sophia went about her sandwich making. She pulled out two slices of bread from the bag and opened the jar of peanut butter.

But that was all she did.

A soft gasp suddenly escaped her throat and the smile of happiness from a moment ago died on her lips. Letting the jars and bread fall haphazardly back onto the counter, she doubled over in pain, gripping her belly as both sides of her abdomen shot off burning sparks.

Fear plunged into Sophia's very soul, threatening to drown her. But she fought the feeling and tried to calm herself, tried to breathe deeply as she prayed for the pain to subside.

But it didn't.

It only worsened.

Every muscle in her body clenched tight as panic gnawed away at her confidence. With each twinge, she felt as though she was being ripped apart, torn apart at the pelvis.

Her gaze clouded with tears as she inched toward

the table, reached for the phone. She had to get to someone, call for help.

God, please don't let me lose this baby.

Again pain blasted into her groin, and she retracted her arm, crying out.

"Sophia?"

Sophia barely heard the doorbell, barely heard the feminine call through the fog in her mind.

"Sophia? Are you home? It's me, Fran."

With every ounce of strength she had left, Sophia cried out for the one person she needed.

"Alex…"

Alex walked into the beach house with a grin on his normally sedate face. He couldn't help it. As it had been from the moment he'd seen her standing on the bow of her sloop, red hair wild and shimmering in the sun, he couldn't wait to see her again.

Perhaps someday that intensity of need would subside. He couldn't imagine it, but perhaps it would and he could return to being Prince Alexander—serious, focused and, alas, unromantic.

He dropped his briefcase at the door and exhaled heavily. If the truth be told, he didn't want to be that man anymore. He didn't like that man. Actually, he never had. Serious, focused and unromantic were what he'd had to be to survive his past.

But Sophia Dunhill Thorne had changed all that.

She had changed him.

"Honey, I'm home," he called, his grin turning a little wicked as he glanced around the living room looking for her.

Yesterday, when he'd walked through the door, Sophia had been sitting at the dining table, totally calm and totally nude. With an easy smile on her lips, she'd made him eat his entire sandwich before he'd been allowed to have…dessert.

Sheer torture.

Well, today, he'd brought *her* dessert instead. Her new favorite: bread pudding with cream. And with it he'd also brought the hope of feeding it to her, watching the sweet confection as it slipped between her full lips.

That was, if she could be found.

His grin widening, Alex stalked from room to room searching for her. As he entered each space, he imagined her waiting for him beneath the sheets in one of the bedrooms or in the bath, doused in suds.

But she was nowhere to be found, he soon realized, as he came to the last room and found it empty.

Slightly vexed, Alex rushed back to the kitchen, hunting the countertops and tables for a note. Perhaps she'd run to the store or set up a picnic on the beach. But surely he would have seen her on his way in, if she'd chosen the beach.

A foolish, premature fear twisted around his heart. One he'd managed to block over the past several weeks. He despised himself for allowing it to return now. But the thoughts came regardless, heedless.

Had he missed something? A sign that Sophia might be unhappy? In their marriage? In Llandaron? After all, she had fought the arrangement at first. And though she seemed in relatively good spirits, she *had* been a bit preoccupied this week.

But surely that was only about the book she was writing.

He plowed his hands through his hair. Of course it was about the writing. Bloody hell, he was losing it. She'd probably gone to pick up a special lunch or maybe she finished the manuscript early and went out to mail—

Alex stopped short as his gaze caught on the blinking light of his message service. Shaking his head at his previous stupidity, he rushed to it and depressed the button; fully ready to hear his wife's voice.

But the message wasn't from Sophia.

"Your Highness, it's around 11:00 a.m." The voice was distinctly male and older. "Your boat has been repaired. Kip had it all buffed and polished and towed to the slip as you requested. And don't you worry about provisions. I personally saw to it that she's all packed and ready for your journey."

The machine beeped. No more messages.

A cold knot pulsed in Alex's gut. And it grew tighter and tighter with each breath he took. He could actually feel his gaze turn hostile as he stared at the answering machine.

She's all packed and ready for your journey.

Like an ocean wave in a storm, his past came rushing back, battering his heart. His mind bombarded with visions, his muscles tensing just as they had when he'd walked into his town house in Scotland and found Patrice gone. No note, no nothing.

Just like today.

Iron fists closed around Alex's soul. Had he really abandoned his vow? Lost all perspective? Had he actually allowed himself to believe that Sophia cared for him, wanted him, was in love with him?

Obviously he had, he thought, seething with anger and humiliation at his lack of control.

But he would get it back—at all costs. He had to. Sophia was carrying his child. His child! And the heir to the throne of Llandaron. That child would remain with him always.

Alex slammed his fist on the counter, curses falling from his lips.

If Sophia wanted out, fine. But she wasn't about to take their child with her.

"Alex?"

Alex whirled toward the door, found Maxim standing there, his jaw tight, his gaze strained.

Alex's lips thinned in anger. Sent to break the bad news to the crown prince. He sniffed sharply. At least

Patrice had had the decency to send a priest instead of a family member when she'd run off.

"What do you want, Maxim?"

"I've been knocking for thirty seconds," Maxim said, a slight hesitation in his hawklike stare.

Alex had no time for his brother's anxiety. "Why didn't you just walk in, then?"

"I was. And I did. Listen, Alex, I have to tell you something. I was going to call, but I didn't want to leave a message and...wait, what's the—" Maxim's eyes narrowed, two deep lines of concern etched between his brows. "You look like you're ready to strangle someone."

Or sink a fist into Maxim if his little brother's jaw didn't cease this bloody small talk. "Do you know where Sophia is?" Alex fairly snapped.

His brother's gaze slipped.

"Speak up, Maxim, for crissakes!"

"Fran came over here to see her today, but when she got here—"

Alex cursed brutally. "I knew it."

"Knew what?"

"She's gone."

"What are you talking about?"

"She's left town, isn't that what you've come here to tell me?"

"Alex, maybe you should sit down."

"I don't want to sit down," Alex bellowed, stalking over to Maxim, jaw clenched. "Just tell me what the hell is going on."

Frowning, Maxim inclined his head. "Alex, Sophia's been taken to the hospital."

Twelve

Ranen sat forward in the bedside chair, his face fixed with tension. "How are you feeling, lass?"

"Much better. The pain's subsided." Sophia shook her head. "Who could've thought that stretching ligaments could be so excruciating?" Easing herself up into a sitting position, she grinned at her great uncle. "You know Ranen, that's the tenth time you've asked me how I'm feeling in the last hour?"

"Pardon me for being worried about my kin," Ranen grumbled good-naturedly.

"Kin, huh? You're acknowledging that now, are you?"

"Tosh! Always have, lass."

"Ranen…"

"Well, not at the first meeting, that's true enough. But I got things right now, don't I?"

Sophia touched the vase of heather beside her hospital bed. "Yes, you do."

"Get on with things, that's what I say now."

"Glad to hear it."

"Me and my old goat of a brother were too damn stubborn to get on with things. I regret that. But it stops right here, you understand?"

A wave of melancholy moved through the private room, scratching at the door of Sophia's heart. "I want to, Ranen. What happened between you two?"

Ranen jerked to his feet, aged bones crackling as he went. "Robbie lived in Baratin until his thirteenth year. Along with our mother and me. It wasn't the happiest of times, mind you. Our father had passed just two years before, and we clung to our mother like a newborn colt to a mare." Ranen moved to the window and stared out. "But she hardly noticed us. She was never the same after my father died, off in her own world most of the time. Robbie and I tried everything we could think of to get her attention, but nothing worked. Nothing until…"

Sophia didn't want to push him, but she felt as though he might need it, as though he'd been holding on to this story and the anger in his heart for too long.

"What happened, Ranen?" she asked softly.

"It's a bleak ending, Sophia."

"Please."

A heaviness settled over the hospital room as Ranen continued. "Robbie had an idea. Let's get ourselves lost, he said. Then she'll be worried and come find us." Ranen's voice grew rough yet weary. "She did come looking. We used to love to play at the beach, and she knew it. It was a wet morning. She slipped on a bit of sea rock and hit her head."

"Oh, Ranen…"

"My aunt who had been living in America came to take us back with her. But I refused to go. I wouldn't leave Llandaron, and I begged Robbie not to go, either. But he said he couldn't stay after…"

"All these years you—"

"I blamed him for our mother's death." His voice broke in misery. "And I hated him for leaving me."

Sophia swallowed, bit back tears. "I am so dreadfully sorry, Ranen." She now, more than ever, understood why her grandfather was such a recluse, why he believed so fervently in living every moment, why he wanted to sail around Llandaron but never go ashore.

When her great-uncle turned to look at her, anger didn't light his eyes anymore. Only sadness. "Thank you, lass. 'Tis over now. I've made my peace with Robbie and with my own dim-witted ideas about the past. We both did what we felt was right."

"You're a very wise man, Ranen. I wish everyone were as forgiving about their past."

"You speak of the crown prince?"

Sophia didn't know what made her do it, maybe she needed the comfort of family or maybe Ranen was the one person who understood her pain right now, but she reached out for him.

Eyes downcast, he moved to the bedside and took her hand. "You sure do love the man, don't you?"

"Yes. More than anything. I just wish..."

"What, lass?"

She shook her head. "My wishes have grown redundant."

"That he would let himself love you?"

A smile tugged at her mouth. "Yes."

"He'll come around, lass. A tree doesn't always fall at first stroke."

She looked up at him with surprise, his words causing her to remember her past, a past filled with love and understanding. "Grandpa used to say that."

Ranen leaned over and kissed her on the forehead, his whiskers tickling her skin. "Who do you think taught it to him?"

"Hello, Sophia."

A beautiful princess with short gray hair and violet eyes moved into the hospital room with a grace she was born into.

Sophia smiled warmly. "Hi, Fara."

The older woman walked around the bed to stand beside Ranen, but her gaze never left Sophia. "You have more color, my dear."

"The doctor said I should be able to go home to-morrow."

"He wants to watch you overnight. Good man. I approve."

"Tosh," Ranen said on dusty chuckle. "She's right as rain, aren't you, lass?"

"Right as rain," Sophia assured them both with a wide grin.

Fara gave a tinkling little laugh, like sleigh bells, then addressed the man beside her. "We should let her rest, Ranen, dear."

Ranen, dear?

What in the world? And when had this happened?

Sophia felt too stunned at the blatant endearment to speak her queries aloud. But when she saw Fara place her hand on Ranen's shoulder and he actually laid his hand over hers, she couldn't be stopped. "What's this all about, you two?"

Ranen only frowned, while Fara winked.

"Rest now. Information later," the older woman said ushering her beau out of the room. She called over her shoulder, "We'll bring Alexander to you just as soon as he arrives, my dear."

Sophia watched them go with a mixture of happiness and melancholy. There was nothing she wanted more for her uncle and her new aunt than to realize their feelings for each other and give in to the love of a lifetime.

It was just that their coming together now made

her pine, made her wonder. Would it be the same with Alex and her? Would they deny their feelings until they were old and gray and unsteady?

Or would the dreams for love, for a future, that they each carried in their hearts be allowed to walk free?

Fear unlike any he had ever known blistered Alex's heart as he shot out of the elevator and onto the hospital's fourth floor. He stalked down the hall toward Sophia's room and grabbed the first person he saw in the corridor.

"Ranen, how is she?"

"Calm yourself, Highness. She'll be fine."

"Fine? What the hell does that mean? Where's the doctor?"

"He's in with another patient." Ranen patted his godchild on the back. "Honestly, lad, she's perfectly well. She just had some rather severe pain in her ligaments, that's all. The wee one is stretching out the uterus, is what the doctor said. 'Tis perfectly normal, he said."

"Oh, thank God." Alex's gut unclenched slightly, and he released the breath he'd been holding all the way to the hospital.

It had been like some sort of conspiracy on the journey over. Satan's plan to drive him mad. Horrid traffic, no cell phone service, terrifying thoughts about loss and fear and words unspoken.

"I must see her." Jaw tight, Alex headed down the

hallway toward Sophia's room. He had much to say, much to apologize for, and it couldn't wait.

Ranen followed him. "Before you go in, I want a word with you."

Brushing off the old man's request, Alex muttered, "I don't have time. I want to see her now."

"You'll make the time, Alexander." And with that, Ranen grabbed Alex by the arm, stopping him dead in his tracks.

Alex whirled to face the man, his eyes no doubt as black as his mood. "What the devil is going on, Ranen? Is there something you're not telling me?"

"No. No. Sophia and the child are fine. As I said, it was just a little scare."

"Then what's this all about? I should be with her, not having a conversation—"

"Sit down and try to keep your mouth shut, can you do that?" the old man barked.

Alex just stood there for a moment, blank, stunned. No one spoke to him in such a way. No one but his father, at any rate. Then again, Ranen had always been every bit a second father to him.

Brushing aside the twinges of defiance that were clawing to get free, he did as he was bid. The bench behind him looked sturdy enough. He sat down and gave the older man an expectant look.

Ranen didn't sit beside him, but put a foot up on the bench and leaned in close. "If you don't love the girl, you should let her go."

"What the hell are you talking—"

"You know very well."

"I will never let her or my child go." Alex's voice was firm, final.

"You sound like a man making up for lost pride, Alexander."

"And you sound like a man who's trying to play the part of grandfather."

"Not trying, Alexander. Doing."

"Is that right?"

"That's right."

"When did this start?"

Ranen pushed away from the bench, but kept his voice low as hospital staff dashed to and fro around them. "Never mind when. She's my blood and I'm going to protect her."

"From what?" Alex demanded hotly. "From me?"

"If I have to."

Alex snorted.

Ranen put a hand on his godson's shoulder, his voice softening for the first time in a long time. "Would you want her going through life as you did? With a spouse who didn't love her?"

The words cut deep, deeper than Alex could've imagined. And they sent well-hidden questions into his mind, as well. What *did* he want for Sophia? He hadn't thought of it until now. He knew what he wanted from her, but *for* her...

Hell, he didn't want to think of it. Because if he did, he'd have to look closely at himself and the true desires of his heart.

His anger piqued, he narrowed his eyes at Ranen. "I will not take love advice from a man who has spent decades denying his own feelings."

The man didn't flinch one bit, didn't back off, either. "That's over now, son. Your aunt Fara knows my heart. I'm not letting fear take any more of my days or nights."

Alex jerked to his feet. He'd had enough conversation, enough lecturing, enough hearing about newly found fantasies. "Good for you," he said brusquely, his gaze impassive and cold. "Now will you let me pass?"

"Stupid…bullheaded…son of a…" Ranen muttered, shaking his head.

But he stepped aside and let Alex go.

Sophia was staring out the window when Alex walked into the room. But she quickly turned and found his gaze. At first glance she thought he looked angry, but as he drew closer, she realized it was angst that darkened his mood.

"Sophia." His voice wrapped around her like the sweetest, warmest of blankets.

"I'm so glad you're here, Alex."

He sat on the edge of the bed, reached for her hand,

then drew back. "I'm sorry I wasn't there when this happened."

"It's okay. I'm okay." Why wouldn't he touch her, she wondered. Why was he so distant and tense? Was it fear over losing the baby? Of course, it had to be. This child was everything to him. "Don't worry, the baby is just fine."

"I know, and I'm unbelievably relieved."

"Then why the long face?"

His eyes swept over her. "Sweetheart, I'm worried about *you*."

The endearment tugged at her heart. "Me?"

He shook his head, his tone heavy with frustration. "I thought I would have a heart attack on the way over here."

"That wouldn't have been good," she said with a soft smile. "Both of us in hospital."

"I'm serious, Sophia. You scared me to death."

With a quick exhale she asked, "Do you know why that is, Alex?"

"Of course I know why," he said, his voice strained. "I just told you how worried I was about you—"

"No." She gave him a patient smile. "*Why* you were so worried?"

"Sophia, I care about you, dammit!"

"And?"

"Well, you're the first person I've been able to talk to in a long time."

"What else." Sophia fought for calm, but it was incredibly difficult. Her heart's desire was sitting beside her finally opening up to her, finally revealing himself and his feelings, and she didn't want to interrupt the flow.

"You're wonderful, intelligent, funny."

"Thank you."

He nodded, absentmindedly took her hand. "I enjoy your company. I can't imagine my days without you."

She squeezed his hand and grinned wickedly. "Or your nights?"

"That goes without saying."

"Oh, Alex." Sophia couldn't stop the laughter that bubbled in her throat.

"What?"

"Don't you know what this means?"

Alex looked totally perplexed.

"You love me."

Sophia had never seen a jaw drop so fast in her life. But the sight didn't bother her. She'd walked a long road with Alex, a long road to get to this place of pure honesty and no regret.

For weeks she'd sat on her hands, kept her mouth shut about her feelings and hopes that he would come to realize his own first.

And he had. In his way he had.

"Don't look so shocked," she said, pulling him

closer until his face was just inches from hers. "You love me, Prince Alexander and I love you."

"Sophia…"

"We were meant for each other, Alex. Look at our history. Your dream, my sailing in Scotland, then later on your stretch of beach. It's kismet."

"I don't believe in—"

She stopped him, kissing him softly on the lips. "Don't be afraid. We'll do this together. I'm not going anywhere." Again she kissed him, whispered against his lips, "I won't hurt you or humiliate you. Don't be afraid to love me, Alex."

His head fell back suddenly and he groaned. "I'm not afraid to love you."

"What?"

"I'm not afraid to love you, sweetheart. Not anymore. I gave up the need to always be in control because I love you so, lass. I've loved you from the first moment I saw you." He kissed her hungrily, then drew back. "I was just too stubborn and too bloody afraid to admit it to myself."

"Then what is it?"

"Dammit, Sophia," he growled, gathering her in his arms, pinning her with his fiery gaze. "I'm afraid you'll stop loving me."

Sophia stared at him, totally shocked by what he'd just said. "Alex, that's not possible."

"Anything's possible."

"Not that," she assured him, gripping his shoulders tightly. "You're my heart, you have to know that."

"I do know. But fear is a damaging beast. And when I heard the message on the machine from the boat works, I couldn't help but think—"

"You mean about the trip?"

"Yes."

Sophia released a breathy laugh, her heart soaring to the rooftops as her husband held her close on the stiff hospital bed mattress. "The trip is for us, Alex. I wanted you with me when I finished the last leg of grandpa's tour." She gave him a tender wink. "I thought it could be a second honeymoon."

"Or a first," he said on a lazy grin.

"Yes."

"I'm such an idiot."

"Hey, watch it!" she warned. "Idiot or not, you're talking about the man I love."

Alex lifted her hand to his mouth and kissed her palm. "Marry me again?"

She nodded. "Okay."

"Just you and me and our child on the beach where we first met in front of the waves and the sun and God."

As she looked into her husband's eyes, she saw her future, so clearly this time and so bright. There were more children for sisters and brothers and grandfathers and great uncles to bounce on their knees. There were holidays and wedding anniversaries. There was wondrous work, writing and giving. And there was family, with a husband who adored his wife and learned to show her just how much a little more every day.

"The beach sounds perfect," Sophia said, curving her lips. "Then we'll sail off into the sunrise?"

Alex released her hand, leaned in and cupped her face. "I love you."

"And I love you."

Turning around and easing back beside her on the bed, Alex gathered her in his arms once again. "Don't ever stop saying that."

"Never." Sophia snuggled close to her husband and let her head fall against his shoulder. "Never, my love."

Epilogue

Baratin
Spring

On the bow of a docked *Daydream*, of that beautiful boat her grandfather had designed and built, Sophia touched her large belly and watched her beloved uncle wait for the woman of his dreams to walk down the deck toward him.

To everyone that had come to witness the event, it was truly a fairy-tale ending, a long time in the making. But to Sophia, it meant so much more. Ranen had come home, had welcomed the spirit and blessing of his brother and was finally finding happiness.

To Sophia, her family was now complete.

Beside her, Alex hugged her close and whispered in her ear, "Does this remind you of anything, sweetheart?"

Sophia smiled broadly. Just a few months back, she and Alex had renewed their vows at the beach as he'd wanted, with only God and their child in attendance. They'd broken with convention and written their vows themselves and given each other matching wedding bands engraved with the date. And the following day they had set off for Baratin to fulfill a promise accompanied by Ranen's wedding gift, his sweet wolfhound pup, Aggie.

Snatching Sophia's attention, the bridal march, played by two violists on the dock—two old friends of Ranen's—started up, and down the flower-trimmed pier walked a woman of such extraordinary beauty, she made everyone on the deck and on the pier stop and gasp. Dressed in a fitted white gown, Fara was finally taking what she wanted, what she deserved, and she'd never looked happier.

"She's so in love," whispered Fran, rocking her little girl in her arms as Ranen and Fara spoke their vows to the proud and beaming king, who was doing the ceremonial honors.

"She's one of us now," Sophia said softly.

Cathy nodded, giving her sleepy little baby a kiss on the forehead. "Looks like we all have our Prince Charming, doesn't it, ladies?"

Fran, Cathy and Sophia all glanced up at the dashing, roguish and undeniably sexy men at their sides and grinned.

And when Ranen took his bride in his arms for a kiss, each lady grabbed her prince and followed suit.

While all around them, the fog rolled in....

* * * * *

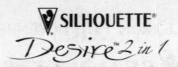
AVAILABLE FROM 19TH NOVEMBER 2004

MIDNIGHT SEDUCTION Justine Davis

Redstone Inc.

When an innocently seductive young woman and asked for his help in solving a deadly mystery, millionaire treasure hunter Harlan McClaren allowed chivalry and male interest to over-rule his good sense...

KEEPING BABY SECRET Beverly Barton

The Protectors

They shared a brief passionate affair and agent Frank Latimer never knew that he'd become a father—not until his son was kidnapped! Once he found his child, Frank was going to 'deal' with too—independent, too-sexy Leenie!

THE HEART OF A STRANGER Sheri WhiteFeather

The Country Club

Lourdes Quinterez and her twin girls tenderly cared for the stranger, but soon Lourdes's feelings changed to a steamy desire for the rugged, mysterious intruder who promised to be her lover, father to her girls and stay by her side.

SECRETS, LIES...AND PASSION Linda Conrad

The night before their wedding Reid Sorrels had disappeared without a trace, leaving Jill Bennett with the ultimate keepsake. Now ten years later, Reid was back and Jill was keeping her secret—she wasn't about to let him break her heart again.

CHRISTMAS BONUS, STRINGS ATTACHED Susan Crosby

Behind Closed Doors

Lyndsey couldn't believe her sexy private eye boss had actually proposed, but it wasn't for real, although they'd be sleeping together! Perhaps if she took his mind off business, she could make him yearn to spend this Christmas with her...

CINDERELLA'S CHRISTMAS AFFAIR Katherine Garbera

King of Hearts

Millionaire tycoon Tad Randolph had befriended and betrayed CJ some years ago and now he wanted redemption. CJ craved Tad's touch and wondered if she dare believe this Christmas affair could last forever...

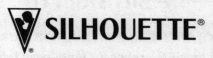

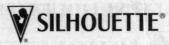
SILHOUETTE®

Sensation™ and Desire™ 2-in-1
are proud to present the brand-new series by
bestselling author

MERLINE LOVELACE

TO PROTECT AND DEFEND

These heroes and heroines were trained
to put their lives on the line, but their
hearts were another matter...

A Question of Intent
Silhouette Sensation
September 2004

Full Throttle
Silhouette Desire 2-in-1
November 2004

The Right Stuff
Silhouette Sensation
December 2004

0904/SH/LC93

SILHOUETTE®
Desire 2 in 1

is proud to introduce

DYNASTIES: THE DANFORTHS

Meet the Danforths—a family of prominence...
tested by scandal, sustained by passion!

Coming Soon!
Twelve thrilling stories in six 2-in-1 volumes:

THE TRUEBLOOD
Dynasty

Isabella Trueblood made history reuniting people torn apart by war and an epidemic. Now, generations later, Lily and Dylan Garrett carry on her work with their agency, Finders Keepers.

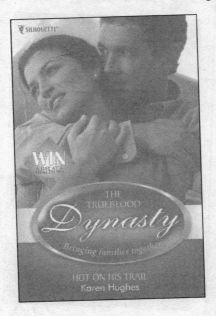

Book Seven available from 19th November

Available at most branches of WH Smith, Tesco, ASDA, Martins, Borders, Eason, Sainsbury's and all good paperback bookshops.

MILLS & BOON

Volume 6
on sale from
3rd December
2004

Lynne
Graham

International Playboys

The Winter

Bride

*A story of passions and betrayals...
and the dangerous obsessions they spawn*

PENNY JORDAN

SILVER

FREE

2 BOOKS AND A SURPRISE GIFT!

We would like to take this opportunity to thank you for reading this Silhouette® book by offering you the chance to take TWO more specially selected titles from the Desire™ series absolutely FREE! We're also making this offer to introduce you to the benefits of the Reader Service™—

- ★ **FREE home delivery**
- ★ **FREE gifts and competitions**
- ★ **FREE monthly Newsletter**
- ★ **Books available before they're in the shops**
- ★ **Exclusive Reader Service offers**

Accepting these FREE books and gift places you under no obligation to buy; you may cancel at any time, even after receiving your free shipment. Simply complete your details below and return the entire page to the address below. You don't even need a stamp!

YES! Please send me 2 free Desire books and a surprise gift. I understand that unless you hear from me, I will receive 3 superb new titles every month for just £4.99 each, postage and packing free. I am under no obligation to purchase any books and may cancel my subscription at any time. The free books and gift will be mine to keep in any case.

D4ZEE

Ms/Mrs/Miss/Mr...Initials ....
BLOCK CAPITALS PLEASE

Surname ....

Address ....

....

....Postcode ....

Send this whole page to:

The Reader Service, FREEPOST CN81, Croydon, CR9 3WZ